BEYOND DESIRE . . .

There wasn't time to think, to control the emotions that filled Frisco as Tom swept her into his arms and kissed her. She responded passionately, unable to control her reaction.

But as the kiss lingered, with his hot breath flooding over her face, her reason began to gain control, and she broke away. "Please, Tom," she gasped desperately, "you mustn't. After all, you promised."

"That was before you said you loved me," he said, his hands caressing her cheek.

"I didn't say I loved you," she protested.

"Perhaps not with words," he told her with a gentle smile. "But you said it with your eyes."

Frisco tried to remind herself that she belonged to Beau, that she loved only him, and that he loved her, but she did not truly believe it. Beau had not pressed his love on her since that first time, at the very beginning of their false marriage. Hadn't he emphasized by every word, by every action, that he wanted his freedom, that he wanted to be free to choose as well? And now he was thousands of miles away.

Slowly she convinced herself that she was no longer Mrs. Beau Tolliver. She was her own person. It was foolish to hope that, when Beau returned, things would be any different. There had been—in her turbulent life—so few chances for happiness. Who could possibly condemn her for grasping at a chance when it came?

Also by Jeraldine Saunders:

Frisco Lady
Signs of Love
Hypoglycemia: The Disease Your Doctor Won't Treat
(with Harvey M. Ross, M.D.)

THE FRISCO FORTUNE

Jeraldine Saunders

PINNACLE BOOKS   NEW YORK

THE FRISCO FORTUNE

Copyright © 1981 by Jeraldine Saunders

An original Pinnacle Books edition, published for the first time anywhere.

First printing, June 1981

ISBN: 0-523-41026-3

Cover illustration by John Solie

Printed in the United States of America

PINNACLE BOOKS, INC.
1430 Broadway
New York, New York 10018

THE FRISCO FORTUNE

PROLOGUE

All was not well. It should have been, but it was not. Graciela now possessed everything she had struggled so very long to acquire. She had regained her freedom, at least insofar as the institution of slavery was concerned. Louis Thiebaud, the man who had claimed to own her body and soul, was now dead, and there was no other man alive who could pursue that claim. Unless perhaps Beau should reveal the story of her escape from New Orleans, in a careless moment telling someone about the sheltered, innocent schoolgirl who had not known the truth about her parentage until the death of her father. Of course, Beau would never intentionally do such a thing.

Graciela had acquired Beau Tolliver as a husband in the same moment she had regained her freedom, and by the same set of circumstances.

1

She had yearned for just such a development in her years of fleeing from enslavement. Graciela loved Beau passionately; when she was apart from him, she ached for him to be near. When she was near him, she longed for his touch. And when he touched her, made love to her, she wanted it never to end.

But their marriage was a lie. That fact had become an obsession with her. Graciela was not really married to Beau Tolliver at all. The marriage certificate dated September 12, 1847, at Cairo, Illinois, was a forgery. Beau had produced it only to prove that she was not an escaped slave, as Thiebaud had claimed.

"You're free," he had told her, when it was all over and they were nestled neatly into the comfortable house he had bought for them. "Only you and I know the document isn't real. I won't hold you to it, except for the sake of appearance. You can do whatever you want, as long as you remember who you are. You're no longer Graciela McGee, escaped slave. You're no longer 'Frisco,' gypsy businesswoman. You're Mrs. Beau Tolliver, and that gives you a place in good society."

Graciela should have spoken up then. She knew Beau was only trying to be fair. She knew it was pride and generosity that prompted his bargain, but she had her own stubborn pride as well, and she had offered no protest. She did not confess to him that she loved him with all her heart,

2

that there was nothing she wanted more than for the marriage certificate to be real and legal. She did not confess it, because she could not be certain that he loved her as deeply. In fact, she suspected he had offered her freedom, because he wanted his own freedom.

That had been the first stone in the wall of silence they had built up between them. Each day that passed added another stone, until now it had become almost totally impenetrable. The months of suspicious, doubting silence had finally set them firmly and inextricably into patterns of resentment and hostility.

Graciela could not be Mrs. Beau Tolliver in name only. She was not capable of hypocrisy. Appearance did not matter to her at all. Oh, of course, she knew how to be a lady. The graces, the manners, the decorum had been drilled into her at the school her father had sent her to, but she possessed a native wisdom that told her these frills lacked substance. The true substance of life was love, and the sham of her life with Beau lacked love. It bound her into as complete and as painful a form of slavery as that she had tried so desperately to escape.

You're free. Those words of Beau's followed her daily in painful irony, echoing in her heart with anguish, building in her soul an angry resentment.

I am not free, she yearned to protest. *A piece of paper isn't freedom. A lie isn't freedom. I am not Mrs. Beau Tolliver. I don't know who I am anymore, but I am not that prim and proper lady you expect me to be.*

But Graciela kept her silence, reminding herself that she must be grateful for all Beau had done. He had risked his life for her. He had bound himself into this false marriage with her, and he did not protest. She had to force herself to do as well.

PART ONE

1

Statehood. It was to be the biggest celebration San Francisco had ever known. Indeed, the people had already begun celebrating, dancing and singing in the streets from the moment the ship had sailed into the bay flying the long streamer from its mast, emblazoned with the words, "California Admitted."

Even more joyous to Graciela was the news that it was admitted as a free state. No Californian could own another human being. Slavery would not be permitted.

Graciela spent much of the day gazing out of her parlor window at the boisterous crowds, longing to be a part of them, yearning to express the feelings that surged inside her, straining at her bosom to break into shouts and song, and mischievously enticing her feet to move into dance.

She spent most of the day alone, however. Beau had come home briefly from his office to inform her, "Mrs. Royce is giving a grand ball this evening, and we're to attend." There was pleasure in his face and in his voice, but there was none of the ebullience she was feeling. His pale Byronic skin held only a slight flush, his green eyes possessed no fire, and his thick red hair was only slightly disarrayed from his trip through the chaotic streets.

"You must wear the new gown from Paris," he ordered. "And you must spend the day resting and working at your hair so that you will be the most beautiful lady present." Then he kissed her affectionately on the forehead and departed, leaving her tantalized by the momentary touch of his lips.

She watched him go from the window, drinking in the heady vision of his powerful and graceful body, wanting to rush after him, to beg him to take her in his strong arms, to offer him the deep passion she felt for him. But of course she did not. That would be unseemly, unladylike.

He was not aware that she was observing him, or at least he did not turn to acknowledge her presence at the window. With elegant nonchalance, he placed one fine boot into the stirrup of his horse and slung the other leg up and over the saddle. Beau's legs were long and muscular, and they strained at the tight-fitting fawn-colored breeches with their broad green stripe that strapped beneath his boot heels. With an automatic flick of his hand, he tossed the brown broadcloth coattails behind him, eased into the saddle, and donned the shiny beaver tophat. With a brisk snap of the reins, he propelled his black gelding down the crowded street and out of her view.

With his going, an emptiness settled over the large house on Telegraph Hill. Graciela was not entirely alone in the house, but she felt terribly lonely. There was nothing for her to do but to sit and be waited upon by others. Alex was somewhere about the house with Lyuba, either upstairs in the nursery or outside in the garden. They were the only ties Graciela still had from the past. Little Alex, her son from her brief and tragic marriage to Shandor, was all Rom, from the top of his dark curly head to the bottoms of his agile, dancing feet He was now over two years old, and he was not only strikingly beautiful but incredibly shrewd and wise for a child.

Graciela was certain that Lyuba had something to do with this latter quality. Lyuba, her faithful Rom companion. Lyuba, who had the Gift. Lyuba, who could read the cards and see the future. Beau had rather reluctantly allowed Graciela to take her in as nurse and companion to Alex, and she had become totally devoted to the child. At times, Graciela suspected they were even closer than mother and son. Certainly, they had their own secrets, which she was not permitted to share. Several times she had come upon them in the garden or the nursery talking quietly but intensely, and they had suddenly stopped each time upon seeing her. She no longer belonged with them. She had become an outsider.

Nor could she feel a closeness with Carlotta, their Spanish cook and housekeeper. Carlotta ruled over the lower regions of the large house with a fierce rigidity, and she maintained a cold distance between herself and Graciela. If the old woman felt any loyalty at all, it was to Beau, who had been responsible for hiring her, and who— Graciela suspected—had asked her to keep a watchful eye on her mistress, to make sure she maintained the decorum of her new station.

Before her "marriage" to Beau, Graciela had possessed more friends than she could count. True, they were not the sort of people who would be accepted in polite society, but they were wonderfully warm and generous, fun to be with. They had known her as "Frisco," one of the most popular and celebrated women in San Francisco, owner and manager of the finest gambling establishment on the Barbary Coast.

But as far as most of these old friends knew, Frisco was dead. She had died in the fire that had destroyed her gambling house, as well as most of the rest of the city. Beau had allowed Graciela to tell only a few of the girls who had worked the tables for her that she was, in fact, still alive and had given up her business for a respectable married life. However, even those few had drifted away from her.

From time to time, Graciela did have callers, but they were her new friends, the other members of the select, elect "Desirable Dozen," the twelve "respectable" women in San Francisco. Graciela was certain that they came only because Beau was a man of some consequence in the city, and because his import business was of considerable importance to their husbands. She felt no affection for any of them, and she sensed that they felt none for her. In no way did their visits allay the intense loneliness and boredom that had come to characterize her days. The thought of spending this evening with them—this grand evening of celebration—filled her with frustration and dread.

Standing at the parlor window, Graciela parted the baize curtains to have a better view of the crowds in the street below her at the foot of the hill. Someone had hastily made a large banner with a bear on it, and a group had begun to form a parade behind it. An elderly bearded man was playing a concertina, and several girls from one of the dance halls were clapping in time to the music and cavorting with the men, some of whom were passing jugs of whiskey.

Suddenly, the air was cut with the sharp cracking of Chinese fireworks, prompting startled shrieks from the women and laughter from the men. Graciela laughed with them, and the brief

11

pleasure echoed in the empty parlor and died in mockery. Silently she cursed the gypsy blood that made her want to join the merriment. Tears of frustration welled up in her eyes. It was painfully difficult to be a lady.

There was no point in torturing herself by continuing to watch the festivities, so Graciela went upstairs to her room. Since she could not do what she wanted, she must at least try to do as Beau had asked. She removed her elaborate day dress and crinolines, loosened her corset, and climbed into her bed. But she could not force herself to sleep.

Finally, after lying in the heavily shaded room for over an hour, she got up and put on the elaborate white lace dressing gown Beau had given her, then prepared to dress her hair. For another hour, she simply sat and stared at herself in the mirror, unable to decide upon a proper style. She knew how Beau would want it done—subdued, simply parted in the middle, pulled back, and either tucked into a neat bun at the nape of her neck, or braided and the braids coiled on top— but that was not her own inclination. The restrained style did not suit her at all; it was really only suitable for the straight-laced matrons whose faces were characterized by narrow colorless eyes, thin tight lips, and rigid chins.

Graciela's was a dusky, voluptuous beauty. Her hair was a thick and lustrous black, with curls that formed naturally into ringlets to frame her soft, oval, olive-complexioned face. Her dark brown eyes were large and sheltered by long dark lashes. Her lips were full and red; if she kept them closed, attempting to be prim, they seemed merely to pout. Her mouth seemed much more comfortable in a laugh or an open smile, flashing with even, gleaming white teeth.

Graciela was still seated at her dressing table, trying to resist sweeping her curls up onto her head, securing them with fresh roses, and allowing ringlets to fall over her ears, when there was a hesitant knock at her bedroom door.

Startled, she did not have an opportunity to respond before Carlotta entered, an irritable frown on her face. "I am sorry to disturb you, señora," the rigid housekeeper announced, "but she will not go away."

"Who?" Graciela asked.

"A lady," Carlotta hesitated. "I should say a woman, not a very nice woman. A *chica*. I tried to tell her you were resting and could not see her. She has been here before, but before she has always gone away when I tell her to. This time she became angry with me. She cursed at me and began to cry. I cannot make her go away, so . . ."

Annoyed at the old woman's tirade, Graciela interrupted, "What is her name? Did she give a name?"

Carlotta stiffened. "Yes," she said. "A Miss Bennett. She insists she knows you. She says she is your friend."

13

"Miss Lillian Bennett?" Graciela asked, with a surge of surprise and pleasure.

"Yes," the housekeeper responded, "but . . ."

"Of course she's my friend," Graciela exclaimed. "Bring her upstairs immediately. I'll receive her in my room."

But Carlotta did not move. "But," she said, an angry, indecisive look crossing her face, "Señor Tolliver will not like it. He has told me . . ." She caught herself, and quickly tried to cover up. "Excuse me. I will do as you say."

"Just a moment," Graciela rose to her feet and moved to stop her. "What did Señor Tolliver tell you?"

The housekeeper hovered indecisively in the open doorway, staring anxiously at the floor, an embarrassed flush on her wrinkled brown face.

Graciela continued to advance on her threateningly. Her voice rose shrilly as she repeated, "What did Señor Tolliver tell you?"

The dark little eyes flashed up at her defiantly. "He say I am not to tell you," she snapped.

"You will tell me," Graciela demanded angrily, "or I will horsewhip you and throw you out into the street."

A momentary fear crossed the old woman's face, and then her jaw clenched again in defiance. "You would not do such a thing," she said. "Señor Tolliver would not permit it."

"Señor Tolliver would not know about it until

it is too late," Graciela snapped. "You will tell me what he said, and then you will show my friend upstairs."

Finally, Carlotta gave in. "He says he does not like to have these women calling at his house," she muttered. "He says I am not to allow them to see you."

"All right," Graciela told her icily. "Thank you. I will settle this matter with my husband. But, from now on, you are to tell me when anyone calls to see me. Do you understand?"

Carlotta nodded, and turned to go.

Graciela was overcome by a furious rage, one she could not control, no matter how hard she tried to calm herself. How could Beau dare to do such a thing? She was not a child, and she could not bear to be treated as one, especially by a man who was supposed to be her husband. Beau would not even treat a slave in this manner, yet he seemed to treat her as if he owned her more surely than a man might own a slave.

Lillian Bennett was one of Graciela's old friends, from the days when she was known as Frisco. Lillian had worked for her, running one of the tables at the gambling house before it burned. Graciela had been close to all of the girls who worked for her, but she had been more friendly with Lillian than with the others. Lillian had been little more than a child when she had come West with her parents in the Gold Rush, and she had barely reached womanhood when both mother and father were killed by a landslide at their claim. Graciela had taken the orphan in and treated her as she would a younger sister.

Yet, as all the others had drifted away after Graciela's marriage, so had Lillian. Now she understood why, and she was determined to do something about it. She did not yet know how or when, but she intended to confront Beau.

Graciela hardly recognized the distraught young woman who was ushered into her bedroom. It was Lillian, but she looked nothing like the friend Graciela had last seen several months before. She had lost so much weight, she looked emaciated. There were dark circles under the pale blue eyes. Her cheeks were hollow, and her soft, wavy, honey-colored hair had become dirty and matted. The tattered blue gingham dress she wore was soiled and much too large for her now thin frame. She seemed almost frightened to face Graciela, but as soon as the shock of her appearance wore off, Graciela rushed to embrace her warmly.

Lillian began to sob uncontrollably. "I shouldn't have come," the words came out in shame-filled gasps. "I tried not to. I knew you wouldn't want to see me. But I had no one else. No place else to go."

"Of course you should have come," Graciela soothed, stroking the limp unkempt hair. "I've missed you very much. I've thought about you every day, wondering where you were, what you were doing, how things were going with you."

The sobs stopped, and Lillian lifted her head to stare childishly into Graciela's. "I didn't think you knew," she said. "It wasn't really like you to turn us away like that, but Beau said . . ." She caught herself in embarrassment. "I'm sorry," she said. "He's your husband, and I mustn't . . ."

"Don't worry," Graciela smiled consolingly. "I have a fairly good idea what Beau must have said. I'll take care of that. I'll see that you are never turned away from my door again."

She took Lillian by the hand and led her to the velvet-covered settee by the windows. "You look like you haven't eaten in days," she said, forcing her friend to sit. "I'll have Carlotta bring some tea and a bit of food. Then you're going to tell me what has happened to you."

Despite her dignified protests that she was not really hungry, Lillian ate ravenously, devouring every crumb on her plate and drinking several cups of tea. Graciela waited patiently until she was completely finished before asking what she had been anxious to know from the moment Lillian had walked in.

"Now," she said, pouring another cup of tea for each of them, "tell me everything."

Lillian lowered her eyes sheepishly. "I don't really know where to begin."

"Well, where have you been living?" Graciela prodded.

17

Lillian still would not look at her. "Until three days ago," she said falteringly, "I was staying in Papa's old cabin up in the mountains." She paused, reached a shaky hand out for her teacup. "I thought perhaps I might try to work his claim again, but I had no money and no provisions, and . . ." She broke off, unable to go on as tears began to well up in her eyes again.

Graciela firmly refused to allow her to break down a second time. "Did you go up there alone?" she asked sharply. "Or was there someone else with you?"

"Yes . . ." she replied, nodding. Then she shook her head, "No . . ." She sighed with frustration. "I went up there alone, but . . ."

"A man?" Graciela queried.

Lillian nodded. "I was trying to get away from him, but he followed me. He wants me to marry him, but I don't love him." She paused and the tears began to flow. "I don't even like him."

"Well, then, you won't marry him," Graciela told her decisively. "It's as simple as that."

"No, it's not," Lillian shook her head, trying to regain her composure. "I don't have much choice. I can either marry him, or I can . . ." She hesitated painfully. "Or I can do what the other girls have done."

"What do you mean?"

Lillian stiffened. Her face became hard with bitterness. "I'm sure you know what I mean," she said grimly. "There are only two things a woman

18

in San Francisco can do. One is to marry, the other is to sell herself. All the other girls who used to work for you have made their choices. For better or worse."

"That's not true," Graciela protested. "It can't be. Most of the girls have found other jobs. They told me so themselves. I know some have had to work as servants, but they've been able to manage."

"Perhaps that's what they told you," Lillian countered. "Perhaps they really believed it at the time. But it's not the way things have turned out. Most have found themselves working as prostitutes. And it hasn't been by choice. San Francisco is a man's town, and women here serve only one purpose—satisfying the men. The only difference is that some are doing it with a marriage certificate, and some are doing it without one."

In her heart, Graciela believed what Lillian was telling her, but her head did not want to believe. "I'm sure Carrie's life hasn't changed," she said determinedly. "She told me she was working the tables at the Golden Slipper."

"She is," Lillian agreed. "But Jim Blaine owns the Slipper, and his rule is that the girls satisfy the customers in every way—both downstairs and upstairs."

"What about the girls who signed indenture papers?" she asked. "They have legal contracts to work as household servants."

"They're worse off than the others," Lillian explained. "Particularly poor little Annie Laurie. She tried to run away from Albert Valery, and now he won't even let her out of the house."

The image that this brought to Graciela's mind was too painful to bear. She could no longer sit calmly sipping her tea. She rose to her feet and walked across to the window, parting the curtains to stare out at the rough, crude little frontier town spread out below. It was indeed, as Lillian had said, a man's town. There were, even now, almost a hundred men for every woman in San Francisco. Out of a population of over fourteen thousand, there were only twelve women considered respectable. Until now, Graciela had thought this a silly distinction, because she was under the illusion that many of the other women were respectably employed.

Graciela knew the girls who had worked for her almost as well as she knew herself. Their hopes and dreams and aspirations would not have permitted them to choose such a life. They had not come to California just to sell their bodies but to find decent work or marriage.

Finally, decisively, she turned from the window and said, "We can't allow this to go on."

"But what can we do?" Lillian looked bewildered.

"I don't know," Graciela admitted. "But I'll think of something. Meanwhile, if you need a place to stay, we've got an extra bedroom."

2

The moment Beau walked into her room, Graciela's resolve weakened. While preparing for the ball, she had imagined that she could stand up to Beau. After all, any reasonable person would be able to see that she had an obligation to the girls who had once worked for her, who had placed so much trust in her in the past. They needed help, and she was the only one who could help them.

It was an attitude of defiance, and it prompted her to a hasty decision. With Lillian assisting her, she dressed her hair in an exotic elaborate manner, sweeping it all upward to a cluster of pink roses and allowing masses of ringlets to fall freely about her face and ears. The effect was breathtaking. She would clearly stand out among the dour society matrons. And she would probably be frowned upon, but in her present mood, she didn't really care.

Lillian helped her to tighten her corset until her back ached from the strain, and her already full bosom expanded by at least two inches. And then she donned the new rose-pink dress Beau had ordered from Paris. It was the latest in fashion, and far more extravagant than anything yet seen in San Francisco society. The bodice was cut very low and fit snugly, helping to accentuate Graciela's tiny waist. Pale pink crepe de chine, trimmed in metallic silver ribbon, was fashioned over the deeper pink taffeta so as to create a rather daring false waistcoat. The sleeves, of the crepe, began tightly just below bare shoulders, growing full at the elbow with a silver-trimmed slit that revealed a pouf of the darker taffeta. The full skirt over crinolines had six loose panels of silver-trimmed crepe that parted when she moved to expose daring glimpses of the dark taffeta underskirt.

Except for her black silk evening mantle, Graciela was fully dressed to leave for the ball, well before Beau arrived home from his office. She hoped to overwhelm him by her stunning beauty, and then to bring up the subject of her friends' dilemma. Sending Lillian to her room, with an admonishment not to show herself until after she had had a chance to talk to Beau, she settled herself at her dressing table to wait.

Only a few moments before Beau was expected, she realized she had forgotten about Carlotta. If the housekeeper should greet Beau at the door, she might say something about the unexpected visitor, and that would spoil everything. Anxiety began to creep in and create doubts.

But then she heard the familiar sound of the front door opening and closing and Beau's footsteps moving promptly and deliberately up the stairs, with no delay for even a brief conversation. Greatly relieved, Graciela rose to her feet and—filled with excited anticipation—straightened the folds of her gown around her.

There was a gentle warning knock before Beau opened the door and stepped into the room. She faced him expectantly, with a smile. His first reaction was a delighted gasp, but before the smile of pleasure took over his face completely, his eyes rested on her hair, and the smile became an angry frown. "What have you done?" he demanded.

She did not move or speak, but stood where she was, staring blankly into his angry eyes, her strength of purpose melting away. Even when quiet, Beau seemed to overwhelm his surroundings, but his anger could blot out the entire world. More than anything she might want for herself or for her friends, she wanted to please Beau. However, she did not want to please him with artifice or pretense or anything false to her own character. She wanted her peculiar, distinc-

23

tive attributes to give him joy. When they did not—as now—she experienced bitterness and frustration.

She could not prevent the shameful blush from rising in her cheeks, nor could she control the tears that stung her eyes. When they came, the sobs took over completely, and she swiftly turned away from her husband to seek shelter in the shadows of the room.

"Tears won't work with me, my dear," Beau said coldly behind her. "You should know that by now. I suggest that you sit down and do your hair again, this time the right way. There'll be plenty of time while I get dressed."

"No," Graciela said meekly. "I won't be going with you."

Beau moved swiftly, took her by the arm, and turned her to face him. "Don't be a damn fool!" he snapped, his jaw rigid. "You are going, and you will look and act like a lady. Remember our bargain. You are entirely free, so long as you keep up appearances."

That was her opportunity to speak, to voice her protest that she was not free, that his form of marriage had enslaved her more surely than the accident of her birth, but she said nothing. She stood silently staring at him through angry, tear-filled eyes, and she continued to stare as he stalked out of the room, slamming the door behind him. Then she sat down at her dressing table and proceeded to do as he had instructed.

24

Graciela maintained her silent, expressionless obedience as they left for the ball, though she seethed with anger and resentment inside. However, as their open carriage set off down the hill, she could not look at Beau, who was seated beside her; she feared, if she did look into his eyes, she might break into tears again. Instead, she watched the festivities that were continuing in the darkened streets.

The night hid many of the reminders of the devastating fires that had destroyed the city three times—the soot, the debris, the few partially charred buildings that remained. But there was still the smell of smoke and ashes that would not go away, tonight heightened by the torches carried by many of the men in the street. Phoenix-like, the crude, sprawling town had begun to grow out of the still-warm ashes after each catastrophe, with hardly a thought to the loss. After the last fire—the one that had destroyed Frisco's gambling house—a few of the people had decided to rebuild their homes and businesses of brick, but most had persisted in their faith in wood, and so the danger of fire remained ever present in the minds of the populace.

As they rode down Battery Road toward Market Street, the crowds grew in size and increased in exuberance. The crude streets and roads were not made for carriages—Beau's was one of only three in the entire city—and so they were difficult enough to traverse even without the shoving and jostling of the people on foot and riding horseback.

Under other circumstances, that might have annoyed Graciela, but tonight the unrestrained enthusiasm and joy buoyed her spirits, and she felt an additional pleasure at Beau's discomfort. He had been trying in recent months to give the impression he was far above the masses of people. Now, caught in the masses, he had difficulty maintaining his composure. "Keep moving," he shouted to the driver. "If they won't get out of the way, run 'em down!"

"I can't do that, Mr. Tolliver," the driver cut back. "There are too many of 'em! If you don't like the way I'm managing, you git up here and take the reins."

As Beau settled back into the seat, grumbling to himself, Graciela had to restrain herself from giggling out loud. The driver was Mike Welsh, a former Sydney Duck who had worked for her at one time as a bodyguard, and who still occasionally did odd jobs for them. He was a brawny, earthy man, incapable of pretensions or fine manners. He deferred to Beau as "Mister" only out of consideration for Lyuba's position in their household. Although he had never spoken to her of marriage, Mike had long had more than a passing interest in the gypsy fortune-teller.

Then suddenly, the fireworks began out over the bay, great streamers of fire shooting up from one of the boats and bursting into brilliant colors, accompanied by the regular booming of cannons and the snap of riflefire.

Graciela was so moved she forgot her silence. "Oh, how beautiful," she exclaimed, as one flowerlike pattern after another lit up the sky. "Let's stop the carriage so we can watch!"

"Don't be absurd!" Beau snapped. "If we stop here, we'll never get to the ball."

"Oh, forget the ball!" Graciela replied irritably. "We could have much more fun here than we could with that bunch of stuffed shirts."

"That bunch of stuffed shirts, as you call them," Beau said coldly, "happen to be our friends. They're expecting us to be there."

"Sometimes I think you're stuffier than all of them put together," she said disparagingly, then turned back to watch the fireworks.

It was not until that moment that she noticed the man staring at her. He was an old man, dirty and ill-kempt and bearded, wearing patched, ill-fitting clothes. He was a familiar type on the streets of San Francisco, a miner in from the goldfields for a brief holiday.

When her eye caught his, he grinned and blushed with embarrassment. Sheepishly he stepped up to the carriage and spoke. "Ma'am, I hope you'll pardon me for lookin' at you so hard, but it's been over a year since I seen a woman, and quite a few years since I seen a beautiful lady like yourself."

Graciela smiled warmly, with full understanding. She had heard that some miners would walk thirty miles when they heard a man had a wife or daughter in camp, just so they could stare at the women's clothing hanging on a line to dry.

"Thank you," she said genuinely. "I consider that a fine compliment."

"If you wouldn't mind my askin'," he again blushed, shuffling his feet hesitantly, "do you think I could shake your hand?"

"Of course," Graciela replied, extending a white-gloved hand. As he took it gratefully, respectfully, she added, "In fact, you can have more than that." And she leaned over from the carriage to give him a kiss on the forehead.

Suddenly a great shout and round of applause broke out around them, and she realized the crowd had been watching.

"My God," she heard Beau groan behind her.

Before he could say more, another man stepped forward from the crowd, asking with a grin, "Ma'am, may I shake your hand?"

Graciela laughed with the joke. "Of course," she replied, extending over to shake his hand and give him a kiss on the forehead.

There was another whoop from the crowd, and the men began to line up by the carriage, each grinning and asking the same, each receiving the handshake and the kiss, until Beau shouted out, "That's enough, Graciela! Your behavior is disgraceful! We must move on!"

There was a loud unanimous booing from the crowd, and one man even threw a half-eaten apple at Beau. Increasing his fury, Graciela laughed. Beau could not bear even gentle mockery. He stormed to his feet, leaped to the driver's seat, pushing Mike Welsh to the ground, and took the whip and reins. He did not sit, but stood in the front of the carriage and slashed the whips viciously on the horse's flanks, causing it to rare up violently and then charge ahead through the crowd, sending men scurrying and stumbling against each other to get out of the way. Several men yelled with pain as they were shoved aside by the horse and by the carriage wheels, but to Graciela's relief none fell beneath the wheels.

She did not scream; nor did she protest Beau's foolhardy action; she was too stunned by the suddenness to do anything except fall back against the seat in terror. The streets ahead were no less crowded than where they had been, but the commotion had caused the crowd to part and allow them through. They were only a block away from the Oriental Hotel on Market Street when the horse slowed its pace, and Graciela could catch her breath. "You're insane, Beau Tolliver," she said loudly, her voice shaking. "You could have killed someone."

"Yes, my dear," he said fiercely without turning to look at her, "and it could have been you. And if you ever do anything like that again, I still might."

3

It was going to be a difficult night. By the time Beau and Graciela arrived at the ballroom of the Oriental Hotel, neither was speaking to the other. They managed to remain polite and gracious as they passed through the reception line, but the anger they felt for each other continued to simmer beneath the surface. In Graciela's view, there was no real difference between the guests at the ball and the people in the street. A distinction was made—in the dress of both men and women—but it was truly a superficial distinction.

As elsewhere, men here far outnumbered women, and most made no concession in manners. They may not have removed their coats out of deference to the ladies, but their speech remained loud and boisterous and filled with obscenities. They used the cuspidors for spitting their foul-smelling tobacco juice only if the cuspidors were handy; otherwise they used the highly polished oak floors or the Oriental carpets. When they drank too much whiskey—as most did—they were just as offensive as other men.

Graciela did not really object to that—refinement had no real place in the crude frontier surroundings. What she objected to was that the women had to pretend not to notice. They had to behave as if they were back East in Boston or New York or Philadelphia, and the men attending were the finest dandies and gentlemen. Since there were only a dozen "ladies," and hundreds of "gentlemen," that was extremely difficult to do.

However, there was one blessing: Graciela could easily manage to see very little of Beau. There would be so many men vying for her attention, she could ignore her husband completely if she chose to. On these occasions, it was expected that wives and daughters would spread their favors around graciously among the single men or those who had left wives and families in their home states. Though many of them undoubtedly found other forms of female companionship at times, these social functions provided their only acceptable contact.

But first it was necessary to greet the other ladies present. As the evening began, the large room was segregated into distinctive clusters. The married couples hovered just inside the entrance on one side of the room, with their young sons

31

and daughters on the other side. The unattached men of good New England families all collected at the far end of the room in a rather restrained group. Those from the Old South—the Virginians and Carolinians—laughed and joked together near the French doors, and just outside on the veranda. Those men of less distinguished heritage who had made names for themselves since the Gold Rush were the loudest and most noticeable group, laughing and joking with each other around the punch bowl, which had obviously already been strongly laced with spirits.

When the orchestra, consisting of a piano and two violins, began to play, the men would choose partners to dance, and the groups would mix.

After a few polite, restrained words to the Royces, Beau guided Graciela to the grouping of husbands and wives. It was here that she could break free of Beau's arm to chat inanely with the two Mrs. McAllisters, with Jessie Fremont and Phoebe Hearst and Octavia Boggs, or, more accurately, to smile and nod pleasantly in response to their inanities.

It was a great relief to Graciela when the music started, and the gentlemen rushed to collect the ladies for the first reel. First in the race to reach Graciela was Nicholas de Peyster, scion of the New York Knickerbockers, a handsome young man, though no less stuffy than Beau.

The winner of the second dance, however, was a stranger to her, though she recognized his name when he introduced himself. "Albert Valery," he said, bowing low to kiss her hand ostentatiously, then leading her into the dance before she could object.

The arrogant little Frenchman was not what she would have expected from what Lillian had told her. He was indeed intimidating, but it was more his manner than his size that created the effect. He was small and wiry, with a narrow, small-eyed face like a ferret. His well-oiled, curling mustache gave him a rather comical look, but the malice in his dark little eyes told one not to laugh. His brocaded vest and his small delicate fingers glittered with jewels.

"We have a mutual friend, I believe," he said with a sly smirk, as he led her into the dance. "Miss Annie Laurie Crawford."

Graciela realized that he was testing her, trying to find out if she knew precisely what their relationship had become. She did not like his offensive manner, and so she was determined to give him little satisfaction.

"Yes," she said coldly. "I understand she has indentured herself as your parlor maid. I have thought about calling upon her to see if she is satisfied with the position."

This response startled Valery. "I hardly think that would be appropriate for a lady of your station," he replied. Then he added snidely, "Your *new* station."

Graciela chose to ignore the implication. "She

was formerly in my employ," she said, "and I am interested in her welfare." She gave him a cold, haughty glare, as the dance required her to step forward, curtsey slightly, then step back. "I trust she is well."

"Quite well," he replied, "though she has a rather rebellious temperament, frequently requiring punishment."

"Oh?" Graciela arched her brow. "That's surprising. I always found her quite eager to please. Is it possible you are not treating her properly?"

That query was clearly unsettling to Albert Valery. A flicker of fear crossed his brow, and he hesitated, not knowing quite how he should answer. Then, quickly, a broad grin covered the doubt. "Mrs. Tolliver," he said in mock reproach, "I fear you have been jesting with me."

"Oh, no," Graciela replied. "I never jest."

As the dance ended and Valery escorted her from the floor, Graciela added, "I am quite serious in my concern for Annie Laurie. Do you think I might call upon her sometime soon?"

Again there was the flicker of nervousness. "I don't really think that would be very wise," he said politely.

"Would you permit me to see her?" Graciela cut back sharply.

His agitation increased. "I am quite aware of your former station in life," he said grimly, "but others obviously are not. They might start to ask questions if you were to call to see one of my . . ." He hesitated. ". . . servants."

"Could I see her?" Graciela repeated, this time more adamantly.

"If you insist," he replied stonily, then took his leave.

The next two dances passed uneventfully, though Graciela had difficulty keeping her mind on her partners. She continued to think about Albert Valery, and about Annie Laurie. The little Frenchman had said nothing directly to confirm what she had been told, yet everything about him told her it was true. His repugnant manner served to fuel the anger that had been simmering in her all day. Within moments, that anger would blaze forth as suddenly and devastatingly as the fires that continually swept through San Francisco.

Graciela took little note of the couple who arrived at the ball late. She recognized Jim McCabe, the owner of the El Dorado gambling house, though she did not know the woman on his arm. She was an attractive woman—well dressed and as elegantly mannered as any other woman present. There was, as far as Graciela could see, nothing untoward in her appearance.

Graciela had just concluded a dance with Charles Fairfax as they entered the room, and was being escorted to her position by the French doors, where other partners were waiting. But halfway across the dance floor, Charles Fairfax stopped suddenly to stare in horrified silence at the couple. It took Graciela a moment to realize that he had reacted just as every other man in the room had done. The women—or at least most of them—were as curious and as confused as Graciela was.

The men obviously knew the woman on Jim McCabe's arm, though the women obviously did not. No one—man or woman—moved to greet them or to welcome them to the ball. Everyone stared in silence—a silence that crackled with hostility. Then the whispers began to hiss through the room.

"It's Mrs. Liz Nivens, the Madam."

"She runs the place on Washington Street. Across from the plaza."

"They say she lured her girls away from the best families in the South."

Sarah Royce made the first move, signaling the band to resume playing. Then, with the couple headed toward her as if to speak, she pointedly turned her back on them and walked toward the refreshment table, her head high and haughty.

To Graciela's astonishment, it was Beau who made the next move. He spoke rapidly to the three men at his side—George Hearst, General Hitchcock, and General Wilson—and the four of them advanced menacingly on the couple.

Several couples had returned to the dance floor, and Graciela was being importuned to join them. "You've promised me this dance," William Botts was reminding her politely but persistently.

However, Graciela could not reply. She could not even look at him. She was too intent upon what was happening across the room. Apprehension surged at her breast; anger began to rise in her cheeks, as she strained to hear what Beau was saying to the couple.

The words came to her indistinctly: "You've made a grievous error, McCabe. I suggest that you correct it." Beau's anger was barely controlled.

McCabe smiled. "I realize we're late, Beau," he said, "but I'm sure everyone will accept our apologies. It's almost impossible to get through the crowds in the . . ."

"That's not what I'm referring to," Beau snapped back more loudly, "and you know it, McCabe."

"Please, Jim," Liz Nivens said in embarrassment, "I think we should go."

"No," McCabe replied, keeping a defiant gaze on Beau. "No one has given us a reason to leave."

"We know what you're up to," Beau challenged. "It's spread all over town, boasting you could take Liz Nivens anywhere. We're here to tell you that you're mistaken."

"If we're to leave," McCabe's eyes narrowed, "you're going to have to give us a reason."

"If you'll just step outside with me," Beau said, "I'll be glad to give you one."

Graciela knew by the tone in Beau's voice what he intended to do, and she was mortified. Her anger now blazed forth without control. As Beau and the other men escorted the couple toward the door, she moved swiftly to catch up with them, silently cursing the swaying hoop of her crinolines for impeding her progress.

They had already left the room before she could reach them. In the hotel foyer, Beau struck the first blow, as Graciela screamed, "Stop it, Beau!"

He turned to tell her, "Stay out of this; it's none of your affair!" As he did, he took a blow from McCabe squarely on the jaw, sending him flying backward.

Graciela rushed to step between the two men. "It *is* my affair," she said hotly, "anytime you try to make a fool of yourself."

Recovering from the blow, Beau advanced on her menacingly. "Get out of my way, my dear," he commanded. "I will not have you interfering in this."

Graciela did not budge an inch. Instead of obeying, she folded her arms defiantly over her breast. In one swift, fierce movement, Beau grabbed her by the shoulders, lifted her off the floor and thrust her aside. Then he lunged at Jim McCabe.

Unable in her fury to watch further, Graciela pulled away from the protective arm of George Hearst to rush across the foyer and out the front door onto Market Street. There she stopped. Faced with the massive, now drunken crowd, she hesitated. Even if she did find the carriage, she would have little chance of getting it home safely without the protection of Beau or Mike.

Tears of rage and frustration smarted at her eyes. Standing on the steps of the Oriental Hotel, she was trapped between two worlds. She could not move forward into the rough masses, and she would not return to the supposedly polite society inside the hotel, where she belonged.

As she stood there helplessly, the sobs breaking over her body, a pleasant motherly voice spoke to her. "Mrs. Tolliver, I want to apologize to you," Liz Nivens said from behind her. "This is my fault really. I should never have agreed to come with Jim."

Graciela was so surprised by the unexpected words that her sobs ceased. She turned and stared at Mrs. Nivens. If she had not known otherwise, it would have been difficult for Graciela to imagine her the keeper of a bagnio. She was pretty, in a plain way, with straight, honey-colored hair and green eyes. Her green silk dress was elegant though not ostentatious. Her manner was dignified, though perhaps a bit more direct and forthright than one would find among polite society.

"You see," the older woman continued, "he made a bet with some friends that he could take me anywhere in San Francisco. He was challenged to escort me to Mrs. Royce's ball. I didn't eally want to come. I know I don't belong among you people."

"Perhaps not," Graciela replied genuinely. "I can't judge that. But if you don't belong here, then neither do a great many of the men in that room."

Mrs. Nivens smiled with understanding. "I agree," she said, "but men expect a great deal more from ladies than they do from each other. Don't judge your husband too harshly. Go back inside and enjoy the celebration."

"No," Graciela said flatly. "I can't do that." She blushed faintly. "If I did, I might just cause a bigger scene than you have."

"Well, you mustn't stand here alone," Mrs. Nivens advised. "And it isn't particularly wise to be seen in my company. Perhaps one of the gentlemen might take you home."

Graciela shook her head. "The only gentlemen I know are friends of Beau's," she explained, "and I don't think any of them would want to offend him."

At that moment, two men stepped out of the door of the hotel.

"Perhaps I can help," Mrs. Nivens suggested, then turned to the men, speaking to the taller of the two. "Tom," she called out, "could I ask you to help a lady in distress?"

The man turned. He was hardly older than Graciela and incredibly handsome, with black hair, a strong lean face, and laughing dark eyes.

Those eyes twinkled mischievously as he grinned at Mrs. Nivens. "Are *you* the lady in distress?" he asked.

"Of course not," Liz Nivens cut back with bemusement. "Mrs. Tolliver needs someone to escort her home safely. Would you mind?"

"Mrs. Beau Tolliver?" he asked incredulously, looking at Graciela for the first time. In his eyes, there was a look she could not recognize. He removed his tophat, swept it down before him, and bowed low. "I would be deeply honored."

His name was Tom Blanchard. Graciela learned that much before he helped her into her carriage and then got in himself and took the reins. Other than that, she knew nothing about the man. He had clearly been a guest at the ball, yet she had never even heard his name.

4

There was something about Tom Blanchard that excited Graciela. It may have been the laughing eyes; it may have been his dark, slender good looks; or it may have been his enigmatic silence. Whatever it was, Graciela wanted to know more about this young man with an air of mystery about him.

As they drove through the dark, crowded streets of San Francisco toward Telegraph Hill, she endeavored to learn more about him. "Are you new to San Francisco?" she asked, pretending only mild curiosity.

"Yes," he replied, offering nothing further.

"How long have you been here?"

He shrugged. "Only a couple of weeks."

"Where do you come from?"

Again he shrugged. "Back East."

Obviously, he had some reason for wanting to keep such matters to himself. This was not unusual among the citizens of San Francisco. The West was filled with men seeking to escape from unsavory or unhappy pasts. Normally, Graciela would not have cared; she accepted most people for what they appeared to be. But inexplicably she wanted to know about Tom Blanchard.

After a few moments she decided to try again. "Are you planning to settle in San Francisco?" she asked.

"I'm considering it," he said.

"Do you have a business or profession in mind?" she pursued.

"Possibly."

His evasiveness was beginning to grow irritating. Graciela emitted a little sigh of annoyance.

Tom Blanchard noticed and flashed his impish smile at her. "I'm not trying to be rude, Mrs. Tolliver," he said. "But I think you will be much better off not knowing much about me. Your husband will be very upset when he learns I have escorted you home."

"You know Beau?" Graciela asked.

"Yes," Tom nodded, "but it cannot be said that we are friends. In fact, the contrary is true. We are rivals in business, if not outright enemies."

Graciela understood immediately. Though she had not heard the name "Tom Blanchard," she had heard Beau speak of the B&B Overland

Trading Company, which had been undercutting almost every item Beau had shipped around the Horn from the East. Beau would be angry that she had left the ball without him; if he knew she had accepted a ride from his greatest rival, he would be furious.

In her present frame of mind, that delighted Graciela, and she began to scheme of how she might reveal this fact to her husband without being too obvious. As it turned out, there was no need for scheming.

They had just arrived at the large, wood-framed Tolliver home on Telegraph Hill, and Tom Blanchard was gallantly helping Graciela step down from the carriage, when Beau rode up. The borrowed horse had clearly been ridden at top speed; its coat was heavily lathered, and it gasped and snorted in resentment. As for Beau himself, Graciela had never seen him so enraged. Slightly bruised and dishevelled from his fight with Jim McCabe, there was murder in his eyes as he leaped from the horse and bore down upon Tom Blanchard.

"What the hell do you think . . . ?" he shouted belligerently, then broke off as he recognized Tom. "You!" he declared grimly. "First you steal my business, and now you steal my wife." Then he moved slowly forward, his body tensed, his pale face burning with crimson.

Graciela stepped defiantly between the two

44

men. "Mr. Blanchard did not steal me," she said haughtily. "He very gallantly rescued me from the mob on the street. Since you were otherwise occupied, I think you should thank him."

"I'll thank him, all right," Beau said between clenched teeth. "I'll thank him to keep his hands off what's mine!"

Tom Blanchard refused to hide behind Graciela's skirts. He stepped aside to confront Beau himself, but when he spoke, his voice was placating. "I have nothing against you personally, Tolliver," he said. "But if I might offer a bit of advice, you'd never have cause to lose anything that's yours if you kept your hands on it."

"I don't need advice from you," Beau snapped back. "But I'll give you some. I suggest you get out of here right now and stay away from my wife and my house."

That mischievous, mocking light flickered in Tom Blanchard's eyes as he tipped his hat and gave a bow to Beau. "Your servant, sir," he said. Then he bowed more genuinely to Graciela. "And yours, madame."

With that, he donned his hat again, straightened his shoulders, and set off with dignity down the road toward the town. Graciela could not prevent a feeling of admiration for the way the young man handled himself, just as she could not help the disdain she felt for her husband's behavior. She did not want to confront Beau right now, because she knew she would melt before his stronger personality. She would give in as she had time after time and never express the complaints she had. Quickly, she turned and—with the same dignity Tom had shown—marched up to the front door of the house, leaving Beau to look after the carriage.

He caught up with her as she was climbing the stairs to her room. "Just a moment, my dear, I want to talk to you."

Graciela paused, but she would not turn to look at him. "But I don't wish to speak to you," she said, her voice quavering for strength. Then she continued to climb the stairs.

"That doesn't matter!" he shouted back, a bit louder this time. "I'll do the talking, and you'll do the listening!"

She hesitated only a moment, then continued her silent climb toward the stair landing. She had almost reached it when Beau came bounding after her, his boots shaking the staircase as he took the steps three at a time. He caught her at the very top, grabbing her by the arm, and turning her violently to face him. His fingers dug into her flesh; his face, only inches from hers, seemed insane with rage. "When I tell you to do something," he growled, "you will do it."

She struggled to find a voice that would resist, that would say no, but the best she could manage was to say meekly, "You're hurting me. Please let go."

He did not respond immediately, but stood there clutching her tightly, angrily, as if he had not heard. Then he hesitated, dropping his eyes to the steps beneath his feet as he released his grip on her arms. "I'm sorry," he said. "I've never wanted to hurt you."

This was Graciela's chance to escape, but she too hesitated. Intuitively, she knew he meant these words more than he meant his rage; this had come from the old Beau, the Beau she loved so deeply. This was the Beau who could destroy all the willpower she possessed with a glance or a single word.

She forced herself not to look at him, and she tried to pretend that she had not heard his apology. She felt as if her feet were struggling with quicksand as she cleared the landing and proceeded up the second flight of stairs, praying that she could make it to her room where she could think clearly.

"Graciela," Beau's somber voice stopped her, "we can't go on like this."

"No," she replied, her voice hoarse with dread, "we can't."

She looked back questioningly, and his eyes finally caught hers and locked them tightly. "What do you suggest we do about it?" he asked.

This was her chance to speak, to voice all her dissatisfactions. He was giving it to her free and clear. But she was so startled by his manner that she could say nothing. She could only stare at him dumbly, her mouth open. Finally, unable to find the words, she simply shrugged her shoulders, and whispered, "I don't know."

He smiled almost lovingly. "Then why can't you live up to our bargain?" he asked.

It took every ounce of willpower not to break then, not to burst into tears and throw herself into his arms. She had to speak. It was now or never. "Because," she said faintly, her voice quivering, "it wasn't the kind of bargain I could ever live up to. I can't pretend to be something I'm not. If I'm not your wife, and if I'm not my own person, then what am I? I'm nothing more than a slave, and that's what I was running away from all those years."

Beau's brow furrowed as he listened to her words. "That wasn't what I intended," he said defensively. "And you know it wasn't."

"Yes," she replied, "I know. But that's the way it turned out." Gathering courage, she proceeded, "I don't really share in your life at all, except to appear on your arm at social occasions. I have no life of my own except sitting here in this house, staring at walls. I can't run the household; I can't prepare the meals; I can't choose my friends; I can't even go out to buy my own clothes. Every move I make is noted and reported to you. A human being can't live that way. Or at least I can't."

Every word she spoke seemed to hit Beau like a slap in the face, but she was gaining confidence, and she would not let anything deter her.

"Beau," she continued, "do you know what has happened to the girls who used to work for me? Do you have any idea?"

His face flushed, and he nodded.

"They are my friends," she said strongly. "They're the people I care about, not this pompous bunch that calls itself high society."

Graciela could see that she had finally provoked Beau to anger. "Just a moment, my dear," he said, his neck stiff, his shoulders set. "You'd better remember that those pompous members of high society now run this town. If you can't think about your own future, think about your son's. He's going to have to grow up in this town, and respectability is one thing you can't gain after it's taken away from you."

"To hell with respectability," Graciela flashed back. "It doesn't mean a thing without self respect. And after what you did tonight, I don't see how you can have any respect for yourself."

"That woman did not belong in that room!" he shot back loudly.

"Then neither did half the men who were there!" she replied just as vehemently. "How do you think I felt having to dance with Albert Valery? He makes his money the same way Mrs. Nevins does."

Beau was barely able to control his fury. His face was suffused with color, and his clenched fists showed painfully white knuckles, as if he wanted desperately to strike her. His voice was cold and passionless, however, when he said, "I suggest we continue this discussion in the parlor, where the entire household won't hear us." Then he turned and walked down the stairs, without even looking back to see if she was following.

Graciela hesitated a moment. She was afraid of what Beau might do to her once he had her alone behind closed doors. His mood was volatile. But she had managed thus far to speak her mind; she might never get the courage again. With her heart beating wildly in her breast, she followed him.

He waited at the open doorway until she was inside the parlor, then he closed the door securely behind them, and gestured toward the ornately carved, tufted-satin sofa. "If you will sit down," he said rigidly, "we will discuss this in a civilized manner."

Graciela sat obediently, and Beau seated himself in a matching armchair across the round oak table. With a sigh of weary resignation, he said, "I should have known I could never tame that wild gypsy spirit of yours. I had hoped that we might be able to settle down into a nice quiet life, and perhaps eventually you might come to love me."

Graciela's heart leaped, urging her to protest, "But I do love you. That's part of the problem." However, she could not allow herself to give up her air of defiance.

"Considering the fact that we are not really legally married," he continued, "I'm afraid a divorce will be out of the question. The only thing I can suggest, if it's acceptable to you, of course, is that we go our separate ways for a while. Perhaps eventually, we can find some honorable way out of the situation."

A terrible sinking feeling came over Graciela. This was not what she had intended. She had wanted simply to have some small degree of freedom to choose how and with whom she would spend her days. But Beau did not give her an opportunity to protest.

"You have voiced your dissatisfaction with our arrangement," he went on. "I have had a few problems with it as well. I have felt obliged to remain here in San Francisco with you, even though my business has suffered as a result."

Graciela was astonished by this revelation. There had not been the slightest hint that Beau had needed to travel for his business. "What do you mean?" she asked hoarsely.

"That young man who escorted you home is a part of the problem," he explained. "This past year, the land routes from East to West have improved considerably. His company is now able to bring goods in more quickly and cheaply than I can by shipping around the Horn. I have an idea for solving this problem, and I have been corresponding with the Colombian government on the matter. A canal or railroad across the isthmus of Central America would make my shipments even faster than his. However, no decision can be made until I can go down to Colombia and Panama to look into the possibilities."

"But you should have gone," Graciela protested. "I have never wanted to interfere with your business."

"Perhaps not," Beau admitted, "but I have felt an obligation." He smiled. "Seeing how you feel, I realize I have been extremely foolish."

Graciela had completely forgotten about her own problems now. She could think only of the fact that she would be losing Beau, and that was a loss much greater than her freedom. After all that she had said and done, she could now offer no protest. She could do nothing but let him go. "How long will you be gone?" she asked.

Beau shrugged. "A month, two months," he said. "Perhaps as long as a year. It depends on what I find there." He paused, then added, "Of course, I'll make sure you are well taken care of. I'll see that you have an income from the business. And I'm sure that Senator Broderick and George Hearst and others will be available in case you need help or advice." He hesitated, glanced down at his lap. "If you decide you want your independence, all of your own money is sitting in the bank in your name."

5

What if Beau should not return? That question plagued Graciela throughout the week he was preparing to depart for Colombia. She would not be able to bear not seeing him again. She thought continually of all the good things about Beau, the things she had forgotten during the months of her unhappiness—of how kind and generous he had been toward her in the beginning, how strong and courageous he was, how patient he could be. And, hadn't it been, after all, her own fault she had not been happy with him? If she had only spoken up at the outset, insisted that she did not want a sham marriage with him—indeed, if she had simply said, "I love you, Beau, with all my heart"—none of this would ever have happened.

She had driven him to this intolerable position

by her silence, and she now felt both guilty and bitter about it. Guilty because she had hurt him, turned him into something not natural to his own gentle inclinations. Bitter because she could not now tell him the truth for fear he might feel compelled to stay in San Francisco and neglect his business. All she could do was remain silent and pray that he would come back to her.

Her fears were increased by Beau's behavior. He seemed to have no regrets at leaving her; if anything, there was only relief in his eyes, and in his manner. He had thrown himself into his preparations with the energy and the enthusiasm of the old Beau. He would come home to sleep and to eat his meals, but always he couldn't wait to get back to his office, even in the evenings.

Graciela now had the complete freedom that had been promised her at the outset of their living relationship, and—like it or not—she had to be satisfied with it. To her surprise, Beau seemed almost pleased to learn that Lillian was staying as their house guest; and, when the two women talked vaguely about the possibility of reopening Frisco's, he offered no objections. "It might be a good thing," was his only comment. "It'll give you ladies something to do."

But Graciela hesitated. Beau was still the center of her world, and she still secretly hoped something might happen to change his mind, to make him turn to her and say, "I love you, Graciela, and I can't live without you."

In one of their long talks during the days of waiting for Beau's departure, she tried to explain that to Lillian, but the younger woman either could not or would not understand. Lillian had her mind on only one thing—the return to the good old days of Frisco's.

Graciela indulged her in these moments, partly because she cared about her friend and wanted to see her happy again, and partly because she genuinely recalled those days with nostalgic pleasure. Gradually, with proper food, rest, and relaxation, Lillian was beginning to restore herself physically. She was gaining her weight back, and the healthy pink glow was returning to her cheeks. The more they talked of Frisco's, the more the happy sparkle appeared again in Lillian's blue eyes.

Graciela knew that with all the money she had in the bank, she could easily rebuild Frisco's. She could put all of the old girls back to work again, or at least all those who yearned to return to respectability. At times, she was tempted, but she was careful not to say anything that would encourage Lillian in her hopes. A decision would have to wait until after Beau was gone. After all, he might yet change his mind.

But he did not. The day of his departure dawned cool and brisk, with lovely white clouds scudding across the autumn blue sky. Graciela lingered in bed that morning, hoping Beau might come into her room to speak to her. Seeing her lying there alluring and inviting, he might sit down beside her, sweep her into his arms, and make love to her as proof that he loved her and would return to her.

As she lay there dreaming of his embrace, there was a knock at the door. In delighted anticipation, she adjusted herself on the pillows and called, "Come in."

But it was not Beau who entered.

Lyuba had a worried scowl on her face as she came into the room. Even normally, with a cheerful expression on her brow, Lyuba's face could not be described as a pretty one. Scowling, she gave the impression of a thunderstorm approaching, her black eyes like twin claps of thunder.

"We have a problem," she announced as soon as she had secured the door behind her. "It is the little one."

"Alex?" Graciela sat up in bed anxiously. "What's wrong with him? Is he sick?"

Lyuba shrugged. "Sick at heart," she said. "He won't get dressed. He won't eat. I cannot get him to do anything. He just covers his head with his pillows weeping because Mr. Tolliver is leaving him."

Graciela castigated herself for being a fool, thinking selfishly that only she would miss Beau. Of course, little Alex would be heartbroken; although Beau was not his real father, he was the only father the child had known. He would be as upset as Graciela was, if not actually more so. He adored Beau and constantly sought excuses to be with him. "I'll see what I can do," Graciela said, throwing back the covers and stepping out of bed and into her slippers.

As she helped Graciela into the white lace dressing gown, Lyuba told her morosely, "I have never seen him like this. Most things he understands and accepts. He is such a wise child. But this . . ." She left her thoughts unsaid.

Graciela knew what she was thinking. She too had long suspected her son had inherited the Sight. It was in his Romany blood, the ability to see and know the future intuitively. And what Graciela feared was that Alex knew he would never again see the man he called "Papa."

The Sight was a power that could fade if it was not used regularly, if it was not recognized and nurtured. Graciela's own abilities had slackened considerably since her marriage; it was something that was discouraged in the world of the *gaje*, and she had tried to fit with their ways.

With Lyuba following close behind, Graciela hurried anxiously down the hall to Alex's room. She really did not have a great deal of confidence that she could do or say anything that would help, especially when Lyuba, who was closer to the child than anyone else, had failed to comfort him. It was perhaps as much for herself as for Alex that she went to him.

If she had not been told he was in the room, she would have assumed it was empty. No painful sobs broke the air. Alex's little bed seemed merely to have been left in disarray for Carlotta or Lyuba to put back in order, with bedclothes and pillows piled up in the very center. However, Graciela knew that Alex was hiding quietly beneath that pile, keeping his lonely pain to himself. She also knew he would not welcome her intrusion into his privacy.

She perched herself tentatively on the foot of his bed. She did not reach out a hand to remove the covers, but merely said gently, "Alex, I'd like to speak to you."

At first, the covers did not even move, but Graciela was willing to be patient. After a respectful moment, she prodded, "I know you're not sleeping, and I know you'd rather not speak to me right now, but it's important. There are some things we have to do to help your papa."

Again, there was only silence for a long contemplative moment. Then there was a slight tremor beneath the covers, and after another moment, a deeper roll. Finally, a slight crevice appeared, and slowly a small dark face, ringed with lustrous black curls, came into view. His big dark eyes glistened with moisture, and they were ringed with painful red circles from weeping. He stared up at her guardedly, suspicious that she was patronizing him. When he had finally decided that she was not, he asked, "What do we have to do?"

"This trip Papa's going on is going to be very

difficult," she explained as cheerfully as she could. "He's had a lot to do to get ready for it. His boat is going to leave today, and he's still not ready. He's going to miss us both very much, so I think we should try to help him."

"How?" Alex asked.

Graciela smiled. "First we can help him make sure he has everything ready to go," she said. "Then, I think we should help him take all his baggage down to the boat." She gave him an earnest, serious look. "But, when we say good-bye to him, we mustn't cry or look sad, because it will make him feel unhappy."

Alex furrowed his brow pensively. "But what if he looks sad?"

"He knows he'll be coming back to us," Graciela said firmly. "He won't look sad if we don't give him a chance to."

"How do you know he'll be coming back?" he asked in angelic innocence. "Something could happen to him."

Alex had asked the question she had dreaded, the one she could not answer honestly. And so she responded with a question. "What could possibly happen to him?"

"I don't know," Alex shrugged. "Just something."

Her heart sank. The child did see something; something dreadful he could not put into words. She wanted desperately to know what it was he saw, but she feared pressing him further, afraid it would upset him again. To avoid confronting the question, she took her child into her arms and hugged him. She could not let him see her eyes when she lied. "Nothing will happen, dearest sweetheart," she soothed. "He will return to us just as healthy and happy as he left. You'll see."

Then her averted eyes caught Lyuba's, and they were disapproving. Lyuba also saw the truth, and she knew—just as Graciela knew—that this form of lying was exactly the way the *gaje* blocked out the Sight, denied the truth to themselves, and deprived themselves of a basic human instinct. In her eyes, it was a crime to destroy this gift in a child of the Rom.

However, Graciela had little other choice in the situation. To make light of the moment, in hopes it would have no lasting impression on the child, she chose to move on swiftly to other matters. She released Alex from the embrace, and adopted a blithe and businesslike manner. "Now," she said, rising to her feet, "we must both get dressed quickly and get downstairs to see what we can do for Papa. All right?"

Alex nodded, and gave a brave little smile.

Actually, once they were downstairs, there was little either of them could do to help Beau prepare for his departure. He had things very well in hand. But Graciela managed to pull Beau aside for a moment to tell him, "Alex feels very much neglected. To lift his spirits I've told him you need his help, so if you don't mind . . ."

Beau understood, and he came up with numerous small errands and tasks for the child. There was a link between stepfather and boy that did not even exist in her blood tie; it was perhaps a matter of gender more than of inheritance. It was something that Alex needed, and she could not give him. That knowledge made her feel even more guilty about allowing the breach between her and Beau to exist.

As she saw the two of them communicating without words, saw them working and laughing together in mystical understanding, she realized that, before Beau left, she would have to do or say something that would encourage him to return to them. But there was no opportunity while they were loading the buckboard and getting the carriage ready. She was so useless, she might as well have been invisible.

The town was bristling with activity by the time they set off down the hill toward the bay. Mike Welsh took charge of the buckboard, and Beau drove the carriage himself. Lyuba came along to take care of Alex, but there was nothing for her to do. Alex rode up front with Beau, and Graciela and Lyuba sat silently in back, mute outsiders, while Beau and Alex chattered away.

"There's the boat I'm taking," Beau pointed toward the forests of masts set starkly against the deep blue sea. "Can you see it? It's called the *Gold Coast*, and it's that one far down to the left, set apart slightly from the others."

Alex insisted he could distinguish the boat, though Graciela could not pick it out. There were literally hundreds of boats there, many of them abandoned by captains who forsook the sea for the gold fields, leaving their charges there simply to rot. Some had been converted into homes or businesses during the housing shortage after the last fire, but most were sad and lonely derelicts, a ghost fleet that would never sail again.

There were only four or five, all of them in that group to the left, that were now used for sailing, and Graciela could not determine which of them would be taking Beau away from them—perhaps forever. In her heart, she wished the *Gold Coast* were not there, she prayed that it had already sailed, or perhaps might sail before they reached the docks. She could turn to Beau and say, "It's an omen. You weren't meant to go, so you might as well stay with us." Of course, that was fantasy. Beau didn't believe in omens.

And the boat was there waiting when they arrived. It would have been waiting even if Beau had been late, not because Beau was such an important passenger—though he was—but because most boats had very few passengers leaving San Francisco, compared to the number who sailed in with them.

Graciela's anxiety had become almost unbearable by the time they had arrived at the noisy hustle and bustle of the ship. She had had no chance to speak to Beau. Now she feared the excitement of boarding would keep them apart or hopelessly caught up with others. In this cacophonous chaos, there could not possibly be privacy. Certainly there could be no tenderness.

In confirmation of her fears, Beau was completely taken up with getting all his baggage aboard ship, talking to the captain about the wind, and showing Alex the myriad mysteries connected with sailing. Graciela was left to loiter in the background with Lyuba.

The sense of foreboding she had felt earlier returned as she followed Beau and Alex about the ship. She did not know what it was, but the *Gold Coast* was taking both her and Beau toward unhappiness, though only one of them was actually a passenger. She wanted to weep from frustration at not being able to tell this to Beau, at not being able to prevent disaster.

All the baggage was loaded aboard much too quickly. The other passengers were saying their farewells, and the ship's crew were quickening the pace of their assigned activities. It was almost time for them to set sail, and Beau had given her no opportunity to say even one word to him. If she now had a chance to speak, she would not have time to pick and choose her words. Whatever she said to him, it would have to be quick and abrupt, and she would be left feeling clumsy and foolish. If she were even to be able to say anything to him at all.

As the captain approached Beau, she felt a

numbness in her head and hands, a queasiness in her stomach. She knew what he was going to say, and she wished she could stop him.

"Mr. Tolliver," the captain told him pleasantly. "You'll have to say good-bye to your guests now. We're just about ready to get underway."

Beau nodded in reply, then turned to Alex. "Well, young man," he said heartily, "you heard what the captain said. You're going to have to get off." He squatted down so that he could look the boy in the eye, and told him with a degree of tenderness, "You know, don't you, that I'm counting on you to look after your mother while I'm away. Try to make her smile when you can. She looks so pretty when she smiles."

Then he gave Alex a big hug and said, "We won't say good-bye. We'll be together again before you know it."

Alex did not cry, but the look on his face was more painful than tears. It was loss, hurt, fear, and loneliness all rolled up into one blank expression.

Beau rose to his feet then and turned to Graciela. At that moment, she could not bear to look straight into his beauty. The sunlight cast a rosy golden halo on his wavy hair, illuminating his pale skin like ivory, and filling his sea-green eyes with an ethereal mistiness. His broad shoulders, straining at the mauve linen coat, had never looked more powerful. His muscular legs, moving toward her beneath the fawn-colored trousers, had never possessed such grace. "I hope you'll write to me," he said, and there was restraint in his voice.

Confusion swept over her. "I will," she replied, fighting back tears. "Every week, and you must write to us. Let us know where you are and how you are."

"Of course I will," he said diffidently. He stood before her, his face only a few inches away from hers, looking down at her, but he did not reach out to touch her. His manner remained distant, businesslike. "And if you need anything, you know what to do. The office and the bank both have instructions."

She could not hold back the tears. "Oh, Beau," she sobbed, "be careful. Please come back to us all right."

Suddenly, he swept her into his arms, lifted her face to his, and kissed her. It was a long kiss, desperate with long-controlled passion. She gave into it completely, trying to tell him with her mouth and her embrace what she had been unable to communicate with words.

He withdrew, gently removing her hands from around his waist and cupping them between them in his. "I'll be back," he said. "Don't worry. I have to come back. We have so much to set right between us." Then he ushered them all swiftly to the gangway. "Don't look back," he called out as they descended.

And Graciela obeyed.

PART TWO

6

Once Beau was gone from San Francisco, the idea of rebuilding Frisco's seemed more appealing to Graciela. The sense of foreboding that she had felt before his departure seemed to have departed with him. In its place, she felt a kind of elation, as a prisoner must feel upon being given a reprieve. After all the talks she had had with Lillian about the old days, Graciela was as eager as her young friend to see her gambling establishment back in operation. It was a love more certain and less tractable than any man could be.

In making plans, in managing money, she could dismiss all thoughts of Beau from her mind. Frisco's would belong to her as surely as she had belonged to him, and there was not the entanglement in owning a place that there was in owning or being owned by a person. If anything, it was a comfort and a sustenance.

Graciela was not blind to the fact that San Francisco had changed greatly since her heyday as Frisco. It was a big town now, and hers would be just one of many gaming places, though she did have one thing in her favor. Frisco's had become legend and she knew that legends always improved upon reality, so she had to make the new place even grander than it had been before.

One thing hadn't changed, however: San Francisco was still a rough town for a woman alone. If anything, it was even rougher than it had been before. For Graciela to move as freely in business as a man, she would have to have bodyguards. Along with some of the other Sydney Ducks, Mike Welsh had served that function in the old days and he was willing—if not actually eager— to return to service.

When she asked him, he let out a wild war whoop, tossed his worn, grease-stained hat high into the air, and did a little dance. "You mean it, ma'am?" he asked when he calmed down. "You really mean it?"

She laughed. "Of course I do, Mike. Why shouldn't I mean it?"

"I don't know ma'am." He was embarrassed. "It's just that your life has changed so much. You don't really have to be in business anymore."

"No," she acknowledged. "I'm not rebuilding

Frisco's because I have to. I'm doing it because I want to."

Her reasons for wanting to go back into business were many and varied, but there were none stronger than her desire to help the old friends she had forsaken for so long. Lillian was, of course, elated, but the girl Graciela wanted to help more than any other was Annie Laurie Crawford.

She had been greatly disturbed by Annie Laurie's plight, as described to her by Lillian, and she had been anxious to call on her since the night of the ball. She had not done so, for reasons that were entirely selfish and very reprehensible. If she had visited Albert Valery's house while Beau was still in San Francisco, Beau would certainly have learned of it and he would have disapproved. There would have been another scene at a time when Graciela did not want to upset him. There was also the fact that Graciela did not want to see her former friend and employee until she was sure she could do something to help her.

Now that Beau was gone, Graciela wasted no time. Through Mike, she managed to learn where Valery's establishment was—in a section near Portsmouth Square that had come to be known as Sydneytown. It did not open its doors to customers until late afternoon.

Naturally Mike had insisted upon being told why she wanted to know about such a disreputable place. When she explained, he had insisted upon escorting her there. "It's tucked into an alley off Drumm Street," he had explained. "And besides, it's no place for a lady, even in the daytime."

She heartily agreed with him once she saw the place. Isolated for so long in her house on Telegraph Hill, she had remained unaware of how deeply some San Franciscans had descended into hell. There was no other description for Drumm Street and its lurid alleyways—a writhing, steaming, human hell. Her first sight of the place swept her with revulsion. She wanted to tell Mike to turn around, to take her back home, but she reminded herself that Annie Laurie was living in this place, a virtual prisoner, and she managed to find the fortitude to go on.

The worst of it was the stench—a mixture of rotting garbage, urine, defecation, and vomit, all of which were visible on the sidewalks and in the gutters. Sickly, dirty men lay about in the filth, some sleeping, some probably drunk, and some with every appearance of being dead. Graciela had no idea whether these were homeless men or men who inhabited the buildings in the neighborhood. If they indeed had rooms in these structures, she could easily understand why some would choose to sleep in the street.

She had never in her life seen such a collection of slapdash structures. Even the temporary shacks thrown up after the fire seemed more sound than these. From their appearance it seemed the slightest puff of wind would send them tumbling to the ground. Charred and rotting pieces of timber had been nailed together helter-skelter with no apparent plan or pattern. No window was glazed. Those that were not gaping open like entrances to dismal caverns had either been boarded up or covered with gunny sacks.

Mike stopped the carriage at the entrance to an impassable alley. Graciela's heart ached as she watched a young boy, his legs bent with rickets, cross the alleyway to a large rain barrel. His eyes were small and expressionless, his manner listless. He peered into the rain barrel, reached in, withdrew a dead, drenched rat, dropped it onto the ground, then reached in with cupped hands and began to drink from the barrel.

A hot, flushed sensation swept over Graciela. She felt beads of cold perspiration breaking out on her forehead. She knew she was dangerously close to fainting, and she forced herself to turn away, gulping air frantically.

"Here, boy," she heard Mike call out, through the ringing in her ears, "want to earn a nickel?"

"Sure," the boy responded, his voice betraying doubts of Mike's sincerity. "What do I have to do?"

"Just keep an eye on the carriage for me."

Graciela was still feeling weak as Mike helped her down and escorted her down the alley toward a door that was easily distinguished from all the others because it boasted paint—faded and peeling, but a bright red.

There was no answer to their first knock, so Mike pounded on the door more loudly. After the third try, a dull female voice called out from the other side, "Come back later! We ain't open!"

"Open the door," Mike called back. "We want to talk to Mr. Valery."

"He ain't up yet," the female voice called back. "I ain't supposed to let nobody in. I just cooks and cleans."

Then there was a faint, distant male voice, crusty with sleep. "Who is it, Lucy?"

"I don't know," the female voice called back.

"I'll take care of it," the sleepy male voice said wearily.

It was Albert Valery who opened the door, his eyes squinting in the sunlight, his hands clutching a purple satin dressing gown around his otherwise naked body. "What do you want?" he asked Mike gruffly, then—as he caught sight of Graciela—his annoyance turned into stunned disbelief. "Mrs. Tolliver?" he asked when he found his tongue again.

"Yes," she replied with a sweet, unperturbed smile. "You promised I might call upon Annie Laurie Crawford. I hope this is a convenient time."

"Well, no," he said, in embarrassment, "as a matter of fact, it's not. Actually, she's rather indisposed at the moment. She hasn't been well, and . . ."

"Would you mind," Graciela cut in, "if we came in off the street to discuss this?"

Taken aback by her bluntness, Albert Valery replied, "Of course not. Come in." As he stepped aside and opened the door wider, he added, "The place is in disarray right now. It hasn't been cleaned after . . . last night."

His statement was an understatement. Disarray wasn't an adequate word to describe the condition. Graciela didn't know what she expected a Sydneytown bagnio to look like, but it was certainly not this. She had to be careful of where she stepped to avoid all the broken bottles and glasses on the floor. There were bits of clothing and underclothing everywhere. And the air was close and thick with the lingering smoke of tobacco and something that had a sickly sweet smell.

There was no pretense whatever toward elegance, no gilt mirrors or red-velvet upholstery or polished floors. In fact, there were hardly any furnishings at all in the hallway or the front parlor, just a few crude straightbacked chairs, a makeshift bar, and a rickety staircase. The grimy wood walls were whitewashed, and the unfinished wooden floors sagged beneath their feet.

"We had a party last night," Valery apologized weakly.

"When can I see Annie Laurie?" Graciela asked curtly, ignoring his explanation.

"I don't know," Valery replied hesitantly. "Perhaps if you came back tomorrow afternoon, she might feel well enough to see you for a few minutes."

"If she is ill," Graciela pressed, "I might be able to be of help to her."

That look of fear or anger, of animal brutality, which she had noticed at the ball, flickered across his face. "We take care of her quite well," he cut back icily. "Certainly we know better than to upset her with unexpected visitors."

"Then she must be seriously ill," Graciela snapped. "I insist upon seeing her."

"I'm sorry." Valery moved to bar the way to the stairs. "It's impossible."

Suddenly Mike took charge of the situation. "If Mrs. Tolliver says she wants to see the girl," he said stonily, threateningly, "she's going to see her, and you can't stop her."

When big, burly Mike Welsh spoke in that manner, he could be very intimidating. Albert Valery was intimidated, but he tried not to let it show. He stood firmly in place at the foot of the stairs, but he was trembling slightly, and his voice shook when he spoke defiantly. "I'm afraid I'll have to stop her," he said. "The girl is indentured to me, and I am responsible for her welfare. Mrs. Tolliver is not. I cannot allow her to interfere."

In one swift move, Mike Welsh grabbed the little Frenchman, pinned his arms behind him, pulled him away from the stairs, and held him.

While Valery shouted in protest, Mike smiled at Graciela and said, "Go ahead, ma'am. I'll take care of things down here while you find the girl."

Graciela moved swiftly. She did not like violence, and she was apprehensive about the use of force, but Valery's reaction to her demands had increased her concern for Annie Laurie. She hurried up the rickety stairs to the seamy, ugly second floor. There were six doors off a dark hallway that smelled of sweat and uncleaned chamber pots. Four of the doors were opened, and two were closed. She checked the open doors first, though she strongly suspected Annie Laurie was behind one of the closed ones. She was right. None of the sleeping women in the horrible little open cells were recognizable to her.

Annie Laurie was behind the first of the closed but unlocked doors, though Graciela almost didn't recognize her at first. In fact, Annie Laurie had been so horribly bruised and battered, she hardly even resembled a woman. She wore only a simple shift, with no sheet or blanket to cover her. Her bare, flat, lumpy mattress was lying on the floor in the corner of the room.

Graciela knelt beside the poor excuse for a bed and touched her old friend gently on the shoulder. The stench was almost unbearable. At first Graciela could not understand why she had been unable to see to her bodily functions, why she had to lie on a wet, dirtied bed, but then Graciela saw the chains and manacles on her ankle, securing her to the wall. "My God!" she exclaimed in horror. "How could any human being do this to another?" And the tears began, bitter angry tears. "Dear child," she whispered hoarsely, "can you ever forgive me?"

Then, beneath her hand, the frail body moved slightly. The red, swollen eyelids fluttered open into narrow slits. And the parched, cracked lips struggled as if to speak. The sound was little more than a whisper, but Graciela caught the words. "Frisco?" Annie Laurie asked in disbelief. "Am I dreaming again, or is it really you?"

"Yes, child," she replied. "I'm going to take you away from here."

"It's too late," Annie Laurie protested faintly. "I'm going to die."

"No, it's not," Graciela insisted. "I'm going to get you a doctor. With care and food and fresh air, you'll get better."

"You don't understand," Annie Laurie whimpered. "It's hopeless. Nothing can help me now."

Still Graciela did not comprehend what she meant. "What have they done to you?" she asked. "Why have they chained you like this?"

"I tried to get away," the girl told her. "Time and again, I would slip out, but they always caught me and brought me back." As she explained, she began to sob. "I couldn't stand it. I thought I was going to be a parlormaid. When I found out what Mr. Valery wanted me to do, I tried to get to you to tell you, to ask you to help.

He beat me for that, and locked me in my room. When I still wouldn't do what he said, he tied me up and forced me. After a while, it didn't matter anymore. All the men were the same, and I didn't feel anything. They came, and they went, and I didn't even bother to look at their faces."

"But how long have you been in this condition?" Graciela asked. "With these horrible bruises on your face?"

"That happened last night," Annie Laurie told her. "Or at least I think it was last night. Mr. Valery had a party, and there were a group of men who . . ." She broke down into sobs again. "Oh, Frisco, there are some things you shouldn't know about. The uses some men—men like Valery—have for women are just too horrible to describe."

Suddenly, there was a loud crashing sound downstairs, followed by shouted curses and the sounds of scuffling. Immediately, she knew that Mike was in trouble. "I'll be back," she assured Annie Laurie and rushed from the room.

The whole house was shaking with the crashing of bodies against walls, and a few sleepy, half-clad women stumbled from their rooms as Graciela reached the top of the stairs and started down. Halfway down the stairs she could see what was happening below.

Two big men were struggling vainly to get the best of Mike Welsh, while Albert Valery stood apart, clutching his purple satin robe to him and shouting, "Kill him! Kill the son of a bitch!"

A fat, bald, witless-looking man, wearing only a pair of pants, had just picked himself up off the floor and rushed at Mike—who was occupied with a tall gangling blond man—leaping on him from behind. With a swift lurch, Mike flipped the bald one over his head to send him sprawling onto the floor again, then he swirled and kicked the blond in the groin.

"What the hell is wrong with you two?" Valery screamed. "Kill him!"

The fat, bald man picked himself up from the floor again, reached into his pocket, and pulled out a long, ugly-looking knife.

As soon as she saw the knife, Graciela screamed, "Stop it! This has gone far enough!"

The suddenness of her appearance, and the command in her voice must have startled them, because they all stopped and stared up at her in amazement.

"I did not come here to cause trouble," she said firmly but haughtily. "I'm willing to pay for what I want. That's the way you do things, isn't it, Mr. Valery?"

He stared back at her, hostility burning in his eyes, without confirming or denying what she said.

"I want to buy Annie Laurie's indenture papers," she said. "You set the price; I'll agree to it."

"They're not for sale," he shot back, "at any price."

"Come now," Graciela smiled and spoke more graciously, as she resumed descending the stairs. "In her condition, she can't be worth much to you."

"It's not the money," Valery said huffily. "It's the principle."

Graciela laughed scornfully. "The principle!" she exclaimed. "You must admit that sounds ludicrous coming from you. What will you take? A hundred dollars? Two hundred?"

Valery sneered. "Preposterous!" he scoffed. "She can make that much for me in a night!"

"A thousand then?" Graciela suggested. "Unless she gets to a doctor quickly, she won't live many more nights."

That frightened, angry look flickered across Valery's eyes again, and this time Graciela realized what it was. It was utter and absolute contempt. Contempt for her because she was a woman. That was Valery's secret. He hated women. In that moment, she also realized that he meant it when he said that he would not sell Annie Laurie to her. To do so, he would have to acknowledge that he had been bested by a woman.

"She's not for sale," he said adamantly. "Now, I suggest you get out. I may be too much of a gentlemen to throw you out myself, but my friends here are not."

"All right," Graciela gave in. "But you haven't heard the last of me. I'm going from here to see

81

Judge Hoffman, and I'll get Annie Laurie out of here without paying you a cent."

"We'll see about that," Valery sneered. "Judge Hoffman happens to be one of my best customers."

7

Graciela was fighting mad. There was only one man who could calm her down when she was in this condition, and he was somewhere in the Pacific on his way to Colombia.

Graciela tried every legal and ethical means for freeing her friend, but to no avail. She went directly from Albert Valery's house to see Judge Hoffman. The crusty old bachelor was polite and gracious toward her, but he was also condescending and inflexible. There was nothing he could do. If Annie Laurie had signed indenture papers, she was inextricably bound to Albert Valery. If Valery did not want to sell the indenture, he had every right. As for the mistreatment, that was Graciela's word against Valery's, and a woman had few rights in a court of law.

Graciela next went to see the sheriff, but he was even less helpful. "Ma'am, why don't you just go home and see to your own business?" was all he would say. "A lady like you doesn't belong down on Drumm Street."

A visit to a man reputed to be high on the Vigilance Committee produced a similar result.

Graciela's last resort was Senator David Broderick, the most powerful man in San Francisco. He was her last resort because he was also one of Beau's closest friends and business associates.

At first, Graciela thought he was going to help her. "That is a sad and pitiful story," he said with what seemed to be genuine sympathy. "California may have its statehood now, but San Francisco has a long way to go to catch up to civilization."

"Is there anything you can do about it?" Graciela prodded.

He shook his head sadly. "I don't know, ma'am," he said. "I'd like to, but I don't know what I can do. My heart goes out to the poor girl, but there's only one way you can look at cases like these. And I have to admit that there are many such stories, far too many.

"Any man or woman who comes to California has to have the soul of a gambler. They have to be prepared to take the hands fate deals them. They can win big, becoming millionaires overnight, or they can lose everything they've got, including their very souls. There is no in-between. The winners can't go trying to help every poor sucker who's lost. There are far too many of them, and they'll only pull you down with them."

Spoken like a true politician.

Graciela left Broderick's office with the realization that playing by the rules would never accomplish anything in San Francisco. The rules were made by men—men like Valery and Judge Hoffman and Broderick, and, yes, by men like Beau—and they were broken by men. Only foolish women like Graciela were expected to live by them.

As Mike took her home, Graciela was swept by uncontrollable rage. There were higher rules than those set up by men, rules governed by the heart, rules of love and caring and friendship. By those rules she would set aside the rules of the law. She would rescue Annie Laurie from Valery's clutches no matter what she had to do, legal or illegal.

The carriage was climbing Telegraph Hill, passing the little village of tents set up by newly arrived fortune seekers, when Graciela made her decision. She leaned forward in the carriage to speak to Mike.

"Mike," she called out, "are any of your old friends still around?"

Mike turned and grinned at her, knowing that she was referring to the Sydney Ducks. "A few," he said. "Why?"

"Do you think they'd be willing to do a bit of work?" she asked.

85

"If it's what I think it is," he beamed, "they'd be delighted."

Graciela's plan was exactly what Mike thought it was, and he was able to contact five of his old friends by shortly after midnight that night. They would raid Albert Valery's establishment shortly before dawn, a time when most of its patrons would be on their way home and everyone else would probably be drunk or just going to sleep. The streets then would still be dark and empty enough to get Annie Laurie to Graciela's house, traveling along the waterfront and coming up Telegraph Hill from the rear with little likelihood of discovery.

Neither Graciela nor Lillian could sleep that night, so they both sat up in the parlor with curtains drawn tightly and only one small lamp lit. It was a chilly night, and they built a fire in the fireplace. When they talked, they spoke in anxious, worried whispers. But mostly they listened for sounds that would tell them that the venture was either a success or a failure.

Graciela had made her decision without thinking, impulsively and perhaps foolishly. Now, as she sat waiting, she could not help but realize the great risks involved. Mike and his friends would be in great danger during the raid and the escape. Graciela herself would be taking a risk by sheltering a runaway indentured servant.

After what had taken place today, her home would be the first place Albert Valery would look. Every legal authority in town would willingly believe whatever he said, because she had, in effect, confessed her intentions. Desperately, her thoughts searched the house, trying to find a hiding place where her friend would be secure.

The only possible place was the potato cellar. It was separate from the rest of the cellar, having its own entrance through the floor of the kitchen pantry. It was one of the odd little luxuries of this house, something that might not occur to the searchers.

The only problem was Carlotta. Could the secret be kept from the housekeeper? And, if not, was there some way of insuring her silence? That Graciela had no way of knowing.

It was almost dawn when she heard the sound of horses and a wagon in front of the house. She rushed to the window, parting the curtains slightly to look out. She could barely distinguish the figures, but she was sure they were Mike and his friends. When she saw one of the men lift what was clearly a small frail body from the wagon, she knew the venture had been a success.

By the time she reached the front door and opened it, the carriage and the other men were gone, and Mike was climbing the front steps with Annie Laurie in his arms.

"Was there any trouble?" Graciela whispered.

"Only a little," Mike grinned. "They'll only find two corpses when they wake up this afternoon."

"Oh, my God," Graciela exclaimed. "Not Valery."

"No," Mike admitted. "Just his two big watchdogs."

"It would have been better if it had been Valery," she told him bitterly. "He'll be coming here as soon as he finds out what's happened. We'll have to keep her hidden."

With her small kerosene lantern, Graciela led Mike and Lillian straight back through the hallway to the kitchen and pantry. She removed the braided rag rug and opened the trap door that was concealed beneath it.

"It's going to be a bit cold and damp," she said, "but she should be okay until after they've searched the place." Then she turned to Lillian. "Go upstairs and get some blankets and pillows," she instructed.

It was difficult getting the small frail body down the steep stairs into the potato cellar, but they managed. Graciela stood at the bottom of the stairs with the lantern, while Mike eased his way down step by step.

The cellar would not be a very comfortable sickroom, but it was at least cleaner than the room Annie Laurie had been stolen from. It had brick walls and floor, and a raised wooden platform to keep the potatoes away from whatever dampness there was.

Annie Laurie was hardly conscious of where

she was. She was aware that she was free, but at times she babbled incoherently. If anything, her condition seemed much worse than it had been less than twenty-four hours ago. "You should have left me to die in peace," she told Graciela while they were waiting for Lillian to return with the bedding. "You could have helped the others. I sold myself, but they were sold on the block. Auctioned off like cattle, with no choice. Animals. Wretched animals. Do you know the auction block?"

Her words made no sense to Graciela. She assumed the girl was raving. "Shh," she consoled. "Don't try to talk now. Just rest, and later we'll get a doctor for you. As soon as it's safe."

Lillian returned with an armload of blankets, quilts, and pillows, and they cleared the potatoes from the platform to make a bed. After Annie Laurie was made comfortable, Graciela instructed Lillian to stay with her while she escorted Mike to the door and then prepared some warm broth and tea for the patient.

"You," she told Mike, "are going to have to go home, go to bed, and behave as if nothing has happened."

Graciela had shut and locked the front door behind Mike and was moving back down the hallway toward the kitchen when the sharp, shrill voice called out from upstairs, "What's going on down there?"

Carlotta was awake and out of bed.

"Nothing to worry about," Graciela called back, trying to conceal the apprehension in her voice. "I couldn't sleep, and I'm going to make myself a pot of tea."

"I'll do it for you," the housekeeper said in her proprietary voice, and there were the sounds of her footsteps beginning to descend the stairs.

"No," Graciela replied a bit too anxiously. "I'd rather do it myself. You just go back to bed."

There was a momentary silent hesitation, then Carlotta said huffily, "All right," and there was a resigned clop-clop-clop of her slippers going back up the stairs.

Graciela heaved a sigh of relief, but her heart was still pounding as she returned to the kitchen and set about preparing some nourishment for the kidnapped girl resting tentatively beneath the house.

The anxiety did not let up the entire morning. Graciela felt she was treading on eggshells; the slightest misstep would mean disaster. The worst of it was that by hiding Annie Laurie in the potato cellar she and Lillian were intruding on Carlotta's domain. It took considerable cunning on Graciela's part to come up with errands and marketing chores that would keep the housekeeper out of the house most of the morning.

Graciela and Lillian took turns sitting beside the patient, whose condition seemed to grow steadily worse. Before she had had moments of lucidity; now there were none. Over and over again, her ramblings returned to speak of the "auction block" and the "poor innocent girls."

Several times Graciela considered taking their patient upstairs to a clean warm bed, so that they could call in a doctor. In the bright light of day, her fears appeared foolish; surely Valery would not dare to intrude upon her respectable home with his accusations. But each time she reminded herself that Valery was not the sort of man to stop at anything. She must wait at least until the late afternoon.

The knock at the door came only a few minutes before noon. Luckily, Carlotta had not returned from her trip to the shops on Market Street. Lillian was sitting with the invalid, and Graciela was in the front parlor. Graciela smoothed her hair and took a deep breath to calm herself before opening the door.

Albert Valery had brought only the sheriff and a deputy with him. The little Frenchman had dark circles under his eyes, and his expression was grim. The sheriff and deputy stood behind him, looking apologetic.

"Mrs. Tolliver," Valery said stridently, "we have reason to believe you have unlawfully taken property that belongs to me."

"What do you mean?" Graciela feigned innocence.

"Annie Laurie Crawford," Valery snapped, "has disappeared, and two of my employees have been murdered. I have come to get her back."

"If you are suggesting I'm capable of murder," Graciela informed him icily, "you are sadly mistaken."

"Mrs. Tolliver," the sheriff cut in, "if you don't mind, we would like to search your house. We're not accusing you of anything, but she may be hiding somewhere about." Then he added apologetically, "We do have a search warrant issued by Judge Hoffman."

"Then I don't suppose I have any choice," Graciela said. "Come in."

She led them through the house room by room. Their search was careful and thorough. They checked cellar, attic, and all the closets, even insisting that she open all wardrobes and trunks. They checked kitchen cabinets, and they checked the pantry. Graciela held her breath as they moved about the small room, opening boxes and barrels. She prayed that they would not think to look beneath the braided rug. Hoping to conceal it with her full skirts, she stood over it, pretending to watch them do their job.

Finally, to her great relief, they admitted defeat, though Valery continued to swear that she was behind the disappearance of his employee. "You've got her hidden somewhere," he accused, "and I'm going to find her sooner or later."

Graciela simply smiled and showed them to the door. However, she would not really feel comfortable until they were gone completely. Surreptitiously, she watched from the narrow hall window as they proceeded down the walk toward the street, counting the seconds anxiously until she would be safe.

Suddenly a buckboard pulled up alongside their horses. It was Carlotta. She spoke to the men with a questioning look on her face, then looked up toward the house with a suspicious scowl. Then there was further conversation. The longer their exchanges, the more worried Graciela became. She silently cursed the nosy old busybody, wondering if she might have seen anything last night. If she had not been suspicious before, she was certainly suspicious now.

Then Albert Valery helped the housekeeper down from the buckboard, and the group started moving back toward the house.

Graciela could see by the smirk on Valery's face that she had lost.

Her mind raced. Should she dare to defy them? Should she try to bar their way inside? There was now no time to try to get Annie Laurie out of the cellar and flee.

This time they did not knock. Graciela was still standing indecisively in the middle of the hallway when Carlotta opened the door and ushered the men inside.

Valery beamed at her triumphantly. "I understand there is one place we have not looked," he announced. "According to your housekeeper, you have a cellar."

"You have already checked the cellar," Graciela cut back.

"Not that one," he smiled. "Another, smaller one, where you keep potatoes."

Graciela began to tremble with a mixture of fear and rage. "You have already searched this house from top to bottom," she said curtly. "You have taken up my time. You have annoyed me. You have even insulted me. Now I must insist you get out."

"I'm sorry ma'am," the sheriff said, "we have the right to search everywhere."

Graciela tried to bar their way, but Valery grabbed her arm and thrust her aside, sending her sprawling against the wall.

Carlotta led them through the kitchen to the pantry. She bent over and pulled the braided rug aside, then cast a vicious smile at Graciela. "Down there," she said, "you will find what you are looking for." To Graciela, she added, "Did you think I was such a stupid old woman not to see what was happening last night?"

As soon as they opened the trap door, Graciela heard weeping from below. Even before they began to descend the steep stairs, Lillian's grief-stricken voice called out, "Go ahead and take her, damn you! She's dead!"

It was a small victory for Albert Valery, but a crushing defeat for Graciela. Her efforts had been too late to help her friend, and she would never be able to forgive herself, never find a way to make up for her neglect.

One thing Graciela could do was to provide a decent burial for the girl. Unable to break free of her indenture in life, she had achieved it irrevocably through death. Valery had no further claims on her or obligations toward her. He was quite willing to let Graciela pay for the funeral.

Another thing she could do was to wreak her vengeance on the traitorous housekeeper. "Get your things and get out of here," she told Carlotta, after the men had departed. "I don't want you to spend another night under my roof."

"You cannot do that," Carlotta replied haughtily. "I was hired by Señor Tolliver. Only he can fire me."

"Mr. Tolliver is no longer running this house," she informed her. "I am running it now, and I say you are to get out. Immediately, with no pay and no references."

She narrowed her eyes, clenched her jaw, and dropped her voice ominously. "I want to see you face the streets of San Francisco the same way my friends—whom you so heartily disapprove of—have faced it. I want you to learn how easy it is to keep your precious respectability when you are cold and hungry and homeless."

8

Annie Laurie's death was a great loss to her, and for days afterward she was overwhelmed by grief, self-accusation, and loneliness. She did have Lillian to talk to and to comfort her, but there was something missing in her consolation. It was almost like talking to herself. When Lillian told her that everything would be all right, that she must pick herself up and carry on, she did not seem to speak with the assurance that Beau would have if he were there with her.

Graciela did not realize how much she missed Beau until his first letter arrived.

She had just written to him two nights before, and so she was certain that their letters had crossed in transit. He had not had time to learn of the tragic fate of Annie Laurie. She was not so much moved by the words he wrote, but by the simple fact that he had written as he had promised.

The letter read:

My dearest darling,

We have arrived safely at Buenaventura, though several times during our journey I suspected we would not. Storms are often lovely on land, but they can be fearful at sea. I did not expect such terrible heat here in Colombia at this time of year, but I am told that it is normal, and that it will be even worse in Panama. The trip to Santa Fe de Bogota will be overland and will require several days. I will write again from there. Tell Alex I will bring souvenirs when I return. I cannot write the words I want to write. It would not be fair to do so from this great distance, since I have not spoken them in your presence. Until I can, I am yours faithfully,

Beau

Graciela was sure she knew what he meant, because it was exactly what she had been feeling. The words that remained unspoken between them were: "I love you." As she read and reread his letter, she wished desperately that she had not let him leave her, that she had forced herself to say the words that would keep him at home.

She did not want to admit that she needed him,

but she did. She was rapidly discovering that a woman could accomplish virtually nothing alone. All the obstacles—or at least all of the major ones—existed because she was a woman, and she was dismissed immediately as not being sincere. True, there were some advantages in being a woman—the law had been much more lenient with her in the situation surrounding Annie Laurie's abduction than it would have with a man— but those advantages had nothing to do with establishing a business.

The most serious obstacle she faced was finding a building to house the new Frisco's. She could, of course, build her own structure, and she fully intended to do so, but that would take six or eight months. She wanted to open her doors as quickly as possible. The incident with Annie Laurie had taught her that delay could have dire consequences.

There was—as there had been from the very beginnings of San Francisco—a severe housing shortage, but it was less severe among business and commercial structures than it was in housing. There were a number of buildings to let. It was just that the owners did not want to lease to Graciela.

Some of the owners lied to her outright when she approached them. "The building is for you?" they would ask suspiciously. Then, when she confirmed that it was, they informed her, "I'm sorry, the building has already been spoken for." She knew they were lying, because their advertisements continued in the *Bulletin* for days afterward.

Others tried tactfully to be honest. "I'm sorry, madame," they would tell her. "Your business isn't really what we would consider a suitable tenant. And I'm sure you would agree it would be unwise to rent from someone who was not in sympathy with you."

Finally she had been forced to admit defeat in handling this transaction herself. However, she still doggedly refused to go to one of Beau's associates to ask for help. Instead, she turned to Mike Welsh, asking him to locate a building and to lease it in his name. But, as it turned out, it was too late for that.

After a week of trying, Mike came to her and said, "It's no use. Word has gotten around. Everybody in town knows I'm working for you. But I've got an idea."

"What is it?" she asked dispiritedly.

"I know it may sound harebrained," he eased into it cautiously. "But it would only be temporary, until you get your own building up, and other people are doing it." He paused, waiting until he could see that her mind was open. "Take over one of the abandoned boats in the harbor. The owners have disappeared; they're just sitting there rotting, and you wouldn't have to pay no rent at all."

It was indeed a harebrained idea, but something about it appealed to Graciela. It was different; having a gambling establishment on a boat would distinguish her from all the other gambling houses that had grown up in San Francisco since her last place had burned.

"Frisco's-on-the-boat." She liked the ring of it. It suggested romance and adventure. It connoted risk and chance and luck far more than any sturdy land-based structure could ever do. Rocked gently by the waves, rising and falling with the tides, tethered only tentatively to shore and safety. It would appeal to gamblers, to the wild-spirited adventurers of San Francisco.

"All right," she beamed at Mike. "Find me a boat, and we'll do it."

In less than twenty-four hours, Mike returned to report success. "She's a three-masted schooner named the *Ellen Jane*, tied up south of the slot off Mission Street. She'll need a lot of work, but so would any building you might have rented. 'Course, you'll have to see her yourself to judge, but I like her. She has a good feel about her."

As soon as she saw the boat, Graciela agreed. If one overlooked the need for caulking and paint, the broken jib, and the rotting rigging, she was beautiful, as sleekly and gracefully designed as any boat she had ever seen. And there was more room below deck than she could possibly need. She would have to tear out some of the bulkheads, carpet the decks, and install lighting, but there were other features she would not need to change. The *Ellen Jane* had been a fine ship, with magnificent panelling unequalled by the homes or establishments of the then crude, little San Francisco. All of the fixtures were brass, which would polish beautifully. And there was a staircase leading into the main saloon that was so grand and graceful it could have been built only out of pure love.

Graciela wondered at what kind of man would have built such a boat and then have abandoned it so callously to seek his fortune in the barrenness of the gold fields. Such a boat cried out for love and caring and company. No matter, Graciela finally decided, she would give it all that, and it would give her the same. They were two of a kind, she and the boat—headstrong, independent, and passionately strong. Together, they could stand up to any man alive, and work with them.

However, until the *Ellen Jane* was made ready, Graciela had to do battle alone. And it was not easy. From her experience with Lillian and Annie Laurie, she had assumed she would have no difficulty getting the old girls to return to work for her. But in their own way, they were as difficult to rescue as Annie Laurie had been.

She accepted defeat easily with the married ones. Whether they were happy or not—and Graciela had the impression that most were unhappy with the men they had accepted out of desperation—they did have a degree of respectability and security she could not offer them. Her visits with them, however, were disheartening. The visit to Margaret Duvall was a particularly painful blow to her spirits.

Margaret had been the effervescent one at the old Frisco's. With her French accent, her vivacious laugh, and the way she had of tossing her jet black hair, she had been the life of every party, always ready for fun. She had had no trouble getting a husband. She had married a man as darkly handsome as she was beautiful, a man she had met while she was working at Frisco's. A gambler. He had had money when they married, and he had had money during one or two other brief periods, but most of the time he had been broke and in debt. Finally he took to drink, and they were now living in a dirty hovel down in Sydneytown, where Margaret supported them by taking in washing

The conditions in their small shanty were not quite as bad as the conditions at Albert Valery's had been, but Graciela still did not consider them acceptable for humans. Margaret, her husband, and their small infant lived in one cramped room, where Margaret also did the laundry that provided them with their subsistence.

At the time Graciela called, Pierre was passed out in a drunken stupor on the small bed. The baby was lying naked on its back on the rough wood floor. And Margaret was bent over a washtub trying to scrub grease out of a workman's overalls. Her lovely clear complexion was mottled with red and streaked with dirt and sweat. Her once lustrous black hair hung in limp strands over her forehead, despite attempts to push them back into place with soapy wrists.

But the biggest disappointment to Graciela was the fact that the laughter was gone from the sparkling dark eyes. Margaret did not even offer her a smile when she looked up and recognized her caller. In fact, there seemed to be only disappointment that it was not a customer bringing work.

While Graciela explained why she had come, Margaret did not speak; she merely grunted noncommittally to indicate she was listening. Finally, when Graciela had finished, she looked up from her work and said, "If you think I'd come back to work for you, you're a fool. In two months, you'll be going back to your husband, Pierre will have left me, and I'll be out on the streets again completely on my own. Thanks for the offer, but no thanks."

Her visits with the girls who had taken jobs were less depressing, but equally disheartening. They, too, distrusted Graciela's intentions, as well as her reliability. Carrie's reaction was typical of all of them. "I've got a job," she told Graciela. "Maybe my life isn't as much fun as it used to be at the old place, but as long as I give the custom-

103

ers what they want, I've got nice clothes, a place to live, and three meals a day. If I walked out on him now, taking a chance on something that might or might not be secure, he'd never take me back."

But the reactions she could not understand, the ones that upset her the most, came from the girls who had been forced to turn to prostitution. "If you were a man," Doris told her, "I would say yes. But you're a woman, no different from me. What you did after the old place burned proves it. You had a setback, and immediately, what did you do? You gave up and turned to a man to take care of you. You didn't give a damn what happened to the rest of us. We were on our own to make out the best we could, and none of us were lucky enough to find a man like yours." She licked a brightly painted lip and cast her still beautiful blue eyes heavenward. "Though thank my lucky stars, my Mack is a good one. He picks his customers carefully and he don't beat me or treat me rough."

"But are you happy?" Graciela ventured foolishly.

Doris shrugged. "I don't ask myself that," she confessed callously. "It's a job. It's got to be done by somebody, and it pays good. I'm managing to save so when I get too old to work myself I'll be able to set up my own place." Suddenly, she smiled at Graciela the way the Doris of the old days used to smile, warm and honest. "Listen,

104

even if Frisco's was able to work out again and it did turn into something permanent, I couldn't make anywhere as much as I do now. And let's face it, once a whore, always a whore. After you've been at it a while, you can't change back to what you was before."

"Doris, dear, people can change if you change the image you have of yourself. My dear dead husband Shandor's grandmother, Pesha, taught me that our thoughts create our world. People treat us the way we think about ourselves. It isn't what a person is that counts. It's what a person wants to be." Graciela stopped talking when she saw Doris yawn and realized she wasn't listening.

Out of all of them, Graciela found only one who was willing to come back, and she had reservations. Julie Farrow was one of the older girls, and she had never been able to settle into prostitution.

"The reason I came out to San Francisco was to be a schoolteacher," Julie explained. "I've got a good education, and I did teach one year back in Boston before I came out. It didn't occur to me that there wouldn't be enough children out here to organize schools. It shouldn't be long, though. And in the meantime, I'd rather go back to working for you than keep on working the streets."

"Will you have any problem with your . . ." Graciela strained to remember the word.

"My Mack?" Julie asked. "No. He doesn't own me. He's just doing me a favor by handling me.

He'd much rather get a girl at the auction, so he can control her."

"The auction?" Graciela gave her a puzzled look.

Julie nodded. "You know about the auction, don't you?"

"No," Graciela admitted. "Annie Laurie mentioned an auction. She kept saying something about the 'auction block' over and over before she died, and it's bothered me ever since. I kept feeling she was trying to tell me something important."

"Poor child." Julie shook her head solemnly. "It's terrible what happened to her. But I think I know what she was trying to tell you. It's only a guess, of course, but it seems likely she was trying to ask you to help other girls who might end up like her."

"That's what I want to do," Graciela said earnestly, "more than anything else in the world. But how?"

"About once a month," Julie explained, "there's a boat that sails into the bay, coming from the East Coast. You can tell which one it is because it flies a big banner that says 'Women Aboard.' And of course there's always an advertisement in the *Bulletin* that says when the auction is to take place."

"Are they slaves?" Graciela asked incredulously.

"No," Julie said, amazed that Graciela was so ignorant. "They're girls like Annie Laurie, girls who have signed indenture papers thinking they're coming out here to be household servants or shopclerks, or even wives. Some of them actually do get what they expect, but they're all sold at auction, and none of them get a choice. Most are sold to the Macks and Madames.

Suddenly it was clear to Graciela what Annie Laurie had been trying to tell her. It had been too late to save her, but she had wanted Graciela to help other unsuspecting young women. It had been her dying wish.

9

The newspaper advertisement literally leaped from the page in big bold letters. It was incredible that Graciela had never noticed it before. It read:

50 WOMEN 50
Arriving Friday on the *Mercy*!
All young, white, and English-speaking,
with indenture papers in perfect legal order.
To be auctioned
Saturday, 10:00 A.M.

Graciela was determined to attend and to purchase as many of the indentures as she could. It would be her way of expiating the guilt she felt because of Annie Laurie, and it would also provide her with the staff she needed for Frisco's.

The work on restoring the *Ellen Jane* was going well. Under Mike's supervision, the workmen were days ahead of schedule. In less than two weeks they would be ready to open their doors. Ready, that is, if Graciela had her staff and they were fully trained.

She would need ten to twelve women to run the tables. At the moment, she had only two—Lillian and Julie. If necessary, she might be able to enlist Lyuba's aid, though Lyuba had already indicated she would be interested only in entertaining occasionally, singing and telling fortunes. Her life now was totally devoted to taking care of little Alex, and she did not want to neglect him for what she considered a foolish business venture.

In short, it had turned out that Graciela was entirely dependent upon the auction in order to reopen. If she were unable to find—and to buy—women who were suitable for her needs, her plans were doomed to failure. Suitable or not, she was going to buy as many indentures as she could, though she had not even considered what she would do with the women if they were incapable of running the tables.

Graciela had no idea how much money she would need to take with her to the auction, or if in fact she would have to have cash in hand. To be safe, she went to the bank on Friday and withdrew three thousand dollars, feeling confident it would be more than enough. She recalled that women slaves in New Orleans had sold for as little as three or four hundred dollars each, and therefore reasoned that indentured servants would sell for less than that.

The auction would be held on the docks, at the point where Pacific and Drumm streets met. It was one of the most unsavory sections of the waterfront, a place that Graciela could not possibly go alone. Of course, Lillian would accompany her to lend moral support, and Mike Welsh would serve as bodyguard, but secretly Graciela longed to have Beau at her side—Beau, who was so strong and sure and knowledgeable in the ways of the world.

Saturday morning was cold and wintry, with wind whipping down from the north in fierce, bitter gusts. The sky was clear, but its blue was pallid and desolate, not a day that would encourage hope.

Graciela was astonished by the crowds that gathered on the docks, over a thousand men of all classes, with a scattering of women. Of the women, Graciela recognized only Mrs. Liz Nivens. She assumed the others were keepers of bagnios as well, all come to add to their stock of merchandise. Of the men, only a few could possibly have been Macks, and only a few others serious buyers, men looking for housekeepers or wives. Most had come simply to gawk lasciviously and to enjoy the carnival atmosphere. A few were probably pickpockets and thieves, eager to take advantage of the milling crowds.

Legitimate bidders were requested to register with the auctioneer, a fat garrulous man with a red face and wispy orange hair, and they were permitted to go aboard the *Mercy* to inspect the merchandise before bidding began. Graciela and Lillian had both strived to dress as plainly as possible so as to remain inconspicuous, but their efforts had been in vain. As they boarded the ship, they were the objects of leering stares and even a few whistles.

But if they were offended by the men's behavior, they were disgusted by what they saw on deck. The fifty women who were to be auctioned were forced to stand up on wooden crates and to endure incredible humiliation. "Ask them anything you want," the auctioneer had instructed. "Inspect them to assure yourselves they're healthy, but don't take any liberties. These are clean, respectable young ladies, every one a virgin."

But the men took liberties, and no one did anything to stop them. Despite protests from the women, they lifted skirts to examine ankles and calves, and they pawed at buttocks and breasts.

Graciela tried to say and do things that would at least make them feel more at ease, if not console them, while—at the same time—trying to gauge their intelligence, resiliency, and willing-

111

ness to learn. To her disappointment, Graciela had not managed to look at all fifty women before the auctioneer called out, "Everybody off now! Return to the dock so we can start the bidding!"

She had managed to make favorable notes on only five out of the fourteen she had approached. She was walking down the gangway, wondering if she would be able to judge the others adequately simply on appearance, when a voice called out to her from behind. "Mrs. Tolliver, how nice to see you."

Turning, she saw Albert Valery's smirking face. He tipped his hat mockingly. She realized instantly that he had come to find a replacement for Annie Laurie in his establishment, and she vowed silently to herself that she would bid against him, no matter what the girls were like.

At the foot of the gangway, Valery approached her. "I heard you dismissed your housekeeper," he said snidely. "So regrettable. Have you come to find another?"

"Yes," Graciela responded, "among other things. I'm sure there's no need to ask why you're here. Good day." And she turned her back on him.

She did, however, whisper to Lillian to keep her eye on him so they would know where in the crowd he was when the bidding began.

Valery positioned himself conveniently in the very first row, directly in front of the auction block, a large wooden crate upended on the dock at the very foot of the gangway. Graciela, with Lillian and Mike at her sides, chose to stand a few feet behind him. Behind them the crowd seemed to have grown even larger since their arrival, with gaping men stretching far back into the two intersecting streets.

Graciela quickly caught onto the fact that the least desirable women were auctioned first, and the best saved for last. But even some of the less attractive ones were going for two, three, and even four hundred dollars. Fear began to creep in that she had not brought enough money with her. At four and five hundred dollars an indenture, she would be able to rescue only a handful of women, not even enough to staff her establishment.

As far as she could determine, the Macks and Madames did not bid at all during the first half of the proceedings. All of the competition seemed to be between miners and shopkeepers genuinely looking for servants. Graciela kept her eyes on Albert Valery and Liz Nivens to know when the serious bidding would begin.

It started at Number 28, a pretty, shy blonde girl about eighteen years old, one that Graciela had not had an opportunity to interview. Albert Valery started the bidding at three hundred dollars.

Graciela immediately lifted her hand and called out, "Three-hundred-fifty!"

Valery turned around and flashed her an angry look, then lifted his hand and bid four hundred.

The bidding went up in fifty-dollar steps. Graciela obtained her first indenture at six hundred dollars.

Her nerves were tingling with a mixture of elation and suspense, so she sat out the bidding on the next two.

Then the auctioneer called out, "Number 31! Her name is Constance! She's twenty years old, and she comes to us from Philadelphia! She can read and write! She cooks, and she does excellent needlework! Someday she'll make some man a fine wife, but for now, she's yours! Who'll start the bidding?"

Again Valery started at three hundred. Graciela conceeded that Constance was a beauty, and probably intelligent as well. She countered with three-fifty. She had to go to seven-fifty to get Constance. Quickly she calculated how much money she had spent. Thirteen hundred and fifty dollars. Almost half of her funds were spent, and there were nineteen more women to be auctioned off. Surely the very best would be the very last. Painfully, she regretted her inexperience in such matters. She should have realized that women were still a premium in San Francisco, and she could not compare them to the plenteous slaves in New Orleans.

Graciela bid on Number 32, but dropped out at four hundred since Valery wasn't bidding, and a Mack over at the side got her for four-fifty. Then Graciela's heart went out to Number 33; a young girl who couldn't have been more than thirteen years old. Something about her reminded Graciela of herself at that age.

"Her name is Natasha!" the auctioneer cried out. "Don't let her shy look fool you! She's got spirit if any a girl ever did! Open your eyes, girl! Lift your head and let them see your face!"

The smooth olive complexion was like Graciela's, as were the large dark eyes and the wavy black hair. For a moment she had a sense of deja vu, but she quickly realized that it was a scene she had witnessed only in her mind's eye, in her imagination, a scene she had expected to occur in her own life—a schoolgirl in New Orleans turned suddenly into a slave, threatened with being sold on the auction block, threatened until Beau Tolliver came into her life to rescue her.

"Three hundred!" Albert Valery called out.

Compulsively, Graciela cried, "Four hundred!" She did not realize until after she had spoken that she had set the pace of bidding at hundreds rather than fifties.

"Five!" Valery shouted forcefully, and Graciela thought she could hear the sound of lust and lechery in his voice.

Frantically, she called back, "Six!"

Was it possible that Valery saw the resemblance between the girl Natasha and Graciela? Was he bidding so eagerly just to spite her?

115

"Seven!" he called.

Fearfully, aware of her rapidly dwindling money, Graciela slowed the bidding. "Seven-fifty."

"Eight!" Valery said, almost before she had gotten the words out of her mouth.

Anxiously, she bid eight-fifty, and he countered with nine. Then there was a long pause while Graciela did some mathematical calculations in her head. If she bid farther, this might be the last indenture she would be able to buy. Not only would she be unable to reopen Frisco's on schedule, but other girls might suffer because of her determination to help this one. Would it really be fair of her to go farther? Certainly, this time Valery seemed set upon besting her at any price.

While she hesitated, the auctioneer called out, in his singsong voice, "Nine! I have nine hundred dollars, do I hear a thousand? A thousand? Just look at this lovely young lady, gentlemen. Such spirit and beauty is worth a thousand."

Graciela stared at the girl Natasha. The girl was staring back, crestfallen. Was there a look of hurt and accusation? Betrayal?

"Do I hear nine-fifty?" the auctioneer droned.

She could not let it happen. "Nine-twenty-five!" she cried, her voice painfully shrill.

"I have nine-twenty-five!" the auctioneer called. "Do I hear more?"

116

"A thousand!" Albert Valery shouted, a smug assurance after Graciela's hesitation that she would not go higher. An excited murmur went through the crowd. Apparently this was higher than they were accustomed for such bidding.

Graciela hesitated only a moment to reason: because she had been slow in her last bid, Valery had seen that her will was flagging; his bid of a thousand was a bluff; what she had to do this time was to call his bluff. "Eleven hundred dollars!" she cried with defiance.

"I have a bid of eleven hundred," the auctioneer whined, a bit incredulous himself at the figure. "Do I hear twelve hundred?"

This time it was Valery who hesitated. He fidgeted, turned around to glare at Graciela, to see just how determined she was. She lifted her head high and stared him down. A glazed look came over his eyes, his shoulders slumped, and she knew she had won.

At the same time, she knew she had lost. She had only five hundred and twenty-five dollars left. She could not fight Valery much longer. She was so wrapped up in misery she hardly heard the auctioneer announce, "Sold to the lady for eleven hundred dollars!"

10

Forced to stop at her limit, Graciela lost the next two bids. Miserably faced with the prospect of going home without even having half the women she needed, a misery that was compounded by the sense that she had let Annie Laurie down. Many of the girls and women that she had made favorable notes on before the bidding were among the last fifteen to be brought to the block.

Number 36 was one of these, a tall statuesque beauty with ash-blonde hair named Laura. She had told Graciela she had grown up on riverboats between St. Louis and New Orleans. She had been around gamblers and gambling all her life. She was perfectly suited to work at Frisco's. But Liz Nivens, Albert Valery, and another Mack were all bidding against Graciela, rapidly driving the price up beyond her limit.

Then someone new joined in the bidding, shouting out from somewhere far back in the crowd, "Seven hundred dollars!"

She turned around and tried to determine which of the multitude of faces had broken in so abruptly, but it was impossible. Was it another Mack? She prayed fervently that it was not. If she could not have Laura for Frisco's, she hoped the girl would be purchased by someone who would treat her decently.

After Albert Valery bid seven-fifty, the man in the back bid eight, and this time his voice seemed a bit closer to Graciela. Again she turned around to try to see who he was, but there were just too many tall men in the way.

The mysterious stranger obtained Laura at eight hundred, and the auctioneer proceeded to Number 37.

"Ladies and gentlemen," the auctioneer whined, "here we have Diana. She's twenty-two years old, and she comes to us from New York City. She can read and write, and she has had several years experience working as a waitress at some of the city's best restaurants. Can I have an opening bid?"

For some reason—perhaps the fevered pitch of the last few battles had worn everyone down—there was a lull. This was one of the women who

119

had impressed Graciela, but she hesitated to start the bidding. However, when everyone else hesitated as well, she decided to try a new tack, opening with a lower bid. Perhaps she might actually be able to acquire a fourth worker. "Two hundred," she called out.

"The lady has opened the bidding at two hundred," the auctioneer announced. "Do I hear two-fifty?"

Albert Valery responded, clearly because he wanted to spite Graciela. There was little enthusiasm in his voice. He seemed preoccupied with studying a list he had made on a scrap of paper, as the price for Diana went up by twenty-five and fifty-dollar increments. Finally, Diana was hers at five hundred and twenty-five dollars, every cent Graciela had brought with her. As far as she was concerned, with this sale, the auction was over, and she might as well go home.

When the auctioneer pronounced, "Sold to the lady," Albert Valery turned around with a triumphant, mocking sneer on his face, and tipped his hat to her, as if to say farewell.

In defiance, she lifted her chin, straightened her shoulders, and decided she would not leave. She would remain standing right where she was, so as not to give him the pleasure of seeing her depart.

Number 38 climbed up on the crate. She was fifteen, with brown hair in braids wrapped around the crown of her head. She had the grace and dignity of a dancer. Graciela ached for her, knowing what fate the child had in store. Suddenly, a deep and resonant voice spoke from behind her. "I know you're out of money, but if you want this one, go ahead and bid. I'll be glad to advance you whatever you need." It was the mysterious voice that had been bidding from the rear of the crowd.

Graciela turned. It took her a moment to recognize the handsome smiling face. It was Tom Blanchard. "Oh, no," she said, flustered. "I couldn't. But thank you."

The bidding started with three hundred dollars from Albert Valery.

"I realize it's presumptuous of me," Tom said apologetically, "but I think I know what you've been trying to do, and I admire you for it. I've heard the gossip about what happened with you and Albert Valery and the girl."

Liz Nivens bid three-fifty.

"I have plenty of cash on hand," he continued. "I just came down here for a housekeeper, and I acquired her first thing. The other young lady I bought for you, when I realized why you were dropping out of the bidding. I really have no use for her. If you are concerned about being obligated to me, you can repay me."

As Valery bid four hundred, Graciela considered: it would be wonderful to foil the wretched Mack; and, after all, she did need more women to staff Frisco's; she was being given a chance to salvage all her plans; and Tom Blanchard did seem to be sincere. "All right," she agreed. "But only on the condition that I repay you in full on Monday."

Liz Nivens had just bid four-fifty. Graciela called out a bid of six hundred dollars.

A murmur of excitement ran through the crowd with a smattering of applause. Apparently everyone had heard the gossip about her and Valery, and they had guessed at what she was doing, just as Tom had done.

Albert Valery swirled around, his face pale with shock and dismay. He continued to bid against her, though Liz Nivens dropped out, and Graciela finally won the girl, whose name was Brenda, at nine hundred dollars.

The rest of the morning, the bidding continued to be heated, but Graciela beat Albert Valery time after time until he finally gave up and left the auction, picking his way through the grinning, laughing crowd.

One man jeered, "Hey, Valery, first time I ever seen you done in by a woman!"

And Valery replied hotly, "Just wait! It's not over yet!"

Graciela realized even before he said it that their battle had just begun. To Valery, pride was very important; he would never accept humiliation. He would be back, and Graciela must be watchful.

By the time the bidding was over, Graciela had

more than enough women to staff Frisco's. She had spent an enormous amount of money, but she considered it well spent. She realized she could not have done it without Tom Blanchard. Once again he had come to her rescue, a stranger with nothing to gain by helping her. If anything, he should have wanted to see her defeated; she was, after all, the wife of his strongest business rival. Surely, if he kept up with the gossip around town, he would know why Beau had left. By giving aid to Graciela, he was actually helping Beau to stay away long enough to complete his business successfully. Unless perhaps there was some hidden reason Graciela could not see. However, nothing seemed hidden in his face. He appeared to be honest, kindly, and gracious; a gentle knight interested only in helping a lady in distress.

As they boarded the ship to make their payments and to collect their purchases, Tom suggested, "Unless you have brought several wagons with you, I fear you may have difficulty transporting all these women to your home. I do have my wagon, and I would be glad to help."

"Oh, no, thank you," Graciela replied. "You've done more than enough already. As it is, I don't know how I can thank you."

He smiled genuinely. "The privilege of spending a few moments in your company is all the thanks I require."

He meant it. She was sure that he meant it. His eyes were so gentle and straightforward. His manner was restrained and correct, without even the slightest trace of familiarity or presumption. No, he was guilty of nothing more than kindness.

It was Graciela who—looking into his eyes—felt a desire for familiarity. She wanted to presume upon his generosity, hoping that he would insist upon accompanying her home, and not just because she had been foolish enough to bring only the one carriage. The thought that, if given a chance, he might offer her a compliment or breach decorum by caressing her hand excited her, sent a chill tingling along her spine.

It was her own behavior that might become dangerous, not his. She had to remind herself to keep her distance. Yet, somehow, she could not bring herself to give him an outright no. And so she compromised. "Actually," she suggested, "if your offer is genuine, you might take half of the girls, and I will take the other half. Lillian can accompany you." Then she realized she had not introduced her companions to Tom. "Excuse me, I've been remiss. This is my friend, Miss Lillian Bennett. And this is Mike Welsh, who works for me."

His attitude toward Lillian and Mike was as kind and gracious as it was toward Graciela, and he did not seem in the slightest disappointed at her suggestion that they take separate conveyances; a fact that pleased her by confirming her rational response and displeased her by reminding her that her heart might be a bit fickle.

She dismissed Tom Blanchard from her mind and set about the business of paying money and signing documents. All told, she had acquired seventeen indentured workers. Only after she read the contracts did she realize what a great responsibility that was. This time she would not be able to give up Frisco's, no matter how strong Beau's objections.

It was while she was collecting the girls and introducing herself to them that Natasha startled her by saying, "You don't remember me, do you?"

Natasha was the dark-haired, olive-skinned child who had reminded her so much of herself. She stared at her dumbfounded.

"There's no reason you should remember," the child blushed. "I was very small the last time you saw me. But I remember you, and I thought—when you bid so much for me—you did recognize me. After you left the tribe, we saw nothing but tragedy. First Butsulo. Then all the rest went, one by one. As far as I know, I'm the only one left."

"You're a Rom?" Graciela gasped.

Natasha nodded.

Graciela shook her head in astonishment. "It can only be fate that has brought you here to me at this particular time. We will be good luck for each other—you and I."

The child cast her dark eyes downward. "I hope so," she said sadly. "But so far I have wit-

125

nessed only bad luck. Ever since the Nail appeared that day, glowing horribly red-hot, and you and Shandor left us, I have forgotten what good luck is."

Graciela realized she must not trouble the child now by inquiring further. Right now, it was much more important to get everyone settled in their new home, to find out which girls could learn most quickly, and to begin to train them so that Frisco's could open on schedule.

PART THREE

11

In the two weeks between the auction and the reopening of Frisco's, Tom Blanchard became an important part of Graciela's life. She had thought she would see him on that Monday to repay him, and that would be it. He would disappear as abruptly as he had appeared. However, under one pretext or another, he had called at her home at least once a day. Usually it was to offer his help in some facet of the organization or business of Frisco's.

Occasionally the calls were purely social, instigated by Lillian, who teased her, "Why shouldn't you entertain him? Beau has no legal claim on you, and Tom is smitten with you. I can tell."

At times Graciela suspected that it was really Lillian who was smitten with Tom, but she denied it vehemently. "I like him," Lillian would admit. "He's handsome and charming and kind. But I'm not going to fall for any man. Anyway, it's you he comes to see."

That, Graciela had to admit, was true. But she continued to deny, even to herself, that what she felt toward him might be love. It was quite simply a physical attraction, mixed with gratitude, and she only felt that because she missed Beau so desperately. She did love Beau, and she was reminded of that every time she received a letter from him. His business had gone well with the Colombian government in Santa Fe de Bogota, and the last she had heard he had sailed to the isthmus of Panama.

She missed him most in the moments when she was entirely alone, in the evening as she was going to sleep, and in the morning when she had just awakened. Those were the times when she could not help but recall his smiling face with its green eyes and pale white skin, when she most ached to have his strong arms about her.

At other times, her life was taken up with things that had to be done. There was so little time, she had finally found it necessary to delegate responsibilities. Mike was given full control over getting the *Ellen Jane* shipshape. Lillian and Julie were placed in charge of teaching the girls the rules of the various games they would supervise, as well as how to cope with difficult situations. Constance was given the task of supervising those who could sew the green smocks the girls would wear when on duty at Frisco's.

Graciela had decided that two of the girls were too young to work the gaming tables, yet were old enough to work. Ruby, the shy blonde girl who had been Graciela's first purchase, and Brenda, the one with the brown braids, were assigned to the household under Janet Brown, the only one of the indentured servants who had had considerable experience as a housekeeper.

There was only one of the girls that Graciela hesitated to press into service. Not only did she feel that Natasha was too young to work a full day, but there were signs that the child was still emotionally upset from the series of tragedies she had endured. So Graciela had placed Natasha in Lyuba's charge, in the hope she might make a suitable companion for Alex. Lyuba was delighted by this, welcoming her like a long lost member of her family, which in a way she was, though they had never met.

Almost daily, Lyuba found some reason to praise Natasha to Graciela. One day it was the games that the girl had taught to Alex. "They adore each other," Lyuba explained, "like brother and sister." The next day it was her voice. "She sings like a little bird." Then it was her dancing. "She does the dances like in the old country."

But Lyuba did not have to tell her about Natasha's most astonishing talent. Graciela discovered it for herself one evening as she went up to her room tired and strained from the difficult day. As she passed the head of the stairs and reached the nursery door, Graciela heard music, the achingly melancholy strains of a violin, sweetly and deftly played. It was an air that was vaguely familiar to Graciela, and it so startled her that she thought at first it must be her imagination. But then the music broke into rapid dancing flight, and there was delighted laughter from behind the nursery door.

The music was real, and it was being played in her own home. But by whom? She eased the nursery door open slightly to peer curiously inside. To Graciela's amazement, it was Natasha who stood in the middle of the room, skillfully playing the violin, while Lyuba danced and Alex sat mesmerized, his eyes wide and incredulous. Graciela stood transfixed by the magic for a long moment before she made the connection. Of course Natasha had learned to play the violin among the Rom; the piece of music she was playing was one of the favorite airs of the Rom. She had danced to it herself many times.

She waited until Natasha had finished playing and Lyuba and Alex were applauding before entering the room. "That was beautiful," Graciela exclaimed appreciatively. "Why didn't you tell me you could play the violin?"

Natasha dropped her gaze to the floor, reflexively tucking the violin and bow behind her skirts. "There was no opportunity," she apologized. "You have been so very busy."

"But where did you get the violin?" Graciela asked. "You only brought the one carpetbag with you."

"It was in the bag," Natasha explained, squirming under the questions. "I had it wrapped up in petticoats so no one could find it." Then she lifted her gaze to look up at Graciela. The child's eyes were glazed with tears about to break. "Will you take it away from me?"

"Of course not," Graciela exclaimed. "Why should I want to take it away from you? It's yours, and you play it beautifully."

"The old woman who sold me to the ship," Natasha explained. "She took it away from me, but I stole it back. She told me it was the instrument of the devil."

"Well, she was wrong," Graciela told her kindly. "Nothing that creates beauty or joy could possibly come from evil. You have a wonderful gift, and you must never believe anyone who would take that gift away from you." She smiled affectionately. "Now, play something else for us."

Natasha played again, one piece after another, and it turned out that she was as skilled at playing the music of great composers as she was at playing the songs of the gypsies and those of common country folk.

133

Graciela had forgotten what a fine magic music was. It restored energy to her tired body and released her soul from its self-imposed bonds. It was something that was sorely missing from the life of this crude frontier town. She said nothing to Natasha then, but she made plans to build the girl's confidence so that she might persuade her to play for the customers at Frisco's. Even if only a few were able to appreciate it, she would be performing a great service.

When Tom Blanchard heard the child play, he agreed with her, and joined Graciela in encouraging Natasha to come out of her shyness. By the time all of the preparations were completed on Frisco's, Natasha agreed to play, at least on opening night.

12

The day of Frisco's opening was one filled with good omens—too many good omens for Graciela's comfort. It was like a gambler's winning streak; she feared it could not last through the evening. The day broke clear and sunny, unusually warm for December. There was a letter from Beau reporting that everything in Panama was going far better than he expected If all continued as well, he might be home by spring. Best of all, his well wishes for the opening seemed to be sincere.

Early in the afternoon was inspection time. Everyone met at the boat for a last-minute check of equipment and responsibilities. Graciela had set the meeting for two o'clock; she had no idea that Lillian had arranged for everyone else to be there half an hour earlier. To Graciela, she had made an excuse about an errand, promising to meet her there. Tom insisted upon escorting her to the boat, suggesting that it was foolish for Mike to come all the way up Telegraph Hill just to get her when he was sure to have his hands full with final spit and polish. Even Lyuba excused herself from riding in the carriage with Graciela, saying that it would be better for Natasha to get adjusted to the boat before all the excitement and confusion began.

She did not think there was anything odd about their behavior, though it did occur to her that they seemed to be conspiring to throw her and Tom together without a chaperone. Tom's manner confirmed this. He was much more high-spirited than usual, his eyes twinkling with some secret amusement.

They arrived at the docks promptly at two o'clock. Graciela was slightly annoyed to find only Mike there to greet her. No one else was anywhere about, and Mike remained up on deck, calling out to her, "Well, she's all finished. What do you think?"

"If you mean the *Ellen Jane*," Graciela called back, "I think she looks lovely."

Mike grinned at her. "If you think she's still the *Ellen Jane*," he shouted, "you'd better have another look."

Graciela looked at the bow. All trace of the original name was gone, and in bright fresh paint were the words, *Frisco Lady*.

A thrill of pride and pleasure swept through her. "I hope you like the name," Mike beamed. "Me and Tom thought it up."

"I think it's perfect," she shouted, aware of the blush rising in her cheeks. "Thank you." She turned to Tom, who was smiling proudly, "And thank you."

"It was nothing," Tom replied. "But she's only your namesake. She has nothing on the real true Frisco lady. No lady could be as lovely as you."

Graciela tried to ignore the compliment. She turned to call back to Mike. "Why isn't everyone here?" she called out. "I told them it was important to be on time."

"I can't hear what you're saying," Mike cried. "Come aboard."

Tom offered her his arm, a mischievous smile on his lips. "May I?"

She took his arm, and they stepped up on the gangway, which was decked in brightly colored bunting. Swiftly, Mike pulled a small silver seaman's whistle from his pocket and began to pipe a signal, standing as close to attention as he was capable.

"What in the world?" Graciela exclaimed.

"That's the signal that the captain is coming aboard," Tom explained. "I had a devil of a time teaching it to Mike. I think he's tone deaf."

As she stepped on deck, Mike gave a rather sloppy salute, which was genuine if not accurate, and said, "Welcome aboard, ma'am."

137

"Thank you," she said, genuinely touched, but her eyes were on the deck of the *Frisco Lady*. She had not been on the boat since early the previous morning, and then it was still littered with workmen and open cans of varnish and tools. Now it was not only spotlessly clean and shining with fresh paint and varnish, but it was gaily decorated with bunting and Chinese paper lanterns.

"Mike," she exclaimed, happy tears welling up in her eyes, "was this your doing?"

"Well," Mike shuffled and scratched his head in embarrassment, "it wasn't exactly my idea, but I done most of it."

"Then who?" she asked.

Mike grinned. "You're holdin' onto him."

Graciela looked up at Tom. "You?"

Tom nodded. "It's an important night," he explained, "and I wanted it to look festive for you."

It was a difficult moment for Graciela. She was moved beyond words. She had the strong urge to throw her arms around Tom and to give him a warm grateful kiss. Tom was also filled with emotion, and she feared that what she saw in his eyes was love. He stared down into her eyes for what seemed an eternity, hesitating to speak words that were fighting to burst from his lips. Finally, he flushed and said, "Perhaps we should go below."

Graciela was slightly dazed as she accompanied Tom to the stairs, her mind racing to control the emotions she was feeling. What meaning was concealed by his words? Was he taking her below deck so that they could be alone? Did he intend to sweep her into his arms and to profess his love?

As they made the turn at the landing and started down the second flight of stairs into the grand saloon, Graciela had her answer. Her first reaction was shock, and then she burst into laughter.

They were all there—friends and employees—waiting for her, all lined up like a navy crew ready for inspection.

Beside her, Tom called out, "Let's have three cheers for the captain! Hip! Hip!"

"Hooray!" they shouted.

By the third cheer, Graciela's eyes were filled with tears. The grand saloon glittered in the mist of her happiness. The lights flickered like stars against the highly polished brass chandeliers and wall sconces and on the brass spittoons lined up neatly along the walls. The warm oak panelling had been polished to a glistening shine, and colorful romantic paintings in gilt frames, paintings she had never even seen before, hung on all the walls. At the far end of the room, the crimson velvet curtains, trimmed in tasselled gold braid, were closed as if waiting for a show to begin. She noticed that Natasha was conspicuously absent, and she suspected the child was waiting, hidden onstage, for her part of the surprise.

Lillian stepped forward from the head of the

139

line to deliver a little speech she had clearly rehearsed very carefully. While she spoke, Janet Brown and the two housemaids, in black dresses with starched white aprons, poured and served champagne for everyone.

"This is a great day for San Francisco," Lillian said, her voice filled with emotion. "After tonight, she will be whole again. One of the great legends of her birth will be restored. For those of you who are new to this struggling little city on the bay, there was, a few years ago, a woman who was synonymous with San Francisco. Her heart and soul captured the very spirit of the place, and out of respect and love, she was called Frisco. After the fire last year, however, she left us, and we have not been the same since.

"Tonight she returns to us." Lillian lifted her champagne glass. "Ladies and gentlemen, I give you Frisco!"

They all raised their glasses to Graciela, and then drank, crying, "To Frisco!" She was deeply moved. The last time, the name Frisco had just grown on her; this time she was officially christened—and with champagne. To her, this emphasized the difference between the old Frisco and the new. In the old days, she had been too young, inexperienced, and probably foolish. Now she realized what a great responsibility she bore. People depended upon her, and she could not ignore that fact. There was no turning back: Frisco she was; and Frisco she would have to remain.

"Thank you, Lillian," she said. "Thank you all very much. I hope I can live up to your expectations. I guess I am now Frisco again, and you must all address me as such. As of now, there is no more Graciela, and no more Mrs. Tolliver. But you must remember that I am not all there is to Frisco. You are all a part of Frisco, and I am depending upon you as much as you are depending upon me." She paused, then adopted a clearly false expression of sternness. "Now, if you are all ready for inspection."

They all returned to attention, straightening up their line and stiffening up their posture, though it was impossible for them to give up their proud and happy smiles.

As she walked down the line, inspecting every detail of dress and hairstyling, Frisco could find nothing in the slightest to criticize. Everything was perfect, from the highly polished shoes, to the neat green smocks, to the ribbons in their hair.

After she had reached the end of the line and declared her satisfaction, she said, "But someone seems to be missing. Where is Julie? I'm sure she knew she was to be here. And Natasha, too."

"They're here," Lillian said impishly, "but they couldn't attend inspection. I'm afraid you'll have to sit down for this."

Lillian led Frisco to a table set directly in front of the stage and insisted she sit. Everyone else moved forward to stand in a group behind her.

141

Suddenly the crimson stage cutrains parted to reveal a grand piano. Nothing else on the stage, but nothing else was needed.

"My God!" Frisco exclaimed. "Where did it come from?" She had never even dreamed of having a piano. They were rare and precious possessions. Until now, there had been only four in the entire city of San Francisco, and even they were uprights. No one had even attempted to have a grand piano shipped out.

She looked across the table at Tom Blanchard, standing looking down at her and smiling proudly. "You didn't?" she gasped.

He nodded. "I hope you like it."

"I love it," she admitted, "but I can't possibly accept it. It's much too precious a gift."

"Of course you can accept it," he replied. "It's much too precious not to."

Before Frisco could protest further, Julie walked out onstage in a simple demure black silk dress and sat down at the piano. She was followed by Natasha, wearing all white and carrying her violin. To Frisco's surprise the child seemed transformed by the stage; she showed no trace of shyness or fear at all. Without preamble or explanation, they began to play, Julie at the piano and Natasha standing beside the piano with her violin. Frisco had never heard anything like the music they played. It was rapturously beautiful, embodying everything Frisco had ever felt, everything she was. There was grandeur in it, yet there was gypsy as well. When it was over, they all applauded wildly, while Julie and Natasha stood center stage and curtsied graciously.

"It was beautiful," she told the performers later. "But I've never heard it before. What was it?"

"It's a piece of music written by a man named Franz Liszt," Julie explained. "He calls it the Hungarian Rhapsody."

"You must play it again tonight," Frisco said emphatically. "In fact, you must play it often. I don't think I could ever grow tired of listening to it."

13

The first sign of trouble came only moments before Frisco's opened its doors. Frisco was in the room she had set aside for her office, a small but comfortable room just off the landing of the staircase, reviewing the guest list one last time, wondering anxiously which of the invited elite of San Francisco would show up. The wives of the select had been invited formally along with their husbands, though Frisco suspected few, if any, of the women would show up. She had forever separated herself from respectable society by going into business, and there were clearly some who would have religious objections to the kind of business she had gone into.

When the knock came at the door, she expected it to be Lillian, come to tell her that everything was ready and that the first guests had arrived on deck. Instead, it was Tom Blanchard. His face was flushed, and there were worried furrows on his brow. "There's trouble brewing," he said anxiously as soon as he had shut the door behind him. "Albert Valery's up to something."

Frisco did not panic. "I knew he would try something sometime," she said calmly. "What does he plan to do?"

"I don't know," Tom replied. "At least not precisely. I just heard the rumors as I was passing through Sydneytown on my way over here. I was told he had hired a few toughs to show up here tonight and cause trouble."

Frisco shook her head in resignation. "Well, there's nothing much we can do except let Mike know so he can be ready for them." She went to the door, opened it, and called out to Mike, who was standing near the foot of the stairs talking to Lyuba. He came inside, closed the door behind him, and Frisco related what Tom had told her.

"Oh, yes, ma'am," he nodded. "I heard about that yesterday, and we're all ready for them."

Frisco looked at him crossly. "Why didn't you tell me about it?"

Mike grinned sheepishly. "I didn't think it was anything to bother you about. Don't worry. It's all taken care of. You should see how nice my old friends look in their fancy new suits. You won't be able to tell them from the upper crust."

"Fine," she said. "I'll be out in about three minutes. You can go ahead and open the doors."

When Mike was gone, Tom smiled at her and said, "I can see that I'm not really needed as much as I thought I was. May I at least have the honor of escorting you tonight?"

"Of course," Frisco responded. She smiled, "And as for being needed, I don't see how I could possibly have done any of this without you. I'm truly grateful, and I don't know how to thank you."

"You know my answer to that," he said. "The privilege of spending a few moments in your company is all the thanks I require."

"I remember," she said. "You told me that after the auction." She hesitated, then added, "But I'm not sure I truly believe it. Especially not after the piano. That is more than just a kindness, more than just a friendly gesture."

"Yes," he replied. "Well . . ." He hesitated, clearly debating with himself on just what precisely he ought to say. "I'm sure you must know by now that I love you."

The word had been spoken, thrust suddenly out into the silence of the room for her to deal with. She regretted immediately that she had pressed him to speak it, because she had no idea how to cope with the situation.

"But you said . . ." She was flustered. "You said you only wanted a few moments of my company."

"And I meant it," he said, his voice gathering strength. "I realize that you are a married

146

woman, even if you and your husband are not on the best of terms. I respect marriage, and I respect you. I have no desire to place you in an embarrassing position."

"I'm afraid you already have done so," Frisco replied.

"What do you mean?" Tom asked.

She could not explain. She wasn't even sure that what she felt for Tom was love. She did feel something when he was near, a desire for his touch, to have him hold her in his arms, to feel his lips on hers. That was surely a physical passion, but was it love? She knew that what she felt for Beau was love, but could a woman love two men at the same time? If she was unfaithful to one, could she truly love either? These were questions she could not possibly answer. And, until she could answer them, she could only try to keep control of her feelings.

"Too much has been said already," she told Tom. "Right now, I think we should go downstairs so that I can welcome my guests." She walked over to the gilt-framed mirror. "Do I look all right?"

"You have never looked lovelier," Tom told her almost passionately. "It is all I can do to keep from taking you into my arms this moment."

She looked back over her shoulder to give him a cross glance. "That doesn't agree with what you said a moment ago. You mustn't go back on your word."

"I'm sorry." His apology was genuine, "but sometimes my heart gets control of my head."

She turned back to the mirror to appraise herself, straightening the folds of her dress, patting her hair into place. Truly, she never had looked better; Tom was right. Lillian had helped her to do her hair the way she liked it, the way Beau had refused to allow her to do it, swept upward and falling down freely in a myriad of ringlets framing her face. And her gown was absolutely perfect for her lush dark beauty. Beau would have voiced strong objections were he to see it. It was a brilliant crimson red silk, with a low-scooped neckline, a tightly fitting bodice, and full, long sleeves that were slashed to reveal black lace undersleeves. Black lace also trimmed the enormous skirt over crinolines.

She descended the stairs to the grand saloon on Tom's arm. All of her employees were waiting at their appointed stations, and they burst into applause as they caught sight of her.

She positioned herself at the foot of the stairs, with Tom on one side and Lillian on the other, to greet her guests. She felt only a momentary pang of fear that they might not, after all, show up, that they might, by now, have forgotten Frisco.

When she caught sight of the first guest descending the stairs, she signalled to Julie to start the music. It was Senator John C. Fremont, and he came without his celebrated wife at his side.

But Frisco was not disappointed; she had not really expected the women. After Fremont, one after another of the notable men of San Francisco appeared—Senator Broderick, Sam Brannan, General Hitchcock, Sam Ward, Judge Hoffman, Judge McKinstry, Harrison Randolph. It was a glittering assembly, and they all welcomed Frisco back without ever mentioning Mrs. Beau Tolliver. They praised her new establishment; they drank to her success; they mingled; and they gambled.

Only the first hour of the evening was for invited guests. After that, the doors were opened to the public. She had placed a large advertisement in the *Bulletin* announcing the time and place of her opening, and so there was no way she could keep track of who came and went. If there was to be trouble, however, she suspected it would be early—after the public had crowded in and before all the prominent invited guests had left.

She was right. The grand saloon was filled with people of all sorts crowded elbow to elbow, when Frisco saw Albert Valery enter, glancing about him nervously. She was near the stage, having just asked Julie and Natasha to play the Hungarian Rhapsody, and so was at the far end of the room from him. However, Mike was standing by the stairs, and she could see that he was aware of Valery's presence. As Valery moved into the midst of the throng, Mike followed him closely, and Frisco continued to watch his movements.

The little Frenchman walked from table to table greeting friends and acquaintances, some of whom were prominent men who would be incapable of making trouble, but others were rough sorts unknown to Frisco. He made a complete circle of the room, then moved toward the staircase as if ready to make his departure. But then he paused, removed his handkerchief, and blew his nose.

As he started up the staircase, a quarrel broke out at the poker table he had just left. Then another started on the other side of the room near Frisco. There were sudden movements at every table, as if men were ready to fight. But before a single blow could be delivered, well-dressed gentlemen—one at each table—grabbed the troublemakers, taking them by surprise and subduing them. A few voiced protests, but Mike's friends told them firmly, "There's to be no trouble at Frisco's."

When the legitimate patrons realized what was happening, they moved to assist. When Albert Valery realized what was happening, he scampered madly up the stairs to escape, but Mike reached him before he could get to the door. "No, my bucko," he shouted. "You've got to stay and watch what happens to troublemakers at Frisco's!"

Mike, with Valery in a hammerlock, led the crowd up on deck. Amid laughter and jeering from Frisco's patrons, each of Valery's toughs were tossed—one by one—overboard into the cold water of the bay.

After all twelve of them were splashing and sputtering in the cold dark water, Mike began to move toward the edge of the deck with Valery, who screamed, "You can't do this to me! It'll be murder! I can't swim!"

"You can learn, can't you?" Mike laughed.

"No," Valery begged, "please!"

The crowd laughed. Someone called out, "This time, Valery, you better learn! You can't beat Frisco! She's too much for one of your kind!"

Valery went screaming into the drink, and the crowd surged forward to watch him flounder in the water, crying for help. After he came sputtering to the surface for the third time, one of his toughs grabbed him by the neck and swam for shore.

When all was quiet again, the guests went back to the grand saloon, and the rest of the evening went smoothly. Frisco's-on-the-boat was a smashing success, with the last guests lingering until midnight.

Then Frisco closed the doors and heaved a sigh of relief. Glowing with satisfaction, and slightly numb with relief, she told the girls who worked the tables, "You were all absolutely perfect. You did your jobs well, and you behaved impeccably. I'm proud of you, and I'm grateful.

151

It's been a hard day for you, and so you can all go to bed now. I'll take care of the money and close up."

The girls accepted her offer gratefully. Most were visibly tired. Cabins for all of the boat's employees had been fashioned on the lower deck, where they were all under the supervision of Lillian Bennett. They said their good nights and departed.

Lyuba had gone home earlier, taking Alex, Natasha, and the household staff, so Frisco was left alone with Mike and Tom, who accompanied her to her office to help her count the money. They had made a good profit, surprising Frisco because all of the drinks for the opening had been on the house.

"You know," Mike said, as Frisco put the money away, "I think we'd better keep a guard posted up on deck at nights. I don't think Valery and his friends will try anything again, but just to be safe I think maybe I ought to hang around here tonight." He turned to Tom Blanchard. "Do you think you could take Frisco home?"

"I'd be glad to," Tom replied eagerly.

14

It was the perfect ending to a perfect day. She was actually pleased to be taken home alone by Tom Blanchard, and she refused to pretend that she was not. She was happy, and she wanted her happiness to linger. Whether she loved him or not, he did make her happy. He was kind and gentle; he was warm and strong. And he had confessed that he loved her. It had been so very long since a man had spoken to her of love.

The town was quiet at this hour of the night. Only a few lights shone from the houses clustered amid the hills that bounded the town. At the moment, she did not see those houses and buildings as shabby and crude; she saw only the lights and felt them to be like stars that had settled to earth. In her fancy, that seemed entirely possible, for the crisp, cold night did not hold a single cloud, making the black, moonless sky an immense canopy of stars.

There seemed to be no one else in the world besides her and Tom. They were together, their bodies almost touching as they sat next to each other in the carriage seat.

For a while, they did not speak. There was no sound at all except for the plop, plop, plop of the horse's hooves and the sound of their own breathing. They were beginning the climb up Telegraph Hill when Tom finally broke the silence. "You didn't answer my question," he said.

"What question?" Frisco asked, startled.

"The one I asked you earlier in your office," he explained. "How have I compromised you?"

Frisco hesitated. She had not answered the question before because she had not wanted to. She had been afraid to answer it, afraid of revealing too much of her own feelings. Now, in this warm, happy moment, still savoring the elation of her success, she was afraid of nothing. She relished her feelings for Tom as a part of all the wonderful magic of being alive.

"By speaking of love," she said.

He stopped the horses, rested the reins in his lap, and turned to face her. "That couldn't possibly compromise you," he said, searching into her eyes, "unless you feel something of the same for me."

"I do care for you, Tom," she said. "But . . ."

She hesitated, and she was lost. In her moment of hesitation, Tom swept her into his arms and kissed her. There wasn't time to think, to control the emotions that filled her and controlled her reaction. Her body wanted his arms about her; her lips wanted his lips. She responded to his kiss passionately, her arms slipping around his waist to cling to his strong broad back.

But as the kiss lingered, with his hot breath flooding over her face, her reason began to gain control, and she broke away. "Please, Tom," she gasped desperately, "we mustn't. After all, you promised."

"That was before you said you loved me," he said, his hand caressing her cheek.

"I didn't say I loved you," she protested.

"Perhaps not with words," he said with a gentle adoring smile. "But you said it with your eyes. In fact, you're saying it now."

"Please, Tom," she begged. "Take me home. I must have time to think."

"All right," he said, and gave a snap to the reins to get the horse going again.

They rode on in silence, a silence that was much heavier than before. Frisco tried to remind herself that she belonged to Beau, that she loved only him, and that he loved her, but she did not truly believe it. Beau had not pressed his love on her since that first time, at the very beginning of their false marriage, and even then he had apologized later when he had made his speech about giving her freedom. And now he was thousands of miles away, trekking through some jungle, seeking his own happiness. Hadn't Beau emphasized by every word, by every action, that he wanted his freedom, that he wanted her to be free to choose as well?

Slowly she convinced herself that she was no longer Mrs. Beau Tolliver. She was Frisco. She was her own person. It was foolish to hope that, when Beau returned, things would be any different. There had been—in her turbulent life—so few chances for happiness. Who could possibly condemn her for grasping at a chance when it came?

They arrived at her home in silence, and in silence Tom helped her down from the carriage to escort her to the door. Except for one dim light shining in the front hall, the entire house was dark. Lyuba, the children, and the staff were all asleep.

At the door, Tom did not sweep her into his arms; he did not kiss her. He simply looked down at her questioningly.

"Come inside," Frisco said softly. She lit a lamp in the parlor and closed the curtains. She started to build a fire in the fireplace, but Tom knelt down and said, "Here, let me do that."

His hands moved deftly and within moments flames leaped forth, sending a warm glow dancing throughout the dimly lit room. She was sitting by the hearth, and Tom turned to her, the fire in his dark eyes reflecting the leaping flames he had just made. He reached out gently and took her hand in his. "I love you," he said softly. "I never intended to say those words, though I have wanted to from the very moment I first set eyes on you. You are the most beautiful and the most exciting woman I have ever met. It is wild and foolish of me to hope, but I have hoped. I would give up everything I own, everything I am just to hear you say you love me."

She was moved by his gentle passion. Trembling, she told him, "That is one thing I cannot do. Not honestly. I don't know what it is I feel, but I do feel something for you, something that is almost more than I can bear. It may be love; it may be gratitude; it may be only the excitement and elation of a wonderful day. Whatever it is, it makes me happy to be with you. And I want very much to be happy."

He dropped her hand and leaned over to kiss her, his body straining across the yards of red silk and black lace. It was a tense, if passionate, kiss. She leaned forward into his arms, and they fell back onto the floor. The whole world dissolved in that kiss. There were no restraints anymore, no fears, no apprehensions. There were only their lips meeting in desire. The two were one in that desire. Their hands, their bodies, their very souls met and moved as one.

She wanted to feel his smooth warm lips on her neck, her breasts, and he promptly began to explore. She shuddered as a chilling heat swept over her. She wanted more, much more; the sheer anticipation of fulfillment excited her. "Perhaps we should go upstairs," she whispered.

Upstairs, in the darkness of her room, she locked the door. They undressed, climbed into bed, and made love wildly, in an ecstasy Frisco had never known before. Or, at least, if she had known it, it had been so long-her body had forgotten it. In some ways, Tom was like Beau; in others, he was like Shandor had been; and yet he was completely different from both. His body had the smooth muscularity and agility of youth that her dead husband had possessed. But his actions had the knowledge and experience of pleasure that came with age, the assurance that she had recognized in her false husband. But neither man had ever made love to her with more obsessive delight.

And never before had she felt so free to explore a man's body, her hands delighting in the touch of his smooth skin with the muscles hard and rippling beneath, as they wandered from the broad firm back down to the narrow waist and the big powerful buttocks, then back again.

It was almost dawn when their passion was spent and they lay quietly in each other's arms. Frisco did not want Tom to go; she wanted to make their happiness last as long as possible, but she knew that it had to be. Their passion had to remain a secret between them.

After Tom had left, slipping quietly out of her room and downstairs to let himself out, Frisco could not sleep. She lay in bed, savoring her happiness. She recalled the many times she had lain here just like this, with the delicate morning light creeping around and through the curtains, aching for fulfillment, aching to be in a man's arms. She had dreamed that it would be just like this.

But she had never dreamed of Tom Blanchard. The man she had dreamed of holding in her arms had been Beau.

15

In the light of day, Frisco questioned her passion, but in the shadows of evening there were no questions. The days and nights passed in rapid succession, turning into weeks of indecision. She wanted Tom's love, but she came increasingly to believe that she did not truly love him. Certainly she was never able, even in the heat of passion, to speak those words to him. Her head and her heart were torn, and the rift began to affect her and Tom and everyone around them.

At first, she thought nothing of the fact that she had not heard from Beau in a while; the vagaries of the mail packets were so uncertain. But after weeks of receiving no letter, she began to wonder and to worry. Was it possible that he knew about her and Tom? Had someone written to him to tell him? Could he somehow have read between the lines of her letters?

The more she worried about this, the more she became determined to put an end to the romance, and the more she believed she was accepting Tom as a substitute for her real true love. In her quiet, private moments, she was obsessed with thoughts of Beau, terrified that she would never see him or hear from him again, jealous that he might have found some other woman, and—recalling little Alex's premonition—dreading that he might actually be dead.

To try to escape her anxieties, Frisco threw herself frantically into her work. She made Frisco's-on-the-boat all that the old Frisco's had been, and more. Rapidly it became the most popular place in town, where the high-life and the low-life met and mingled. Gradually many of the respectable wives began to accompany their husbands, and they complimented their hostess on the respectability of her establishment and the quality of her entertainment.

Eventually it was running so smoothly that there was little work for Frisco to do. The girls handled the tables with no problems; Lillian managed the girls and the money; and Lyuba, Julie, and Natasha looked after little Alex and took care of the entertainment. Mike looked after the bar and managed the security force. Frisco had nothing to do but mingle as hostess and sit quietly in her office; and almost always, Tom was in her company, following her about adoringly.

That was when she decided that Frisco's would have to have a permanent structure. The boat would not last forever, and eventually people would tire of the novelty. She was making money faster than Lillian could count it, and so she could afford a fine brick building, something permanent and fireproof. Building it would also give her something to do, something that would take her away from Tom. She began to make plans. She still owned the property on Nob Hill, where the old Frisco's had been, and that seemed the ideal place.

Tom resisted the idea, resenting the time it took away from him. "You're making a mistake," he told her. "Part of the success of this place is the romantic aura of the boat. You're just wasting money—and time."

"Time you think belongs to you," she snapped at him. "It's my time and my money! I can spend it any way I want to!"

"And you don't want to spend your time with me," he scowled bitterly. "Is that it?"

She hated herself for hurting him, and she softened guiltily. "That's part of it," she told him. "Oh, Tom, don't you see that we can never be truly happy together? We've had our brief moments of happiness, but I can never love you. It's sheer foolishness to go on this way. One day Beau will return, and meanwhile we're tearing each other apart. I know your business is suffering because you're spending so much time with me."

"I've told you I don't care about my business," he said shrilly. "I will give up everything for you if I have to."

"But that's wrong," she said. "You may give up everything and still not have me, and I couldn't bear to have that happen."

After these fights, Tom always went to Lillian for consolation. She had known about their romance almost from the very beginning, and he took advantage of that fact by pouring out all his troubles to her. Only Frisco knew how much this hurt Lillian, because only Frisco knew how much she was growing to love Tom. Certainly Tom never suspected.

Frisco was as much troubled by the situation as Tom was, but she had no one she could turn to for advice. She was the rock, the foundation, that everyone else depended upon, and she could not even allow the appearance of weakness. She suffered all in silence, or at least she did so for as long as she could bear it.

The winter passed in isolating turbulence, and there was still no word from Beau. With the first signs of spring, she and Tom seemed always to be lashing out at each other. Finally, in desperation for some form of comfort or solace, she went to Lyuba and asked her to read the cards for her.

The wise woman simply nodded, as if she had known for some time that this request was coming. "Come into my room and sit down," she said. "The cards are on the table."

They were the old familiar Tarot cards that Lyuba had carried with her for years. They were now worn and slightly frayed at the edges from much use. As she stared down at the cards, memories of other times, other places flooded over her, and she remembered Lyuba's way of reading. She did not always require the person's presence to read for them. Often she read and kept her silence, aware that there was little she could do to alter fate. Of course, Lyuba probably knew everything that had been happening to Frisco, as well as everything that might happen. She had been foolish not to come to her before this.

Lyuba sat down across the table from her and shuffled the cards, an act she performed as automatically and as routinely as breathing, her thin bony fingers extending, bending, flexing—now touching, now releasing the cards in a ritualistic dance. When she was satisfied with the mix, she extended the deck toward Frisco. "Take a card," she instructed.

Frisco picked one and laid it down in the center of the table, face up. It was the Hanged Man. Frisco knew enough about the Tarot to realize that was not good.

Lyuba simply nodded, as if that was what she had expected, and proceeded to lay out the mystical pyramid and circle, nodding as each card appeared. Good or bad, they were telling a story, as the cards had told stories to the Rom for centuries.

Frisco recognized many of the cards and knew their meaning, but they did not tell her stories. There was Justice, and there was Judgment. The Sun and the Moon. There was the Devil, the Lovers, and the Wheel of Fortune. There was Force, and there was the Fallen Tower. And finally, there was the Grand Reaper—Death. Frisco knew that most of those elements were in her life, but she did not know the outcome. That could be told only by Lyuba, from the placement of the cards, the direction they faced, and from a mystical, intuitive relationship she had acquired with the cards over the years.

In an expressionless voice, Lyuba began to read. "Everything you seek," she said, "is within your grasp, but nothing will come easily, and there will be much pain and suffering. There are two men in your life, one dark and one fair, both of whom love you."

"You're sure of that," Frisco interrupted. "*Both* do?"

"Both," Lyuba repeated. "But you must make a choice between them. Your indecision is destroying both of them. Only by choosing can you save both and yourself as well."

She paused, then continued. "One of the men is far away, but he will be returning soon. If you cannot make your decision before he returns, there will be disaster. Even if you do, you will be punished for your mistakes.

"You will build much, create great things, but you will also destroy and risk everything. Death and destruction are very near.

"Finally, you will have to give away all that you have in order to get all that you want."

"You speak of death," Frisco said hesitantly. "It is not one of the men who will die, is it?"

"No," Lyuba said, "it is not, but I cannot say who it is. It would not help you to know."

Frisco did not understand most of the card reading, but she did grasp one fact and allowed it to buoy her spirits—Beau was coming home, and soon. That meant he was alive and safe. And, according to Lyuba, he loved her.

Lyuba had implied that it would be difficult for her to make her choice. But the knowledge that Beau loved her made it easy. The thing that was going to be difficult was telling Tom and getting him to accept it.

Frisco remembered Shandor's wise old grandmother, Pesha's words, "My dear, use your imagination to solve problems, for the imagining ability we all possess is our most powerful tool." She would try not to dwell on her fears.

16

With spring's full flowering came resolution. Frisco planned carefully how and when she would tell Tom. She wanted pleasant, happy surroundings, an atmosphere in which she could talk to Tom and make him understand, without either of them being tempted to shout or hurl accusations. She also wanted people around.

The occasion of the picnic seemed ideal. The girls had worked hard all winter making Frisco's-on-the-boat a success. To thank them, Frisco planned a picnic. To make it a celebration, she planned it for the day the walls would be raised on the new Frisco's on Nob Hill. There were already a few structures built on Nob Hill, but for the most part, it still had the feeling of the country, and the construction site would be ideal for a picnic.

The entire group started out from the boat early that Monday morning, a long caravan of buckboards and wagons, led by Frisco's carriage. All were loaded to overflowing with food and provisions, topped with the girls dressed in bright-colored gingham dresses and carrying little matching parasols to protect their complexions from the sun. Some had invited their beaux to join them, and there was a great deal of laughter and fun. As they rode through the town and up the hill, Natasha, who was riding in the carriage with Frisco, Tom, and Alex, played songs on her violin, while the other carriages sang along to the music.

The weather was delightfully warm, with balmy breezes and great white cumulus clouds scudding across the sky. Everywhere, flora and fauna were breaking forth in new life. It was a time for ends and for beginnings.

The workmen were waiting at the site, having spent the early morning hours completing the foundation and putting the sills in place. They had been invited to join in the food and festivities, and they welcomed the wagons eagerly, helping the girls down and then assisting in unloading the food and setting up the tables. There was much excitement and much merriment. Mike, Lyuba, and Janet supervised the setting up of tables. It took only a few moments for Mike to declare, "Would everybody stop trying to be so helpful! You're just getting in the way! Go for a walk, or dance, or something!"

The newly laid floor was perfect for dancing. Two of the girls set Natasha up on a platform fabricated with two sawhorses and a couple of boards, and she played her violin, while couples paired off to dance.

Now seemed the ideal moment for Frisco to be alone with Tom with no interruptions. She was not needed for preparing the food, nor did she have to look after the children. As long as she knew where Natasha was, she could be sure that Alex would be in the same place. Alex had come to adore the older child, had in fact become her shadow. When Natasha played her music, he would sit absolutely entranced watching and listening.

Frisco pulled Tom aside and suggested, "Let's go for a walk. I want to talk to you."

They climbed up to the crest of the hill, where they could look out toward the bay, with the town of San Francisco at their feet. There was a bit of grass and a few scrubby pines, and they found a shady spot to sit down.

Frisco had decided she would not break her news to Tom gently. She had tried the gentle approach before, and it had never worked. He had grown immune to gentleness. At the same time, she had to be careful not to be offensive, because that would only start a fight. She had to be careful to be straightforward, direct, and cold.

169

"Beau is coming home," she said bluntly.

"You've had a letter from him?" Tom asked, surprised.

"Yes," Frisco lied. "So this has got to end now, Tom. Today. We must not see each other anymore."

Tom got to his feet and walked off a few feet to stare out toward the peaceful blue water. There was a ship sailing into the bay now. He stared at it miserably as if it were the ship that was destroying his happiness by bringing Beau home. After a long time, he spoke, but he did not turn back to look at Frisco as he did so; he continued to stare out at the water and the ship slipping gracefully toward the docks. "I understand," he said. "For your sake, whatever we have had together must end, at least for now. But I want you to understand that I still love you, and I cannot stop seeing you entirely."

"You must," Frisco persisted. "It's the only way. If you continue, you'll only be torturing yourself, and me as well."

"I couldn't live if I could never look upon your face, hear the sound of your voice, ever again," he said morosely.

"You can and you will," Frisco replied, "because you have to."

He turned to face her. Beneath the hurt, Frisco could see a trace of anger and resentment in his eyes, like a child. "You cannot keep me from coming to the boat now and then," he said. "Simply as a customer."

Frisco hesitated. She realized, in some ways, Frisco's-on-the-boat was his creation as much as hers. True, he had given her things, claiming that she must feel under no obligation to him, but she did feel obligated.

"No," she said equitably, "I can't stop you from coming there. But I do think it's unwise, and I can't promise that you'll see me."

"You can't shut me out of your life completely," he protested. "We mean so much to each other. I don't think you realize how much."

"I do," she said coldly, realizing how cruel she was being. "But there is someone else who means more to me."

He ignored her cruelty, began to move toward her. "I don't think you can be sure of that," he said. "You haven't seen him in months." Then he pulled her to him, trying to hold her in his arms, extending his lips to kiss her.

But Frisco fought back, jerking out of his embrace. "No, Tom!" she said strongly. "It must end now! No more! I want you to turn around and walk down that hill, and not look back."

He looked at her, still determined, his dark eyes filled with passion, his lithe body straining desperately for hope. And then his shoulders fell in resignation, and a sad smile crept across his lips. "All right, my love," he said, "But I will not say good-bye."

He turned and began to walk down the hill. Frisco looked at his back for only a moment, then quickly averted her eyes to gaze out to sea. If he did turn, she did not want to see. It was not as clean or as definite a break as she had wanted, but at least Tom had not fought with her. At least he had accepted it. She stood there, gazing out to sea, until she was certain that Tom had rejoined the group down the hill. Then she returned as well.

She arrived at the construction site just as the food was being served. She noticed that Tom had not gone home; he was talking to Lillian, and he did not even look her way. Frisco felt a slight pain of regret, but she quelled it immediately and set about filling a plate with food. Everywhere around her, couples were pairing off to share the repast. Love and romance were blossoming— some of the girls with the beaux they had brought along, some with the workmen. Even Lyuba and Mike, with their on-again, off-again romance, seemed quite distinctly on again, as they sat beneath a tree bantering and teasing affectionately.

Frisco ate her lunch in the company of Alex and Natasha, feeling strangely like an outsider in the face of their special friendship. After the meal, there was an hour of blissful, almost somnolent quiet, when some of the couples wandered off and the others simply rested quietly in the shade or basked in the warm spring sunlight.

Tom disappeared with Lillian, and Frisco played games with Natasha and Alex.

At two o'clock, everyone gathered at the construction site for the raising of the walls. The four frameworks for the four outside walls had already been hammered together by the workmen. All that was required was to lift them into place, attach them to the sills, and nail them together. Not really a very complicated procedure, but Frisco had decided that this would be the ideal stage in construction for making a little speech that would call forth a blessing on the endeavor.

The workmen could have raised the walls themselves, but the girls and their beaux wanted to participate, and so the entire group divided into four teams, each headed by a carpenter. They were going to make a game of it, a race to see which team could get its wall up the fastest. The signal to begin the race would be given by Natasha. The moment she began to play the Hungarian Rhapsody, they were to start.

The girl stood on her platform, violin poised, with Alex and Frisco alongside her. The bow struck the first chord, and the race was on, with everyone laughing and shouting challenges to the other teams. Suddenly one of the carpenters, who was hammering on the wall to Frisco's left, screamed out in pain, releasing his hammer and sending it flying into the air. At first, everyone thought he had accidentally hit a finger, and a few people laughed. But he continued to scream and clutch at his hand, saying, "It's burned! I don't understand how, but the damned thing is burned!"

They all stopped what they were doing and crowded around to stare at the workman in puzzlement. Then one of the girls—Diana—pointed at the nail he had been hammering and exclaimed, "Look! The nail is glowing! It's red hot!"

The crowd stared at the nail. It was indeed glowing with heat. The wooden stud it was only partially hammered into was beginning to smolder as if, at any moment, it might burst into flames. A murmur of horror and amazement rippled through the gathering. Only three people understood its meaning. Frisco, Lyuba, and Natasha. Frisco and Lyuba simply stared at the glowing nail in silent dread, but Natasha began to scream. "No!" she screamed. "Not again! I can't stand it anymore! No, no, no!"

The crowd was stunned. With the exception of Frisco and Lyuba, no one knew why the child would respond in this way. The wounded workman was forgotten as they all stared at Natasha. As soon as the immediate shock was over, Frisco moved toward the girl to try to console her, but Natasha writhed out of her arms screaming, "No, don't touch me! I'm cursed!" Then she rushed at the nail, which by now had managed to set the

174

stud afire, with small flames licking eagerly at the wood.

Frisco could not stop her from grasping the hot nail in her hands and trying desperately to pull it from the wood, though she tugged at the child, shouting, "Leave it alone! You can't do anything about it! Let go!"

The flames now began to move rapidly across the wooden framework. Someone in the crowd said, "My God! We've got to get water!" And a number of men moved off to gather up the tablecloths and find a water supply.

Natasha continued to grasp at the nail, trying to pull it free, but it held firmly. She was now screaming hysterically, her words making no sense at all. Frisco slapped her. "Stop it!" she shouted at the child. "Let it burn! It's the only way!"

She slapped her again, and this time Natasha released her grip on the nail. She fell back, whimpering and staring in shock at the badly burned palms of her hands. This time the child did not fight off Frisco's embrace; she let her hug her and try to soothe her. "Don't worry," Frisco told her with a desperate urgency. "It's going to be all right."

Natasha began to whimper as the shock wore off and the pain in her hands hit her. Lyuba rushed to the food baskets to get ice and butter to treat the injury.

Only then did Frisco realize that the men were now attacking the burning framework with wet tablecloths trying to extinguish the flames. She handed Natasha over to Lyuba for treatment, and turned her attention to stopping the men. "Let it burn!" she told them frantically. "You mustn't try to stop it! You mustn't interfere! The Nail is the gypsy's curse, and there's no way to fight it!"

The men ceased their efforts, but only because it was her building and she seemed to want to let it burn. They could not understand her reason, however; it made no sense to them at all.

"What do you mean by the gypsy curse?" the young carpenter with the burned hand asked. "What has it got to do with this building and that nail?"

"It is a long story," Frisco told him. "But, among the Rom, who are my people, the glowing hot nail always presages great tragedy. It is the most terrible omen that can confront a gypsy; it brings sorrow and death."

"But why a nail?" the workman asked.

"It is said," Frisco explained, "that it was a gypsy blacksmith camped outside the walls of Jerusalem who unknowingly made the nails for the crucifixion of Yeshua ben Meriem, whom you call Jesus. The fourth nail the gypsy made would not cool down no matter what he did, and the Roman soldiers were forced to use only three nails on the cross. The fourth nail has haunted the Rom ever since. It is a curse that none of us can ever escape."

Only after she had finished explaining did Frisco realize that Natasha and Alex had been listening in stony silence. "It's my fault," Natasha whimpered. "I brought the Nail to you. It has been following me for years."

"No, child," Frisco said gently. "It is not your fault. You must believe me. The Nail follows all of us. It has appeared for me long before you ever arrived in San Francisco."

She took Natasha's hands and examined them. The butter and ice had helped to ease the pain, but they had also helped to raise great blisters on the palms. "You're going to have to be treated by a doctor," she told the child. "I think we'd better get into the carriage right now and go back to town."

Frisco and Lyuba helped the two children into the carriage and gave instructions to the others for taking the baskets and supplies back to the boat. Tom came forward and asked Frisco if he could escort them home, but Frisco insisted that Mike would be able to take care of them.

Just as they were about to leave, the carpenter who had been supervising the work came forward and said sheepishly, "Beggin' your pardon, ma'am, but what should we do about the building?"

177

She looked at the charred, blackened framework, still burning and smoking, then looked back at the carpenter. "Let it burn itself out," she told him with a wan smile. "Then tear it down and start over." She paused for a moment, reflectively, then asked, "Do you think you could construct a building without a single nail? Perhaps using wooden pegs?"

The man gave her a puzzled frown, but he said, "Well, I suppose I could, but it would take a long time, and it would cost plenty."

"Don't worry about the time or the money," Frisco told him decisively. "Just do it."

As they rode back down into town, Frisco was worried, but she tried not to let Natasha or Alex see her concern. She was worried about the portent of the Nail. Because of the Tarot reading Lyuba had given her only a few days ago, she was sure the old woman had some idea of what was to happen. But every time Frisco looked inquisitively across the carriage at her, Lyuba's eyes were averted.

The silence was agonizing torture. What was it that lay in store for them?

PART FOUR

17

Frisco did not have long to question: at least a part of the answer was waiting on her doorstep. It was almost dusk by the time the strained, exhausted group arrived at the house on Telegraph Hill. There had been a long wait before the doctor could see Natasha, and then he had spent considerable time in treating the burns and bandaging her hands carefully. To Lyuba and Frisco, the kindly doctor had explained, "I'd hope to keep permanent scarring at a minimum. I've heard her play the violin, and I'd like to see her continue."

The possibility that Natasha might not be able to play again had not occurred to any of them, and it was a very sobering thought. Little Alex had seemed close to tears. It was a somber group that Mike delivered to their front door, each withdrawn into a private anxiety.

None of them saw the man waiting quietly by the door until after they had started climbing the stairs. He was a small man with dark hair, a dark beard, and a swarthy complexion. His face had a gaunt, haggard appearance; his clothes were ill-fitting rags, patched and dirty; and from the stench, Frisco realized he clearly needed a bath. Her first thought was that he was one of the numerous low-life beggars who haunted the docks and Sydneytown, and she started to order him away from her doorway.

But then the man spoke, and, despite his heavy Spanish accent, she recognized a quality of nobility and education. "Señora Tolliver?" he asked.

"Yes?" Frisco responded cautiously.

"I am Juan Pablo Martinez y Guitterez," he said softly. "Please forgive me for coming to you like this, but it is a matter of grave concern, and there is little time for formalities."

"Yes?" Frisco again questioned cautiously. "What is this grave concern?"

"It is Señor Tolliver . . ." he began, then hesitated, glancing questioningly at Mike, Lyuba, and the children.

Frisco's mind began to race: Beau; he has heard from Beau, and there is something gravely wrong. She moved quickly, taking her keys from her purse and striding toward the door. "Come inside, please," she said. "We can talk in the parlor."

The man refused her invitation to sit down,

with a vague apologetic smile that indicated he was aware of his unpresentable appearance. "No," he said. "I will give you my message quickly and then go."

When he did not sit, Frisco herself stood, facing him anxiously, waiting for his news.

"You must understand," Juan Pablo began hesitantly. "Señor Tolliver did not ask me to come. I came of my own choosing. You see, he is sick. I do not think he knows how truly sick he is."

Fear gripped Frisco. "Where is he?" she asked.

"He is in the harbor," Juan Pablo told her. "On board the *California*. We just arrived this morning. He was not well when we left Panama, but I did not know he had the fever. Now he refuses to leave the boat, and I fear he may not survive another night."

"Is it the Yellow Fever?" Frisco asked.

"I do not know," Juan Pablo shook his head. "But I think it is the malaria. We have much of both in Panama. He has the chills first, and now the fever."

"How many people know of his illness?" Frisco asked.

"Only the captain, and a few members of the crew," Juan Pablo told her.

"If none of the authorities know," she began to think aloud, "we must try to get him off the ship and bring him home before they find out. And then we must get him a doctor."

183

"I do not think Señor Tolliver will want to leave the ship," he said with a frown. "And he will be very angry with me for coming to you."

"Better angry than dead," Frisco cried.

She then went to see if Mike was still in the house, found him in Natasha's room with Lyuba and Alex. She explained the situation to him and asked him to try to fashion a litter as quickly as possible. "Also," she added, "see if you can borrow a wagon. This would happen when all of ours are in use!"

From the moment that Frisco learned of Beau's problem, an intense energy and determination took possession of her. She recognized this was a crisis as severe as any she had ever faced, and she refused to give in to weeping or worry. She acted quickly and decisively. During it all, one thing sustained her. In the card reading, Lyuba said that *she* must choose; that meant that she had it within her power to save Beau, and she intended to do it no matter what obstacle presented itself.

It was night by the time they reached the docks, and all was quiet aboard the *California*.

Before she went below to Beau's cabin, Frisco spoke to the captain to see if the authorities had been notified of Beau's illness.

"No," the captain winked. "I'm sure he's just got a bit of the seasickness, and I wouldn't want to see my ship quarantined. You're free to take him home if you can carry him."

184

Quickly, she instructed Mike to pull the wagon onto the dock, right up to the gangway. "Then you and Juan Pablo bring the stretcher down to Beau's cabin," she said.

The *California* reeked of illness. As Frisco went below and worked her way along the narrow corridor to Beau's cabin, the odor and the lack of air were stifling. But Beau's small cramped room was the worst; it was suffocatingly close. The body that lay on the small cot was virtually unrecognizable as Beau. His clothes were filthy rags, and beneath them his body was thin and emaciated. He had grown a beard, and it was dirty and matted, as was his hair. His skin was mottled with a fevered crimson flush. Everything about him—his clothes, his cot—was soaked with sweat.

There was one small lamp beside his cot. Frisco lifted it to survey his condition more accurately. As she did so, his eyes opened. Despite the fever, she could recognize Beau in those eyes. His body may have been felled, but his fierce fighting spirit was unchanged beneath those green luminous orbs.

For a moment, he simply stared up at her without speaking, without even giving a sign of recognition. Then his eyes narrowed and flashed with anger. "It really is you," he said, his voice hardly more than a whisper. "You should not have come. You must go away."

"Be quiet," Frisco replied. "You're going to be taken care of, whether you like it or not."

"No," Beau whispered in protest, "mustn't spread the disease."

"Nonsense," Frisco told him, "treating you isn't going to spread anything. It's just going to help you to recover."

Beau did not have enough strength to protest when Mike and Juan Pablo lifted him onto their makeshift litter and carried him from the boat to the wagon that was waiting on the dock. The bumpy ride home must have been agony for him, but he was too weak to complain.

The other members of the household had returned from the picnic by the time they arrived. Frisco sent everyone scurrying to fill one order after another. Mike was sent out to fetch the doctor, Janet to the kitchen to make tea and broth. One of the housemaids was sent to burn Beau's clothes, the other to heat water to be brought to Beau's room in buckets so that she could give him a bath.

The doctor confirmed Beau's condition as malaria. There was little Frisco could do except try to keep the patient cool and comfortable. "We don't understand these tropical diseases," he told her, shaking his head sadly as they stood outside Beau's room in the hallway. "Some patients live and some die, and there's no way of telling which will do what. Sometimes I think it all depends on how badly they want to live."

Frisco sat at Beau's bedside all night, keeping a constant watch. While he was awake, she fed him broth and tea. While he slept, she bathed his face continually with a cold damp cloth, and she kept up a long, low monologue, telling the man things she would never even have considered saying had he been conscious.

"Dearest Beau," she cooed softly and lovingly, "you must get better, because there are still many things I have to tell you, still many things I want to hear you say. Things like 'I love you.' Yes, Beau, I do love you. I have loved you from the very first moment I set eyes on you in that house in New Orleans, sitting there with the girl on your lap, looking startled and just a bit angry at the intrusion.

"I loved you like a schoolgirl then, a schoolgirl who could never have believed that love might be returned. But later on, when I saw you again here in San Francisco, I hoped. I was more experienced then in the ways of love, and I thought perhaps—just perhaps—that you might come to love me as I loved you. When you risked your life to save me—when you risked your reputation and everything you had—I was certain of it.

"You claimed me as your wife, presenting that false marriage certificate as proof that I could not possibly be a slave. You took me home, and you made love to me, and I was blissfully happy. For that one night, I believed you truly loved me.

"But then, suddenly, you changed. You told

me you did not expect me to live up to that false marriage license. You suggested we live under the same roof, appearing to be man and wife, but not sharing the same bed. I was mortified, afraid that I had not pleased you as you had pleased me. As deeply as I loved you, I was angry because it was clear you did not love me. I resented it when you gave me orders as you would give a slave, and I rebelled, but I never ceased to love you, and to hope that someday you would love me."

She continued to speak to his soul even though she knew he wouldn't remember when he gained consciousness. Secretly, she was hoping that he might somehow hear what she was saying, because she knew that she would never be able to be this honest with him when he was awake.

She kept up her monologue all through the night, her voice droning on and on until it was hoarse, her hands patting the damp cloth on his face until his fever had drained all moisture and coolness from it, then dampening it again and repeating the procedure. By morning, she was completely exhausted, but she kept going, determined that she could last as long as the fever did.

But her head was nodding wearily, fighting off the inevitability of sleep, when Lyuba came into the room, slipping quietly up beside her and saying, "You must rest."

"No," Frisco protested.

"I will take over for a while," Lyuba insisted. "If there is any change at all, I will call you."

"All right," Frisco gave in, "but call me if he awakens."

Lyuba agreed.

As Frisco turned to leave the room, she saw Alex hovering in the doorway, fear and grief in complete possession of his face. "Is Papa going to die?" he asked her, with tears welling up in his eyes.

"No," Frisco assured him. "I'm not going to let him die. And you mustn't either. You must say prayers asking God to let him live."

"But he's very sick, isn't he?" Alex frowned.

She nodded. "Yes," she said faintly. "He's very sick."

"And Natasha's hurt very bad, isn't she?" Alex pursued, with some private connection between the two problems.

"Yes," Frisco admitted, "but she's going to get better, too. Don't worry, she'll play the violin again."

"Is this all because of that nail?" he asked.

She shook her head wearily. "I don't know, child . . . I don't know."

18

By the following evening, he was conscious again and able to talk for a few minutes. The first thing he said to Frisco, however, was, "You should have let me die."

Gradually, Beau's physical condition improved, but his spirit seemed completely broken. It took days for her to learn the full story of what had happened to him in Panama, and to understand the reasons for his despair. The mission had been a complete failure. "It was a foolish dream," he told her one afternoon as she sat by his bedside. "I had no idea what the place was like before I went. I don't see how human beings can live in that terrible oppressive heat and humidity. And the insects—they're indescribable. They attack your body, while the natives attack your soul. Together they devour you body and soul."

Frisco tried to lift him out of his despair. She suggested, "Perhaps, after you're feeling better, you can try again."

"No." He remained adamant. "No one will ever be able to cut a canal through that jungle. And I don't think it would be worth it to try to build a railroad. It would cost too much, both in money and in human lives."

On another occasion, he confessed, "This venture has cost me a fortune. And the business here is almost bankrupt; I don't know if I can salvage it at all. Tom Blanchard has bested me at every turn. I don't know how he did it."

For a whole week, Frisco stayed by Beau's side, looking after his every need. During that week, she did not once go to the boat to work, leaving everything to Lillian and to Mike. She tried to avoid mentioning her own work to Beau, partly because she knew he disapproved of it, and partly because it was such a success that it would only rub salt into his wounds.

However, after a few days, he brought up the subject himself. "Aren't you neglecting your work by staying home with me?" he asked.

"Not really," she replied. "There aren't any problems that Lillian can't take care of."

Later she regretted having told him that much. The fact that she wanted to stay home and take care of him did not register with Beau; what registered was that her work had been a success, while his had been a failure. After that—at every opportunity—he made sarcastic cutting remarks about that fact.

He had always objected to hearing her called "Frisco," and had only called her "Graciela." Now he would use the nickname, but he would always give its pronunciation a slightly cynical, disparaging edge. In the morning, when she would come into his room, he would call out, "Well, *Frisco*'s come to take care of her worthless husband!" or "How many million have you made this week, *Frisco*?"

She did her best to endure his barbs, realizing they hurt him as much as they did her. She could not ignore them, however, though she pretended to. It would only aggravate the situation if she protested or responded in anger. She told herself that he said these things only out of frustration at being an invalid, that his attitude would change when he was able to go back to work himself. But she did not fully convince herself that this was true. There was no longer even the slightest suggestion of love in Beau's manner, not even a flicker of caring in his eyes.

She managed to endure for a week before breaking, and even then she did not allow him to witness her display of emotion. His words were particularly vicious that morning. "I wish to hell you would leave me alone," he accosted her, as she brought in his breakfast. "I'm getting sick of your damned cheerfulness, and I can't stand any more of your pity!"

Frisco controlled herself and replied calmly, "I don't pity you, Beau. And if I'm cheerful, it's because I'm glad to see you're getting better."

"No, it's not!" he snapped back. "It's because you're glad to have me flat on my back! You're getting your revenge!"

"Revenge?" She could not help displaying her incredulity. "Revenge for what?"

"Don't pretend you don't know what I'm talking about," he spat out. "Before I left for Panama, you were always complaining about the way I bossed you around, forced you to do everything my way. Well, you're not my slave anymore! I'm your slave!"

That accusation was more than she could stand. She did not reply to it, because it was so preposterous there was no reasonable reply possible. She simply turned and walked out of the room. She got halfway down the stairs before she broke into helpless tears. She sat down on a step, unable to find the strength to go farther, leaning her head against the railing and letting all her frustration pour out in great sobs.

She was blinded by her tears, and she did not realize she was not alone until she heard sobs echoing from the foot of the stairs. Looking up, she saw Natasha standing below her looking up at her, weeping pitifully, her helpless, bandaged hands held stiffly out at her sides. "Oh, Natasha!" she exclaimed. "Why are you crying?"

193

"Because you're crying," the girl said. "And because I know it's my fault."

Frisco held out her arms to her. "Come here, child," she said.

Meekly, Natasha obeyed, allowing Frisco to enfold her in her arms, to cradle her head on her shoulder. "What makes you think it's your fault I'm unhappy?" she asked softly.

"I've brought you the Curse," the child replied woefully.

"But I've already told you that's not your fault," Frisco said, pulling her back to look sternly into her eyes. "You haven't brought me anything but beautiful music and a lot of happiness."

"But the Nail has followed me everywhere I've gone," Natasha persisted. "Now I've brought it here with me, and look at what it's done for you and Mr. Tolliver. I love you, and I don't want to harm you. I think I should run away or kill myself. That way you would be free of the Curse and happy again."

For the first time, Frisco realized how truly disturbed Natasha was, and she was shocked and horrified. She again clutched the child to her breast tightly, holding her in a desperate desire convey her feelings. "Don't even think such things," she said. "If you should ever do anything of the sort, I could never be happy again. The Curse does not follow any one person. No one can bring it to another. You must believe that."

The child pulled back and studied her face intently, as if trying to decide if Frisco really meant what she was saying or if she was simply trying to console. Finally, deciding that Frisco was sincere, she said, "Then you must try not to be unhappy. You mean so very much to me, I can't bear to see you cry."

It was a reminder of all those who depended upon her. When she had opened Frisco's-on-the-boat, she had made a commitment to them. Since Beau's return, she had neglected them. Even though they could get along without her very well, they needed to see that she still cared, while Beau clearly did not want her caring.

She vowed then that she would go back to work. She would divide her day, giving her mornings to Beau, her afternoons to the construction of the new Frisco's, and her evenings to Frisco's-on-the-boat.

Perhaps if Beau saw less of her, he might appreciate her more.

19

Frisco's energy seemed boundless. With the single exception of lifting Beau's spirits, everything she attempted was successful. Business at the boat could not have been better. The pegged construction of the new Frisco's moved more swiftly than anyone had expected; within weeks, the outer shell of the building would be complete. Under Janet's supervision, the household could not have been run more efficiently.

With Frisco out of the house most of the day and evening, Beau did have more freedom, and he began to invite his friends and business associates over to see him, with the intention of going back to work as soon as he was able. But the more he tried to involve himself in salvaging what was left of his shipping business, the more it seemed to fail. There was one loss after another to the B&B Trading Company, and he became obsessed with the belief that Tom Blanchard was out to destroy him.

Tom continued to visit the boat every night, and he continued his pursuit of Frisco, though she stood firm in her resolve that all was over between them. She gave him no encouragement; she tried to pay even less attention to him than she did to her other customers. Always he sought comfort and refuge in the company of Lillian. He did not see, though Frisco did, how deeply and passionately Lillian was coming to love him. If only he could see that, perhaps half of Frisco's troubles would be over.

If only Beau could love her as deeply as Tom did, she would be blissfully happy. She kept thinking of the Tarot reading that Lyuba had given her. She was certain that she *had* made the choice the older woman had spoken of. Why then could she not have Beau's love as the cards had foretold?

Early one morning after a sleepless night, she went to Lyuba to ask for another reading. "No," the gypsy told her firmly. "The cards have not changed, and they will tell you no more than they have."

"But the cards lied," she said. "I have made my choice. I want Beau's love. The more I try to deserve it, the more he despises me."

"You have not really made your choice," Lyuba said with a sad understanding smile. "Remember, the cards also said that you must forsake everything you have to gain what you want."

"You mean the boat?" Frisco asked in horror. "But I can't do that. I have obligations. So many people depend on me."

"You have not truly chosen," Lyuba nodded.

"That's a choice I can't make," she said angrily.

Lyuba shrugged, as if to say there was no other way.

It was an impossible situation. Time had changed nothing. The dilemma she faced was the same as it had been before Beau had left for Panama; the only difference being that now Beau's very survival as a man depended upon her returning to slavish subjugation. It was his spirit or hers; the two of them could not exist in one love, equally free and strong.

"I refuse to believe that," she snapped angrily. "Beau is not such a weakling that he has to see me destroyed in order to recover his will to live."

"No," Lyuba agreed. "Beau's spirit will recover, but without any help from you."

That much of her prophecy proved to be true. It was the children who began to revive the old Beau. Frisco did not even know that he had begun to spend his afternoons in the company of Alex and Natasha, because she spent her afternoons at the construction site.

One afternoon, however, she came home early. There was no one downstairs in the house, but there was the sound of music coming from the back garden, the Hungarian Rhapsody played on the violin. Joyously, the thought entered her mind: "Natasha has begun to play again; her hands have recovered." And there seemed to be no loss of quality.

She moved purposefully down the hall toward the sound, filtering in through the back door. Janet and the two maids were standing on the small back porch, shaded by the grapevines that climbed over the latticework. When Janet saw Frisco standing in the doorway, she gave her an amazed smile, lifted a finger to her lips, and beckoned her to join them surreptitiously.

As she stepped out onto the porch, she could not see the children, but she could see Beau sitting in a chair in the sun, suffused with light and happiness. There was a glow of the old Beau about him. There was color in his cheeks, a broad smile on his face, and his feet tapped joyously in time to the music. Cautiously, she stepped forward to watch Natasha playing.

She was stunned by the scene that met her eyes at the far end of the garden. It was not Natasha playing so beautifully. It was Alex! Little Alex, who could not yet even read or write. While Natasha looked on proudly, her injured hands clasped in her lap, the child performed every gesture, every note, precisely as she had done before.

The music swept over her, chilling her with its beauty and power and grace. Could this little child possibly understand all its nuances? Of course, he could. She thrilled realizing that her precious son was a musical genius. As he played, his eyes did not leave Natasha. He loved her no less deeply than a grown man would love a woman. He was playing for her, for her alone, though he probably did not even realize it.

Her gaze returned to Beau. He did not even know she was standing there listening and watching. All of the passion she had identified with this piece of music was passion she felt for him, yet had been unable to give to him. As it began to sweep toward its most intense climax, she did not pause to think. Impulsively, she slipped across the grass at his feet. Mesmerized by the music, he did not protest, but simply cast a glazed joyous glance at her and extended his hand for her to hold. She took it gratefully and prayed that this moment could last.

Of course it could not. The music ended, and Beau withdrew his hand to applaud enthusiastically, just as Frisco did. But Beau's joyous enthusiasm did not cease. The child and the music had revived him.

A few days later, he started going back to his office to work. It was then that he began to hear the rumors about Frisco and Tom, though he said nothing to Frisco for several days.

Late one Friday evening, Frisco came home from the boat to find Beau waiting up for her in the parlor. She was in the front hallway, removing her hat and gloves, when he opened the parlor door and said stiffly, "I'd like to speak to you, my dear."

There was in his manner all the angry intensity of the old Beau, and she was taken aback. Warily, she seated herself on the sofa across from him. Whatever it was he wanted to talk about, she knew it was going to be difficult.

"I'd like you to tell me," he said archly, "everything you know about Tom Blanchard."

She realized instantly what he meant. He had heard about their romance, but he wanted her to tell him directly.

She did not cower before his demanding scrutiny. Nor did she intend to lie to him, though she would phrase her response her way. "I know Tom Blanchard very well," she said with dignity. "I won't deny it. We saw a great deal of each other while you were in Panama."

"My God!" he exclaimed. "Then it's true! I didn't really believe it!"

"I don't know what you've heard," Frisco said strongly. "But I have no doubt that it has been added to considerably by gossip and rumor. I owe Tom a great deal; I don't think I could have made a success of the boat without him."

"Are you in love with him?" Beau broke in abruptly.

"No," she replied. "He is in love with me, but I am not in love with him. Nor have I ever been."

"Has he made love to you?" he snapped.

"Yes," she replied truthfully. "But it will not happen again. It's over. He knows there is only one man that I love, and that is you."

Beau chose to ignore that statement. "You are incredible," he said bitterly. "I have one enemy in all of San Francisco. One man in the whole city who is out to destroy me completely, and you choose to take him for a lover! Until now, I had no idea what a bitch you were!"

His cruel words hurt, but more painful was the realization that he despised her, that he refused to understand. In her defense, she said simply, "I made a mistake. He's a very kind man, a very good man. For a very brief time, I thought I might have loved him. But I found out very quickly that what I felt was only a longing for you to return. He means nothing to me."

"Then why did you let him read my letters?" Beau snapped suddenly.

She was so startled by the accusation that she was stunned speechless for a moment. "I didn't," she said finally, incredulously. "I never even discussed your letters with him." But then she began to wonder if she had dropped an incautious word from time to time.

"You're lying," he said. "I've checked everything, and that's the only way he could have known what I was doing and what the company was doing. He used you and through you my letters to destroy my business bit by bit."

"That's impossible!" she exclaimed. "Tom wouldn't do that."

Beau shook his head in disgust. "If you believe what you're saying, then you're a fool! Either way, bitch or fool, I don't want to have anything to do with you!"

And he walked out of the room and out of the house. He did not return at all that night, nor did Frisco see him the following morning. She had no idea where he had gone nor whether he would ever return to her or not. She was completely devastated by his accusations and by his departure. There now seemed no hope at all that they could be reconciled. The breach between them was much too wide. Of course she had only herself to blame for what had happened, but that knowledge made it all the more painful.

She kept going over and over the developments in her mind to try to see if there was any salvation for her whatsoever. Her mind kept coming back to the one accusation Beau had made that was totally unjust—that she had shared his letters with Tom. The more she thought about it, the more she recalled Tom asking about his letters, asking if she had had news from Beau. But she could not recall ever having said anything indiscreet.

Finally, in desperation, she decided that she would confront Tom with the accusation. It was the only way she would know just how guilty she was of betraying the man she loved.

Saturday night was always the busiest night at Frisco's-on-the-boat. Miners came in from the camps and mingled with the town men, both high and hoi polloi. Winnings were big and losings were big, but no one really cared because the excitement was worth it. Frisco moved through the crowds, chatting and joking with old friends, and making strangers feel at home.

As always, Tom came to greet her the moment he arrived on the boat, his dark eyes beseeching her with that hurt, accusing look. His words never strayed from the glib, the casual, but his eyes always begged for privacy and intimacy. Tonight, she saw those eyes light up with delight and expectation when she told him, "I'd like to see you in my office." Her invitation was misleading, because it was charming and gracious.

Her manner changed once they were alone together in her office, with the door closed behind them. Her back stiffened; her shoulders braced to attack. "I've heard some very disturbing things," she said with a trace of anger in her voice. "Now I want to hear you tell me why you sought to become intimate with me."

Tom looked puzzled. "You know why," he said with a wan smile. "Because I'm in love with you." He began to move toward her, with his lithe casual grace, passion still burning in his dark eyes.

"Stay where you are!" Frisco snapped. "That's the reason you've given me! I want to know the reason you've given yourself!"

Tom paused, remained standing a few feet from Frisco. He cocked his head quizzically to one side. "I don't understand," he said. "What are you trying to suggest?"

"Wasn't there a business reason?" she asked. "Wasn't there some profit to be gained by making a fool of Beau Tolliver's wife?"

"No!" he protested immediately, his voice rising sharply. Frisco wasn't sure whether it was in fear or in anger. "That's absolutely untrue! I love you, and I want you for my wife, but I would never . . ." He left the rest unsaid, either from genuine reluctance or from inability to put the lie into words.

"Perhaps," Frisco nodded, softening only slightly. "But once you had gained intimacy with Mrs. Beau Tolliver, wasn't it easy to take advantage of that situation to drive Beau Tolliver slowly into bankruptcy? To learn all the details of his business plans and then turn them to your profit?"

Tom paled. His mouth dropped. He stood totally speechless before the accusation. It was the first time Frisco had ever seen his glib words and his smooth manner fail him, and it was all the answer she needed. "It's true then," she said.

Tom recovered his poise quickly. He moved toward her with desperation to cover up his lie. "No," he said. "You've got it all wrong. I love you." His arms grasped her waist firmly.

She struggled to break free, but he was too strong for her. His hot, firm lips bent down to kiss hers; she turned her head to avoid them. "Get out of here!" she screamed at him. "I hate you! I never want to see you again."

"You mean everything to me." His voice was passionate. He began to kiss her frantically on her neck. She clawed at his face, digging her nails into the soft smooth flesh.

"We belong together, Frisco," he continued, as if he did not even feel the pain she was inflicting. "We're two of a kind!"

"No!" she screamed, breaking into bitter sobs. "No, damn you!"

Suddenly her office door opened, and Beau stood there on the threshold, his green eyes flashing like a jungle cat's, his muscular body poised as if ready to attack. It took him only a moment to grasp the situation. He leaped across the room, grasped Tom by the arm, pulled him away from Frisco, and sent a clenched fist smashing against his jaw.

Tom fell sprawling onto the floor. He lay there, too stunned and shocked to move. Beau stood over him, a satisfied smile on his face. "I wanted to do that the first time I ever saw you with my wife," he said. "But I restrained myself

206

then, for her sake. I'm glad this time I didn't have that excuse."

He glanced malevolently at Frisco, then—his body relaxing—he looked back down at the helpless Tom. "I'd like to kill you," he continued, "but that would be too easy. I have other plans for you, and by the time I'm finished you'll wish you were dead."

In the same grim attitude, he turned to speak to Frisco. "As for you, my dear," he said, "you can go to hell with him!"

And with that, he departed.

20

Frisco was shattered: she was a woman who had everything and yet had nothing. She moved through the ritual of her days as one without a soul or spirit, following her routine, as if departing from it would bring on a complete collapse of will. She continued to perform her duties at the boat, but the sparkle was gone from her eyes, the joy absent from her manner. She greeted her guests with a smile, but it was strained and forced, and she feared that they recognized the fact.

Her behavior was much the same at home with the children. They felt the absence of Beau as much as she did, yet they did not have the benefit of understanding why he had left. It was clear that they considered themselves somehow to blame, and Frisco could not find the words to explain that they were not.

Music no longer filled the house. Alex refused to play the violin, and Natasha insisted she could not play. The burns on her hands had healed, but her palms were badly scarred, and Frisco often found the child sitting and staring at the scars in despair. The dark, sad eyes that would look up at her in these moments mirrored her own emptiness. She longed to do something or to say something that would ease Natasha's suffering, but she could find nothing in her heart because there was no hope there.

Yet she continued in the pattern of her life with the excuse that she was living for others. It was the one thing that sustained her and enabled her to keep going—the belief that others were dependent upon her. The children needed her to remain firm and reliable now that Beau was gone again. And the girls on the boat: where would they be if she were to forsake them? She had taken on that responsibility, knowing that she must never again give it up.

There were moments, though, when she doubted that resolve, times when she could not avoid looking at herself with the eyes of truth. In the evenings, when all of her meaningless work was done, she would be alone in her room and she would sit down before the mirror to brush her hair before going to bed. She could not avoid seeing the face that stared out at her from the mirror. She could not lie to it, because it did not lie to her. It told her things she did not want to hear.

The eyes were strange to her: they were dull and lackluster, with dark circles beneath. There were tiny lines beginning to form at the edges of the eyes and around the mouth. She wondered if it was a hard face, and a cold one; did it speak with derision and with bitterness? She felt it said: Alex and Natasha do not need you. They need warmth and love, joy and laughter, companionship and understanding. They need a mother, and they need a father as well. They do not need a living legend, and that's what you are—a creature made entirely of myth, lacking substance, too selfish to give anything of real human value.

It went on relentlessly: You delude yourself if you think the girls on the boat need you. It is true that they need Frisco, but Frisco is a legend, a myth, a symbol. You are not Frisco. You are Graciela McGee and no one needs you, because no one even knows who you are anymore.

Finally, inexorably, it reached the heart of the matter: You expect Beau to love you, yet you have given him no reason to do so. You have done nothing but make demands on him. You tell yourself you love him, but always you translate that love into need—your needs. What about his needs? If you loved him the way you say you do, you would want to give to him, not take.

210

But she could stand no more. She hated the face in the mirror for telling her these things, and she turned away to avoid hearing more. She sought comfort in tears, lying down on her bed and sobbing into her pillow, begging for sleep to come and blot out her misery. Instead, what came were agonizing questions: Where had Beau gone? What was he doing? Would she ever see him again? Was there anything she could do to get him back?

Eventually, she was able to drift into sleep, but it was a fitful sleep. When she awakened in the morning, the night's agony seemed nothing more than a nightmare, and she forced herself once more to face her ritual of obligations.

Her days and nights passed in this manner until they ran into weeks. Weeks of loneliness and despair. Occasionally during those weeks, she caught glimpses of Tom Blanchard on the boat, but he did not speak to her. He spent his time with Lillian, and he avoided even looking at Frisco. Of course she had no desire to speak to him, but there was something in his manner that puzzled her.

His spirit seemed to be deteriorating as steadily as hers. His poise and confidence seemed less sure each time she saw him. The bright, enticing smile seemed increasingly more false. His head and shoulders, once so proudly erect, were beginning to stoop. And there was that same hollow, haunted look about the eyes that Frisco saw in her mirror. However, it was only in passing that she wondered what private hell he was going through. She had too many problems of her own, and he had made his hell just as she had made hers.

For some reason, Frisco's-on-the-boat was not running quite so smoothly as it had been. The problems were minor, but they were irritating. One night, it was a drunk disrupting things; the next, a sea captain, new in town, claiming the cards had not been dealt fairly. Another night, two prostitutes came in with the intention of working the saloon and protested fiercely when Mike threw them out. The prominent men of San Francisco gradually stopped patronizing her place, and word began to get about that Frisco's-on-the-boat was going downhill rapidly. Certainly, profits were dwindling.

There were even problems with the new Frisco's. Construction of the brick exterior was almost complete, and work was scheduled to begin on the interior. But for some reason, she could not get supplies. The merchants she dealt with gave her one excuse after another, until work had to be halted completely.

Frisco began to worry that her business might go under completely. She couldn't bear that thought; it was all she had. A part of Lyuba's Tarot reading came back to haunt her: "You must forsake all that you have to gain all that you want."

Much of that reading did not make sense to her. She had not forsaken her work, yet she was now in danger of losing it. The reading had said that she must choose between Beau and Tom. She had chosen Beau, and yet she had lost both. Was there some nuance, she wondered, that she had missed?

She went back to Lyuba, and this time she was insistent about another reading. "I need help," she confessed to her old friend and companion. "I'm losing control of my life. Nothing is sure or certain for me anymore. Life is going on all around me; things are happening, but I'm not a part of them. I'm merely drifting. Perhaps the cards can help me."

Lyuba was sympathetic, but she said sternly, "The cards cannot tell you how to live. They can tell you only what choices you have, and what you may expect from those choices."

"But I need something," Frisco insisted. "I cannot go on like this."

"Child," the woman shook her head chidingly, "you should know where to turn. You have the Gift. You were once trained to be a *phuri dai*. You must look inward for the kind of answers you seek. The cards can tell you but a little of what you want. The same is true of the palm and the stars. Your heart and your spirit have to tell you the rest."

"I have lost the Gift," Frisco confessed miserably. "I have become a *gajo*."

Lyuba smiled and shook her head. "You only think you have."

"Please, Lyuba," Frisco begged, "read the cards for me."

Finally, she agreed. "I will read them," she said. "But this time, you must try to hear what they tell you. You must look inward, to your heart, and understand."

Frisco sighed. "I will try."

The old woman removed the deck of cards from the pocket of her apron. They were wrapped neatly in a piece of black silk. "Sit down at the table," she said, "and try to reach your heart. Forget your thoughts, and let your spirit take command." Her voice droned on monotonously as she began to shuffle the cards. Frisco began to relax. "Select a card," Lyuba said, extending the deck.

Frisco obeyed. It was the Fool.

Lyuba nodded. "Choice," she said. "It is as before, but now the card has become you. The choice has become of vital importance."

Frisco felt an ache of frustration, a desire to cry out in protest, but she forced herself to relax, to accept. She lay the card in the middle of the table. Lyuba crossed the card with a second card. It was the Lovers. "Again a card of choice," she nodded. "It is a choice between the needs of the spirit and the needs of the body. It is a choice of two loves."

214

Next came the triangle of six cards. Lyuba made a little keening sound as she laid them out. The three points of the triangle were the Nine of Swords, the Tower, and Temperance, the last in a reversed position. The cards forming the sides of the triangle were the Eight of Swords, the Seven of Cups, and the Two of Pentacles reversed.

"This is what your inner heart knows and must accept," Lyuba said ominously. "The Two of Pentacles reversed: you cannot handle two situations at one time. The Tower: all you have built may be destroyed. The Seven of Cups: your black thoughts will haunt you and prevent you from obtaining what you want. Temperance reversed: your business desires conflict with your personal needs. The Eight of Swords: you do not know which way to move, but you will be forced to move. And finally, the Nine of Swords: because you cannot make a choice, someone you love will die."

"No!" Frisco protested. "Can't I alter that?"

Lyuba shook her head. "I doubt it," she said, "but let us see what the rest of the cards say."

She began to lay out the circle of twelve cards, moving clockwise from twelve o'clock—the High Priestess, the Chariot reversed, the Three of Swords, the King of Wands reversed, the Sun reversed, the Five of Cups, the Four of Pentacles reversed, the Ace of Wands, the Queen of Wands, the Knight of Pentacles, the Eight of Cups, and the Ten of Swords.

215

In reading, Lyuba moved in reverse order: "The Ten of Swords. Misfortune and ruin will come suddenly, but it will bring an end to confusion and indecision. The Eight of Cups: you will abandon something you have only begun; a structure will not be completed so that you can have inner joy. The Knight of Pentacles: a man with dark hair and dark eyes."

"Tom Blanchard," Frisco nodded. "But I have already given him up."

"He still plays a part," Lyuba told her. "Temperance points toward him, the choice between business and personal. He lies between the Eight of Cups and the Queen of Wands, a fair-haired woman who is fond of him."

"Lillian," Frisco recognized.

"Next to her," Lyuba continued, "is the Ace of Wands, a new undertaking that will not materialize. And next is the Four of Pentacles reversed, the loss of all earthly possessions."

Frisco had known such a loss before. The image of the fire came to her mind with such overpowering fear that it seemed almost real. Her false marriage to Beau had begun with a fire. Could it possibly also end with one? A fire that would destroy everything she had built?

"The Five of Cups," Lyuba went on. "Another card of loss. Then the Sun reversed: it represents a contract or an agreement that must be cancelled."

That meant only one thing to Frisco: the false marriage license to Beau. It had stood between them from the very beginning. Immediately, Lyuba confirmed this.

"It is related to the next card, the King of Wands reversed. A fair-haired man with whom you have a quarrel. He judges you harshly, and he will never give in. The Tower, which is the overthrow of all that you have built, points to him."

Of course—Frisco acknowledged—Beau is a stubborn man; he won't give up until he has things his way. But I am stubborn, too.

"The next card suggests that you love this man," Lyuba went on without pausing. "The Three of Swords: the man you love will flee from you and his going will bring you sorrow."

Frisco was puzzled. Beau had already left her. Lyuba spoke as if this was yet to happen.

"Next is the Chariot reversed. It has two meanings: one is revenge, and the other merely confirms other cards, indicating that there will be a collapse of all your plans."

Before the last card, Lyuba paused, her objectivity gone, grief filling her face. "The High Priestess," she said, "with the Nine of Swords pointing to it. The death of someone you love cannot be altered. The Priestess is a power beyond human control."

"What do you mean?" Frisco asked. "What power?" And, as she asked, an image came vividly to her mind—the image of the Nail, glowing red hot and smoldering. Lyuba did not answer, but her eyes met Frisco's, in heavy silence. "The Nail," Frisco gasped.

Lyuba nodded.

21

Slowly the Gift began to return to Frisco. It seemed to come completely unbidden as she grew more and more to accept her fate as inevitable, grew less and less to fight it. She would be busily occupied with something, and then suddenly there would be a moment of Sight—an image flashing into her mind and then out again with lightning speed. Almost before she had caught its presence, it was gone.

There were images of Beau laughing and holding a woman in his arms—a woman who was not Frisco, a woman with blonde hair. There were images of fire, with the sounds of crackling timbers and screams, a carriage dashing through the streets; and through the flames came the ghostly images of Beau and of Alex and Natasha, their faces stained with soot and sweat.

But the image that came to her most often was that of the Nail, glowing red hot and smoldering, lying in the middle of a table filled with playing cards. A table like those on the boat. That image haunted her, because it was the one thing she was most afraid of, the one thing she wanted to fight, to resist. But even that she accepted as inevitable.

Her outward manner altered along with her inner spirit. The dark circles disappeared from her eyes, and the anxious little lines were going from her face. Those who had noticed her strained appearance of the past weeks, and who had commented upon it among themselves, now commented upon how content she was, how cool she seemed in the face of mounting problems, how genuinely happy she was to greet them.

The problems on the boat did not lessen; in fact, they seemed to increase. What changed was her attitude toward them, and that made them much easier to deal with. Intuitively, she knew that Beau was behind them. It was his way of wreaking revenge. He could not possibly have the satisfaction of his revenge if she did not allow the problems to ruffle her composure. What if he did hire a man to start a fight, to destroy a bit of furniture? Frisco didn't mind; she knew that—in time—she would be losing the place anyway. She felt there was nothing she could do about it.

Oddly enough, there was a certain comfort in the problems. They told her that Beau was still alive and fighting her, something she would not otherwise know, since she still had no idea where he was. They were like greetings he sent her, greetings that said, "Hello, I'm still angry." As long as she knew that, she had hope. Anything was possible. The time to worry would be the time when he no longer cared at all.

There was only one facet of her life that Frisco could hope to deal with, and she threw all of her revived energy into it. The children needed her. Like his mother, Alex was learning to live with the loss, but Natasha was taking it personally, growing dangerously withdrawn. She moved about the big house in silence, slinking shyly along walls or clinging desperately to furniture or objects.

Frisco had noticed Alex trying to draw Natasha out of her misery, valiantly attempting one unsuccessful ploy after another. Natasha meant so much to him he would try anything— relentlessly sloughing off the hurt of rejection and failure, eternally hoping he would be able to return her to normal.

One Sunday evening, after dinner, the three of them were sitting in the parlor. Alex excused himself from the room and returned a few minutes later with the violin, which had not been played in some time. He extended it to Natasha. "Play the song for me," he said. "You know the one. I don't know how to play it yet."

Natasha cringed away from the instrument, shaking her head silently.

"Please," Alex begged. "I want to learn it."

"No," Natasha said. "I can't play anymore. My hands."

"Your hands are all right," Alex cajoled. "You're just afraid to play."

"No," she shook her head. "You play something."

Deviously, Alex said, "This is the song I want to learn." He lifted the violin to his chin and began to play a sweet, happy tune, but after the sixth note the strings screeched painfully offkey. "You see," he said, "I can't go any farther."

"You're just pretending," Natasha said. "You know how it goes."

The child continued to try other approaches, with no success. She persistently refused to touch the violin, finally telling him, "It's yours now. I'll never play it again."

Alex looked at the gift with mixed feelings. Clearly he coveted the instrument. "No," he refused it. "I won't accept it if it means you'll never play again."

"If you don't take it," Natasha said grimly, "I'll smash it to pieces!"

Tears crept into Alex's eyes. Natasha had never spoken to him so harshly. "All right," he said, hurt. "I'll take it."

Frisco did not attempt to interfere in their exchange, but it did give her an idea. She thought she understood the girl's problem. Natasha had retreated into herself because she believed she had brought harm to those she loved. The one thing that might help her was to feel needed. Little Alex understood that intuitively. The problem was that the need could not be a contrived one. Natasha's music had been sorely missed on the boat. As the business had been dwindling, a number of patrons had mentioned the absence of "the girl that plays the fiddle."

She confided her plan to Mike and Lyuba, and all three of them scoured San Francisco in search of another violin. Finally, Frisco herself found the right one in a pawnshop. It was beautifully made, a much finer instrument than the old one, and with a bit of polishing and new strings it literally gleamed with a plea to be played.

She waited for the right moment to bring up her plan before Natasha. That opportunity came on a morning when Frisco was attempting to reconcile her account books. She had brought them home from the boat the night before, and she was sitting at the little desk in the back hallway, trying to figure out where a discrepancy had occurred. The solution kept eluding her, and she was beginning to suspect that Beau had somehow played another of his tricks on her. Several times she had made angry sounds venting her exasperation.

After one of these loud sighs, she looked up to see Natasha standing in the back door watching her silently. Frisco smiled at her affectionately, and said, "Hello, Natasha. Have you been out-side?"

Natasha ignored the pleasantry. "What's wrong?"

"Oh, it's just one of the problems I've been having with the boat," she said, trying to make light of it.

"I see," Natasha said sadly. "Then I guess there's nothing I can do to help."

That was Frisco's opportunity. "Well," she said hesitantly, determined not to break the idea too hastily. "There is something you could do to help me, but I don't think you would want to."

Natasha looked slightly offended, resentful. "If there was something I could do for you," she said, "you know I would do it. After all, you've done so very much for me."

"I don't know if you've been aware of it," Frisco began to explain, "but business on the boat has been very bad lately. One of the reasons, I think, is that the customers miss the music."

Until that point, Natasha had been looking at her with happy anticipation, but then suddenly her face fell. "Oh," she said, "I see."

"Some of the customers used to come just to hear it," Frisco pressed.

"Alex could play," Natasha suggested.

"No," Frisco shook her head. "Alex is too young to play alone. He would be too frightened by the crowd. And besides, some of the people have specifically asked for you."

"I'm sorry," Natasha fought back tears. "But I can't play anymore."

"Have you tried?"

Natasha shook her head. "Anyway, I've given the violin to Alex."

"I have an idea," Frisco suggested. "But you don't have to do it if you don't want to. You could practice all by yourself, with no one listening, just to see if you can still play. My idea is to offer the public two violinists playing duets. If I advertised in the newspapers, I'm sure people would come. Business would be back to normal in no time."

Natasha considered the proposal seriously. "But where would we get another violin?" she asked.

"I have one," Frisco said, smiling. "Would you like to see it?"

Natasha nodded.

When Frisco returned with the violin, Natasha's eyes lit up with loving admiration. "It's beautiful," she said, "much nicer than my old one."

For the next few days, music filled the house again, not just the strains of one violin, but the full-bodied sound of two, leaping and dancing and playing off each other in harmony. There was even laughter as Alex and Natasha each tried to find ways to vary their parts. But most important, the fearful shyness began to melt away from Natasha.

Frisco placed large advertisements in all the San Francisco newspapers:

FRISCO'S

Is Proud to Announce

Its Two Child Prodigies

Alex and Natasha

Playing Violin Duets!

Beginning Friday, May 7.

On that evening, the boat was filled to over-flowing. There had never been a larger crowd at Frisco's. Everybody came. The prominent men, with their wives and families, the regulars, miners and ranchers from miles around. Whatever Beau had been doing to keep people away, it was obviously not enough to prevent them from coming to see the new attraction. Then, a few minutes before the show was to begin, even Beau himself appeared. He did not sit at a table, nor did he spend money on a drink. He simply stood back under the shelter of the bar to watch as unobtrusively as possible.

Frisco was tempted to go and speak to him, but she restrained herself. This was the children's night, and for their sake she was glad he was here. She could withhold snide remarks until a more suitable time. And so she did her best to ignore him. However, she could not help noticing how good he looked. He had gained his weight back, and there was color in his cheeks. He even looked prosperous in a new suit of clothes, which showed off his tall, powerful figure.

The entertainment began to a smattering of applause. The curtain parted with Julie already on-stage at the piano. Then the children came on, looking slightly nervous. Frisco had dressed them both in gypsy costumes. Natasha wore a lovely white peasant blouse, a colorfully embroidered black skirt with white ruffles, and a bright red sash around her waist. Alex wore black knee-pants, with long white stockings, a white shirt with beautiful billowing sleeves, an embroidered vest, and a red sash.

When they began to play, all signs of nervousness vanished. Their music filled the grand saloon, and they gained confidence from the sound. There was an excited murmur from the crowd, then a hush of raptured attention. At the end of each piece, the applause was deafening, accompanied by whistling and stomping from the cruder elements.

They concluded their entertainment with the Hungarian Rhapsody. It was obvious to Frisco what delight the two had had in arranging their parts for this, so that it was not so much a violin duet as a violin *duel*, each vying with the other in virtuosity. The audience went wild as it realized what the two children were doing, applauding each little display, then hushing to catch the next.

Just seeing the happiness on the faces of Alex and Natasha made Frisco happier than she had been in months. At least in this important part of her life, she had been successful. At least she had been able to restore Natasha's will to live.

But, almost before she had completed the thought, an image flashed swiftly through Frisco's mind—the image of a nail glowing threateningly.

22

Tom Blanchard was not as resilient as Frisco. He appeared to have very few inner resources to depend on. Frisco had noticed him on the boat, looking increasingly haggard. He had taken to drinking, and much of his time was spent in the bar, despite Lillian's efforts to lure him out.

Frisco still did not speak to him, but she was beginning to feel pity as much for Lillian's sake as for his. It was obvious that Lillian was now hopelessly in love with the man; even she recognized it. And Frisco cared very much for Lillian. Because of her own experience with Tom, she did not think it wise to interfere, but neither did she want to see her best friend and most valuable employee dragged down by his drinking.

For the most part, she kept her silence, but one evening—after the doors of the boat had been shut for the night and the two women were in Frisco's office counting the receipts, Frisco decided she had to say something. "You've been looking very tired lately," she tried to sound casual. "I think you need to get more rest."

"I know," Lillian replied, "but it seems, even when I do go to bed, I can't sleep. I've had so much on my mind."

"Has it occurred to you," Frisco plunged timorously forward, "that you're worrying about things you can do nothing about?"

Lillian stared at her, knowing full well what she meant. Her eyes betrayed the mixture of emotions she was feeling—hurt, resentment, anger, apprehension, and finally despair. She succumbed to this latter emotion with a sinking of her shoulders and with tears welling up in her eyes. "I know," she said flatly. "But someone has to try to help him." There was a note of accusation in this last, but her manner quickly became apologetic, plaintive. "Frisco, try to forgive me and understand if I take Tom's side in all this. I realize he's made things difficult for you. He's done some pretty bad things, but it wasn't really the way it appears. He never really meant to harm you. He was in love with you. He still is."

Her voice broke with a note of bitter resignation, as tears began to flow down her cheeks. Frisco moved to her friend to embrace her. "I would never judge you, Lillian," she said comfortingly. "I know how you feel about Tom.

Maybe I don't think he deserves someone as good as you, but I wouldn't begrudge you happiness with him, if you could find it. I wish there was something I could do to help you."

"You could help," Lillian sobbed, "if you would."

"How?" Frisco asked.

"See Tom," she replied. "Talk to him. He's wanted so much to talk to you since . . . since that last time. But he's been too ashamed to ask."

"I don't know," Frisco hesitated. "I don't really see how that would help."

"It would help him just to know that you don't hate him." Lillian's eyes were begging.

Frisco turned away to think without having to see the pain in her friend's face. Did she hate Tom? She wasn't sure. She turned back to confront Lillian. "But would that help you?" she asked.

"Yes . . . No . . ." Lillian hesitated, sighed wearily. "It doesn't matter. It would help me just to see him less miserable."

"All right," Frisco gave in. "I'll see him. But that's all. And I don't want to see him alone. I want you to be here."

The meeting took place the following night. Frisco asked Lillian to bring Tom into her office as soon as he arrived on the boat. She did not want to give him any time to gather his liquid courage at the bar before the confrontation took place.

It was painful for Frisco to look upon Tom's face close up. It was like looking upon a fine classical sculpture after it had been mutilated by barbarians. In her bitterness, she had forgotten how much joy he had given her, how much she had cared for him, how desperately she had once wanted his body to hold hers. The beauty that had entranced her was still there in his face, and in his body, but the spirit that had so tantalized her was gone.

As he stepped hesitantly into the room, his eyes cast downward, Frisco realized that she did not hate him. Hate was the other face of love, and she had never felt a passion that powerful for Tom Blanchard. She had found comfort and warmth and excitement with him, but had committed nothing from the depth of her heart. So now she could feel only betrayal and coldness and pity.

"Hello, Frisco," he said sheepishly. "How have you been?"

"As well as can be expected," she shrugged. She glanced from Tom to Lillian, whose strained, anxious face was pleading for kindness, and then back to Tom. "How have you been?"

"I've been having a rough time," he mumbled. "But I guess it's what I deserve. I try not to complain."

He was leaving the initiative to her, waiting for her to say or do something that would ease his misery. She recognized that as a symptom of his weakened and depressed mental state. However, she had grown sufficiently wise to know that she could not give him the strength he needed. No one could. He had to find it in himself.

"I've noticed you here in the evenings," she said not unkindly. "I don't like to turn away business, but it's disturbed me that you've spent so much time in the bar."

Lillian looked shocked and angry, and Tom flushed with embarrassment. But then, surprisingly, he smiled. It was an embarrassed smile, but somewhere in it was a sparkle of spirit. "You're right," he said. "I have spent too much time in the company of bottles, but bottles don't talk back."

"I don't know," Frisco said. "If you give them time, they do."

Lillian fidgeted. She clearly didn't like the direction the conversation was going.

"Maybe," Tom nodded, growing more comfortable in Frisco's presence. "I haven't gotten that far yet." He arched a brow, and his mouth curved in a wry smile. "But I haven't found a drink yet that packs a punch like a man . . . or a woman."

His look was ingratiating; his words were beginning to cover ground that Frisco wanted to stay away from. "Tom," she said, suddenly becoming serious, "you and I both deserved what we got."

He looked hurt at the rebuff. The embarrassment returned, but only for a moment. He stiffened. "Yes," he said. "I suppose we did ask for trouble." He cleared his throat, looked down at his feet. "But I didn't come here intending to reopen old wounds. I came to apologize to you, to tell you I'm sorry for hurting you."

"Tom," she began, "I didn't expect . . ."

"Please don't interrupt me," he said with surprising strength. "There's something I have to say to you. You can refuse to believe it if you wish, but at least hear me out."

Frisco nodded, admiring his determination and realizing that perhaps there was hope for Tom yet.

"I want you to know that I did not seek your friendship in order to line my pockets. Everything I said I felt for you was true—is still true. I loved you, and I still love you."

Lillian looked painfully at the carpet. Frisco started to speak, to suggest that these were words Tom should not speak in front of someone else, but decided it was too late.

He continued: "What I said at the very beginning—that I expected nothing but the pleasure of your company—was true. I accept the fact that the pleasure is over. To try to make it continue would only hurt you more. And God knows I have already hurt you more than I can bear."

"Tom, please," Frisco interrupted. "You've hurt yourself more than . . ."

"Let me finish!" he persisted. "I have to clear

234

my conscience. I want you to know that I only attempted to lie to you once—that last day, when you confronted me with the truth. I honestly did not realize until that moment what I had done to you. It began very innocently. When we were together, you would mention the news you had had from Beau. And without even thinking, I began taking advantage of the knowledge when I found it useful. It was that simple. I didn't even realize what I was doing when I began to ask you what news you had of Beau."

"It's all right, Tom," Frisco said. "I believe you. What's done is done."

"No, it's not," Tom said. "Somehow I've got to make it up to you. I realize now that you really do love Beau, and that I was only fooling myself when I thought I had a chance with you. In trying to find happiness for myself, I've destroyed your happiness, and I can't live with that."

"You didn't do it alone," Frisco told him. "I have to take most of the blame myself."

His intensity was making her uncomfortable. She was grateful for his confession and for his apology, because it made her realize she had not been quite such a fool as she had thought. Her initial judgment of him had been the correct one. But she could not allow their relationship to continue in this way—with the constant building and balancing of debts.

"I'm grateful to you for coming," she told him. "And I'm grateful for what you've said. It means very much to me. But you owe me nothing more."

"I feel that I do," Tom persisted. "I feel that I owe you happiness. That's what I've taken away."

"No," Frisco replied. "The only happiness you owe me is your own. My happiness is my affair. If you want to help me, lift yourself up by your bootstraps; help yourself."

"That's impossible," he said, shaking his head. "At least here in San Francisco."

"Why?" she demanded. "The city hasn't changed that much in three weeks."

"Yes, it has," he said. "I'm being driven out of business by a man. Beau Tolliver. If I fight him, I'll only be hurting you more."

"Balderdash!" Frisco said emphatically. "You can fight Beau Tolliver all you want to! I'll even help you! He's trying to run me out of business, and I'm not sitting by and letting him do it!"

As she spoke, an image came to her mind. Hanging over Tom's head and glowing red hot was the Nail. For a moment, it shook her, but then it was gone as suddenly as it had appeared.

"In my case," Tom said, "it may be too late. I don't have much business left. Of course, I could always go to him on my knees and beg."

"No," Frisco said emphatically. "Don't you dare do that!"

"But he *is* your husband," Tom said, shaking his head.

Frisco had the urge to speak, to confess that Beau was not in fact her husband, that they had never really been married, but she could not. This was her secret, her problem to work out. Hers and Beau's. It would never do to confess it now, especially to Tom Blanchard.

"At the moment," she said, as a compromise, "there is only a piece of paper linking us together. We are hardly husband and wife."

23

It was only a piece of paper, yet it threatened to destroy Frisco's life, and possibly many others as well. The meeting with Tom had started Frisco thinking about the forged marriage certificate again. It was the one thing that continued to link her to Beau, and it was the root of all the troubles between them. It did not really bind them together as man and wife, but it did bind her to him. As long as that document existed, Beau would look upon her not as a free and independent spirit, but as his possession.

He had never had to woo her and win her in the traditional way of man and woman. In the mating of almost every species, there is a ritual through which each partner establishes rights and prerogatives before agreeing to unite as one. Frisco realized that she and Beau had been denied that ritual, and therefore they had been denied fulfillment together.

In its place, there was an unnatural bondage. No matter where they were on the face of the earth—either together or thousands of miles apart—Beau Tolliver could reach out to her and control her life, either intentionally or by chance. He was doing it now, and it was clearly intentional.

There had been a brief respite from his malicious tricks for the first few nights of performances by Alex and Natasha. However, as soon as Beau had realized that the music was bringing back all her patrons, his efforts had begun anew. He did not, himself, return after that one visit, and Frisco still had no idea where he was living, but she recognized his hand in the petty disturbances that happened night after night.

Frisco had been determined not to be ruffled by these little annoyances, but after a while she could not help it. They were a constant reminder of him, and it plagued her that she did not know his ultimate object in disrupting her life. Did he want to ruin her so that she would come begging to him for help? Did he want to see her penniless and sleeping on the street? Or did he simply want to remind her that he owned her, body and soul?

But the most annoying thing for her was that she could never be quite certain which of her problems were ordinary ones and which were planned by Beau. Was he responsible for the pickpockets that had begun to haunt the boat on crowded nights? Had he hired the man who had slipped by the guard on deck after hours and managed to find his way into the girls' private quarters? Had he arranged the vandalism that had broken all the glass windows in the new building? Each time she had to face a problem, her mind automatically went to Beau, and that made her furious.

If she only knew where he was living, she would turn the tables on him, but all Mike's efforts had failed to locate him. He obviously did not want her to know where he was, for even his close business associates claimed not to know.

Her irritation reached a peak on a Saturday night when there were two incidents, one following closely on the other. Later she was to learn that they were not really related, but that evening she connected them in her mind and believed that Beau was behind both.

The first involved a young miner in San Francisco for a weekend spree. Despite her house rules, he was both drinking heavily and betting heavily. He was playing poker and losing one hand after another. He was at Laura's table, and she was one of Frisco's best dealers. Having grown up on Mississippi riverboats, she could sense trouble coming long before it happened. After the third hand, she signaled Frisco to keep an eye on her table.

There was something decidedly strange about

240

the young miner. He did not have the hardy, roughhewn appearance of most of the men who worked the fields. Of course, his skin had been baked full brown, and his hands were worn and callused, with chipped cracked nails, but there remained a delicacy in his look and his manner, a frailness of spirit usually associated with a poet. He was thin to the point of gauntness; his thick shock of chestnut hair was fine and wavy; and his pale blue eyes had the look of madness, of instability, of holding some secret vision that no one else could see.

Frisco eased quietly up to the table to watch. The miner had just ordered another whiskey from the bar. "If you're going to continue playing at the tables," Laura told him, "this will have to be your last drink."

"I can hold my liquor," the miner said with a scowl.

"That doesn't matter," Laura said pleasantly. "It's a house rule." She smiled at him. "I must also warn you that the house also has a rule about the amount of money one person can lose in a single night. If you continue to lose at the rate you are now, you will reach that limit very soon."

"No matter," the miner said flippantly. "My luck will change. You'll see."

They played another hand, and again the miner lost heavily, but he shrugged it off. "That's the way my luck goes," he said with a twisted smile. "When I lose, I lose big; but when I win, I win big. And when it changes, it changes like that." He snapped his fingers. "You'll see."

"If it doesn't," Laura said, "this will be your last hand."

"I've got plenty of money," the man said sullenly. "I can cover my losses."

"I'm sorry," Laura repeated sternly. "House rule."

There was tension at the table as the next hand was dealt. The miner threw every bit of money he had in his pockets on the table, running the stakes incredibly high.

It was then that Frisco broke in. "I'm sorry," she told the man, "but we can't allow that. You must keep enough money in your pockets to cover a day's lodging and food. It's a rule we have here, and we don't break it for anyone."

"But you don't understand," the man said wildly. "I can't start to win until I've lost everything. That's the way my luck is. It turns, and then I win much bigger than I lost."

"That may be," Frisco told him, "but we don't make exceptions. I'm sure some other house— perhaps the Golden Slipper—will be willing to take everything you have, but not Frisco's."

"You can't stop me from finishing this hand," the miner insisted.

"No," Frisco said, "we can't, but we will return any money that's over your limit."

"That's not fair," he replied sourly. "You're jinxing me."

They finished the hand, and the man lost. In anticipation of trouble, Frisco had already signalled to Mike to have a couple of the men ready, and they had joined the crowd standing about the crowd watching.

"That's it for the night," Frisco announced. "You're a hundred and fifty dollars over the limit. We'll refund that, but you'll have to leave."

"No," the man said. "I've got to stay in. My luck will change now."

Frisco shook her head firmly. "You have no more money. It's impossible."

"I still got my good-luck piece," the miner said shrilly. "I can bet that." He reached into his coat pocket and drew out an object, casting it down onto the table amid the scattered cards. As the object rolled across the ace of spades, it flashed brilliantly, like fire.

The object was a nail, large and glowing.

Frisco caught herself before she screamed, startled by the *deja vu*. She had witnessed this scene before; it was one of the images that had flitted through her mind, prophecying the future—a nail flashing and glowing among the cards.

It took her several moments to realize that the nail was not glowing because it was red hot; it was glowing because it was fashioned of solid gold. Strained by fear, she ordered, "Pick that up, sir, and go!"

"It's worth money," the man said angrily. "It

weighs a good two pounds. It's not an ordinary nail."

"I realize that," Frisco told him. "But we have no use for it."

When he still made no move to go, Mike reached out for the nail and slipped it into the miner's pocket. The man turned on Mike then, as if ready to fight, but two of the guards grabbed him and held him securely. As he struggled to break their firm grip on him, Frisco counted out a hundred and fifty dollars and slipped it into the pocket with the nail.

"No!" the man screamed insanely. "You can't do this to me! I won't let you!"

Frisco nodded to the guards, and they ushered the miner swiftly up the stairs to the deck and then down the gangway. They stood there and watched while he walked off the dock, still shouting back his protests.

No one saw the man return, but Frisco would learn later that he did. For some mad reason of his own, he came back to hammer the gold nail into the rope that kept the *Frisco Lady* securely moored to one of the pilings of the dock.

Frisco had no idea of the meaning of this strange occurrence, but it had shaken her. It was not Beau's doing, but she assumed it was. The only rational explanation she could think of was that he had hired the man to do it in order to upset her. He knew about the Curse of the Nail, and while he did not take it seriously, he knew that she did.

She was still trembling from the shock when the second altercation took place.

It was almost midnight when the old man came stumbling drunkenly onto the *Frisco Lady*. There was little to distinguish him from the hundreds of other down-and-out habitues of Sydneytown and the docks. He was shabbily dressed, and from all appearances, he had not had a bath in weeks. The top of his head was completely bald, but surrounding the shiny pate was a mass of grizzled gray hair. His two upper front teeth were missing, and his remaining teeth were yellowed and crooked. His nose was red and his eyes were puffy from drink.

He stumbled down the steps into the grand saloon, then looked around him in amazement. "What the hell is going on here?" he bellowed. "None of you people belong here! This is my boat!"

All activity at the tables ceased, while everyone turned to stare. Mike and the other guards moved stealthily across the room to take charge of the man and quietly eject him from the place.

"Whoring and gambling," the man continued to rave. "The sins of Babylon! Oh, sweet *Ellen Jane,* what have I abandoned you to?" He glanced heavenward with outstretched arms, then spread his arms outward to take in the entire as-

245

semblage. "Get off my boat!" he cried in the booming voice of a preacher. "Every one of you! You have defiled it!"

Mike and his men grabbed him then and started to drag him up the stairs, but in his drunken state the old man was more difficult than they had expected. He swung and kicked at them wildly, bellowing, "Oh, no! You can't get the best of me! I know my rights! This is my boat, and I want it back!"

Frisco had never truly felt that the *Frisco Lady* belonged to her; she had always wondered about the real owner, the man who had abandoned the sleek, proud *Ellen Jane*, and she considered the boat simply a loan from him. She had imagined the owner as a young, powerful figure of a man, handsome and shrewd and adventuresome. Now, confronted with a man claiming to be the owner, she was puzzled, disappointed, chagrined.

"I'll get the law on you," the man continued. "I'll take it to court! I'll make you regret this!" With one foot, he sent one of the guards sprawling down the stairs. With a flail of his arm, he sent another back against the stair railing.

Suddenly, Frisco was concerned. The man probably had little legal right to the boat, after abandoning it for years, but he did have a moral right to it. And he could create a great deal of bad publicity if he wanted to. She hurried over to the stairs. "Stop, please," she said. "We can discuss this reasonably in my office."

Mike and the guards relaxed, but the man's anger did not abate. "There's nothing to talk about," he said sourly. "This boat is mine, and you're trespassing."

Frisco remained calm and courteous. "I'm sure, sir, if this is your boat, you would agree that you have treated her shabbily. It took a great deal of work to get her back into shape. If I am to give her back to you, I want some assurance that she is indeed yours and that you will treat her more kindly in the future."

The old man stared at her in astonishment. "You mean you *will* give her up?"

"Of course," Frisco replied. "I admit that I've borrowed her. But I think we should discuss the situation privately in my office."

The old man looked a bit embarrassed, confused. He followed her into the office, and Mike followed him, keeping a watchful eye on him, in case he should decide to get surly again. However, his vigilance proved unnecessary. Frisco's politeness had changed the man's manner entirely. He remained heavily under the influence of strong drink, but the drunken reeling and the slurred speech disappeared, and a keen intelligence was now perceptible behind the swollen, puffy brown eyes.

"I take it you're Mrs. Tolliver?" the man asked as Frisco stepped behind the desk.

"Yes," Frisco nodded. "But here on the boat I'm known only as Frisco. And now, if I may, I'd like to know something about you. What's your name?"

"Wellington," the man replied. "Captain Phil Wellington. The *Ellen Jane* was my ship, named for my wife. Dead these ten years, bless her soul."

"What was the *Ellen Jane*'s home port?" Frisco asked.

"New York," Captain Wellington told her with a note of sadness, "but she hasn't seen home in nearly five years. Like as not, she'll never see home again."

"When did you abandon her in the bay?" she pursued.

"Forty-nine," he said with a regretful shake of his head. "In October. I brought passengers and cargo from New Orleans. There was so much talk about the gold out just lying in the fields waiting to be picked up, I decided to stay and try my luck. But my luck hasn't been no good since my wife died, back in forty-two. I lost everything I had except the *Ellen Jane*, and I couldn't put her back out to sea without money."

At first, Frisco had not known whether to believe Wellington or not. Whether he was or not the captain of the *Ellen Jane*, he could easily have been sent by Beau just to make trouble. She now suspected the man was telling the truth. He knew everything she had managed to learn about the ship, and more. The captain's name had been Philip W. Wellington, and his home port had been New York, though the last voyage, which had ended in October of 1849, had begun in New Orleans.

"Captain Wellington," she said, in a very businesslike manner, "what would you consider an adequate fee for the rental of the *Ellen Jane* for the past six months? Of course, I expect you to make some allowances for the repairs we have made, but I want to be fair."

The captain was flustered. "Rental, ma'am?" he stammered. "Why, I don't know. I know nothing about things like that."

"Would five hundred dollars be suitable?" she suggested. "I think I could arrange to move out within six weeks. And for that I would pay you another two hundred."

"Seven hundred dollars!" the old captain calculated. "Ma'am, you don't know what you're saying! I'd be willin' to take a bottle of whiskey and call it fair!"

"I thought you said you wanted your ship back?" Frisco prodded. "Seven hundred dollars would be a good start toward getting her in operation again."

Captain Wellington looked down at the carpet. "Ma'am, I was just blowing off. You should know better than to take a drunkard serious. Just look at me. Do you think I could ever command a ship again?"

"That's for you to say," Frisco replied, not unkindly. "I simply want to be fair about this. If you don't really want the ship back, I want to sign a lease agreement and pay you a monthly rental. If you do want the ship back, I will hand her over as quickly as feasible."

Captain Wellington stared at her pensively for a long time. Tears began to drift aimlessly down his cheeks, and he did nothing to stop them. "I don't deserve nothing like this," he said finally. "You've been better to the *Ellen Jane* than ever I have. I want you to keep her. But maybe you could give me a job, scrubbing her and keeping her clean. That would make up for the years I've neglected her."

"I'd be glad to do that," Frisco said with a smile. "But I would want to pay you a rental as well."

Wellington looked sheepish. "You may not want to do that, ma'am," he said guiltily, "when I tell you what I got to tell you." He took a deep breath to sustain his courage and announced, "The *Ellen Jane*'s my ship all right, but I've known for a long time you was using her. I was glad about that; I liked knowing she was in good hands again and being looked after. I came here tonight because a man paid me to make trouble for you. I did it for the sake of a bottle of whiskey."

"What man?" Frisco asked, knowing the answer as she asked.

"A Mr. Beau Tolliver," the captain told her. "He said he was your husband."

Frisco's back stiffened, her eyes narrowed. "Do you happen to know where this Mr. Tolliver lives?"

"Yes, ma'am," Captain Wellington nodded his head. "But it ain't no place for a lady like you to call on him."

24

Beau was living in Albert Valery's bagnio!

"Valery ain't got that run-down place on Drumm Street no more," Captain Wellington explained. "He's built a fine new house over on Montgomery. On the outside it looks respectable, but inside it's the same old whorehouse." He blushed and looked down at the floor. "Beggin' your pardon, ma'am, for plain-speakin'."

"And Beau is living there?" Frisco asked incredulously. "How is that possible?"

"Valery calls the place a hotel," the old sea captain explained. "And he keeps a few rooms for men, just to make it look like it's respectable."

That was the one place on earth that Frisco would never have thought of looking for her husband. No matter how angry he was at her, she did not think that he would join forces with her worst enemy, the one man in the entire world she most despised. Humiliation and anger stirred within her. This was more than she could endure in silence. Beau was showing utter contempt for her, and her spirit—her dignity—would not accept that under any circumstances.

Her face was set in grim determination, when she asked Captain Wellington, "Where precisely is this new place on Montgomery Street?"

"It's just off the corner of Bush Street," the old man told her. "You can't miss it. He's got a door painted red, just like before."

She turned to Mike. "Is your horse saddled?" she asked.

"Yes, ma'am," he replied. "You want me to go someplace?"

"No," she told him. "I want to borrow it."

"You ain't thinking of going to . . ." he began to protest.

But Frisco interrupted him, saying, "I certainly am!" She strode from behind her desk and moved toward the door. At the door, she paused, turned back to Mike. "Captain Wellington is working for us now," she said. "Find him a place to sleep and put him to work. I'll be back with your horse before the night's over."

She walked out the door swiftly, before Mike could protest further, and she rushed up the stairs onto the deck. She was halfway down the gangway before Mike called out from behind her. "Wait, ma'am! I'm coming with you!"

"No, you're not, Mike!" she called back to him. "This is something I've got to do alone!"

She quickly found his horse, a familiar strawberry roan, untied it, hiked her skirts, and hoisted herself into the saddle, seated astride like a man.

Mike rushed down the gangway. "At least let me take you there," he shouted. "These streets is dangerous this time of night!"

This time she did not even bother to answer him, but wheeled the horse around skillfully, kicked it in the flanks, and went racing off down the darkened street. The fury she was feeling found outlet in the horse's fine muscularity and sturdy power. Under other circumstances, she would have been frightened of traversing these streets alone at night, but her rage blotted out all fear. In her present state of mind, she knew she was more to be feared than frightened; to have justice and vengeance, she would stop at nothing.

Everything about her seemed to feed this obsessive passion—the horses' thundering hoofbeats, pounding out, "Tolliver, Tolliver, Tolliver," racing closer and closer to her destination; the long, distorted shadows of buildings reaching out to her like arms clamoring for her success; the dim figures on front stoops and the backlighted figures looking out from windows that watched her in encouraging silence as if aware of her mission. They were all a part of her power tonight.

The cool night breeze tousled her hair, whipping curls in wild abandon, but it also released her from vanity, and so she did not care. Nor did she care that it blew her skirts awry in a mass of lace petticoats, revealing her shapely ankles and calves; propriety was only a silly nuisance at the moment.

Mike's roan seemed to sense her all-consuming heat, and it never flagged in its pace. After she made the turn onto Bush Street, Frisco leaned forward, making her torso become one with the powerful lunging neck as it stretched, and stretched again, onward, relentlessly, time and again, forcing one sluggish, indolent denizen of the street to leap suddenly and fearfully to life to escape their path.

The horse was breathing fire and glistening wet with sweat as Frisco reined it in to a sudden halt in front of Valery's house on Montgomery Street. It stamped restlessly and snorted in protest as she tied it to the railing, as if it knew that their mission was not yet complete and it resented being left behind.

Frisco stalked briskly and unhesitatingly up the front steps to the bright red front door, and rapped sharply with a tightly clenched fist. There was no immediate answer, and so she rapped again more insistently.

When the door opened, she was startled by the face that greeted her, but no more startled than the face was at recognizing her. It was Carlotta—eyes hollow with defeat, cheeks sunken and lined with despair, hair and clothes now carelessly askew, but still the same viciously judgmental housekeeper who had once so disapproved of Frisco. The old woman's eyes widened and her jaw trembled at the sight of the mistress who had cast her into the street to end up finally as housekeeper at a bagnio. Then self-righteous shame consumed her as she gasped, "Señora Tolliver! *Madre de Dios*, it's you!"

But Frisco lapsed into surprise for only a moment. She sensed that this confrontation was only one of the minor victories she would have tonight, and she quickly squared her shoulders and demanded, "Where is Mr. Tolliver, Carlotta?"

The old woman broke into obsequious wailing, falling to her knees and clutching at Frisco's skirts. "Forgive me," she wept. "I have learned my lesson! I see now that you were right! Please, señora, please forgive me and take me back!"

Frisco was dignified, but disdainful. "Stop snivelling, woman!" she commanded. "Get on your feet and take me to my husband!"

Carlotta obeyed, but she did not stop her pleading. "I will do anything you say, señora, but only . . . please take me from this place! You have no idea what horrible things go on in a place like this!"

"Will you shut up and do as I say!" she snapped. "There is nothing you can tell me that I don't already know!"

Carlotta obeyed, opening the door for Frisco

to enter, but she did not stop sniffing or dabbing pathetically at her eyes. "This way," she said, and led Frisco down a large gaudy hallway toward an even gaudier staircase, carpeted in red with gilt-trimmed bannisters. The walls were hung with rather dubious copies of classic nude paintings, all in gilt frames that overwhelmed the canvases.

To her left, just before climbing the stairs, Frisco noticed a large pair of sliding doors, opened slightly. From this room, laughter and loud talk emanated. She could not help glancing through the opening and seeing in the haze of cigar smoke half-dressed women clinging to drunken, flushfaced men, whose hands caressed naked thighs and shapely lace-covered buttocks.

In the midst of the crowd, one face looked out at hers, his small ratlike eyes narrowed, a superior leer on his twisted mouth. Albert Valery showed no sign of surprise at seeing her or any desire to prevent her intrusion. He merely gave her a mocking bow as she passed. In her present frame of mind, he did not ruffle her composure at all. She knew clearly what she was going to do, and there was no way she could be demeaned by it. Even if she lost, she would win.

Beau's room was on the third floor, and it meant climbing two steep flights of stairs. Frisco climbed vigorously, her pleasurable anticipation mounting with each step, but Carlotta's energy flagged halfway up the second flight, perhaps because she had begun to realize that Frisco's ap-

257

pearance might mean trouble, and she did not want to be caught in the middle.

"Señora Tolliver," she said breathlessly, "you must go on alone. I can go no farther. I am old and weak. Señor Tolliver's room is the third door on the left." The old woman sat dejectedly on the step, and Frisco slipped by her swiftly and quickly reached the third floor landing.

She counted the doors and found the third on the left. She paused only a moment to smooth her hair and skirt before knocking. From beyond the door, she heard Beau's familiar voice call out, "It's unlocked! Come in!"

She opened the door slowly but steadily, and without hesitating stepped inside. Instantly, she was flooded with *deja vu* by the sight that confronted her.

In the room, Beau was sitting in a leather wing back chair, wearing only pants and shirtsleeves. On his lap was a tray of food obviously just brought in by a cheap looking blonde. Her lips were brightly painted and her cheeks overly rouged. Her arms were about Beau's neck, and she was staring at Frisco with a peevish scowl.

The first time she had ever set eyes on Beau, the scene had been similar. Then she had been a frightened runaway slave, with her master following close on her heels. Now she was a woman of dignity and a certain degree of wisdom, and the man she was seeking to escape was Beau himself.

Somehow it seemed fitting to her. It had all begun with a game of cards, and she intended it to end with one. On that first occasion, now only a strange and distant memory, Beau had challenged Thiebaud, her master, to a game of cards, with her as the prize. She now intended to issue the same challenge to Beau.

But there was one thing that was unsettling: she had also seen this precise scene before, Beau in this room, with this very woman. She had seen it with the Sight, as one of the images that had haunted her with their swift and unexpected intrusions into her consciousness. And now, as she stared at the real scene, the image of the Nail, hot and smoldering, slipped into her Sight, and she knew that what she was about to do was not out of free will, but upon the call of destiny. She was following her fate as surely as if she had no choice at all.

"Well, good evening, my dear," Beau smiled at her with smug amusement. "This is a pleasant surprise. I don't believe you know my friend Sally, do you?" He kissed Sally on the neck. "Sally, this is my wife."

For a moment, Sally looked frightened. Then, when she realized that Beau had not asked her to leave, she smiled with an air of triumph. "How do you do, Mrs. Tolliver," she said. "Won't you sit down."

"I didn't come here for polite conversation," Frisco said briskly. "I came here to discuss a business proposition."

"Perhaps you'd better go, Sally," Beau said, patting her on the rump to feign an intimacy they didn't have.

"That's not necessary," Frisco said. "She can stay. I'll be only a moment."

Discomfited by Frisco's composure, Sally lifted the cover from Beau's tray, placed his napkin on his knee, then left the room, with a perplexed, "I'll be back later."

When she was gone, Beau cocked his head to one side, and gestured to Frisco to share his food, to which she shook her head no; then he arched an eyebrow quizzically, and asked, "Now, to what do I owe the honor of your company?"

Physically, Beau was as enticing as he had always been, but Frisco was pleased that his physical presence was no longer intimidating, that her will did not melt upon gazing at him. "I think you know the answer to that," she told him curtly. "The differences between us must be settled, one way or the other. We cannot keep on quarreling forever. We are hurting ourselves, and other people as well."

"Like Tom Blanchard?" Beau queried maliciously.

"Yes," she replied. "Tom, among others."

"Can't your lover fight his own battles?" he dug in deeper.

"He is not my lover," Frisco cut back sharply. "And this is my battle. Mine and yours. And you're fighting it like a coward, hiding away in a whorehouse and sneaking up time after time to attack me from behind. That is not the way gentlemen settle things."

"No," Beau said archly, "it's not. But if I may pay you a compliment, my dear, you are no gentleman."

"Obviously neither are you!" Frisco snapped back. "I never cared much for such things as duels, but I find myself understanding how useful they are and how really admirable the Gentleman's Code of Honor is. Right now, I wish that I were a gentleman so that I could slap you across the face with my glove and we could meet with pistols at forty paces. There would be dignity and honor in settling our differences face to face, swiftly and decisively."

Beau looked at her with genuine amazement. "Do you wish, then, to challenge me to a duel?" he asked. "I don't think I would find much honor in facing off with a woman."

"No," Frisco assured him. "I realize that. But I do have a solution that should satisfy your sense of honor as well as mine. We can face each other directly and settle our differences once and for all. Not with sabers or pistols, but with cards. It is the way you won me years ago in New Orleans. It's only fair that you grant me the chance to win my freedom in the same manner."

The suggestion took Beau by surprise. "I don't understand," he said. "You couldn't possibly be more free than you are now. There isn't a woman in San Francisco—or anywhere, for that matter—who lives the way you do."

"Perhaps not," Frisco admitted, "but there is still the matter of my so-called 'marriage' to you. I am not free from your malicious meddling, and you know it."

"I see," he said, scowling contemplatively. "You want to marry Tom Blanchard."

For the first time in this altercation, Frisco lost her composure. "No, you don't see," she raised her voice shrilly. "I do not want to marry anybody. I don't want to be owned by anybody. I want to own myself."

Beau frowned as he mused, "There will be complications, of course. I assume what you want is a divorce, but that won't be easy. It's not easy even under normal circumstances; but with a marriage license that's forged, I don't know."

"It doesn't matter to me how it's done," Frisco informed him breezily. "If a false marriage can be arranged, then a false divorce should be equally easy for a man with your resources. After all, there are plenty of crooked judges around, and they're all friends of yours."

He nodded acknowledgement. "I suppose so," he said. "But what am I to get out of all this? You've told me what your stakes are if you win. What if I should win? Surely you don't expect me simply to walk away and accept things as they are now?"

"No," Frisco said. "I've thought of that. If you

262

win, you own me and everything I have, without any reservations whatsoever."

"That's rather vain of you, isn't it?" he asked cuttingly. "You're placing a rather high value on yourself, aren't you? Hasn't it occurred to you that I might not consider the stakes worth it? That I might not want you at all?"

"I am not just body and spirit," she said arrogantly. "If you don't want me as wife, mistress, servant, or slave, you can discard me easily. Just toss me out onto the street or sell me to someone else. I happen to be a very rich woman, as well. My assets at the moment are valued at close to a million dollars. They're all yours if you win— everything. I think you will agree that's at least worth what I might get should I win."

"Yes," he nodded, "that's more than fair." His eyes were studying her in something akin to awe, as if he did not quite believe that she would be willing to risk so much for what he considered to be so little. "All right," he said finally, "I'll agree. When and where is this to be?"

"Tomorrow night," she said, "the boat will be closed. We can have complete privacy, if that's acceptable to you."

He nodded. "Of course," he said with a mocking smile. "If this is to be a duel of sorts, we'll have to follow rules. We'll have to have seconds as witnesses, and it's my prerogative to choose the weapon—or in this case, the game."

"Agreed," Frisco nodded.

PART FIVE

25

Beau had chosen five-card draw. Lillian would deal the game. Frisco had selected Mike and Lyuba as her seconds, and Beau—obviously intending to intimidate—had picked Albert Valery and Sally.

However, Frisco was not unsettled by his maneuver. There was something else that had upset her on leaving Valery's house after the challenge—and that had continued to upset her all that night and the following day. The Sight had plagued her with a single vision that occurred and recurred in increasing frequency. It was the image of the Nail, no longer just hot and smoldering ominously, but flaming violently, accompanied by the crackling of wood and the screams of terrified people.

Because of that vision, she had been unable to sleep or to rest, and she was anxious that her mind would not be clear for the crucial poker game.

Only she and Beau knew what the stakes were to be. All that Lillian and the others were told was that it was to be like a duel, intended to settle a private dispute. But Frisco suspected that Beau had broken their agreement and had told the entire story to Albert and Sally, because their faces—when they arrived on the boat—were filled with secret amusement. Mike, Lyuba, and Lillian were waiting on the boat, downstairs in the grand saloon with Frisco, when the others arrived.

It was a hot evening, so oppressively dry that Frisco's skin itched and chafed under the burden of her heavy gown. An unusual heat wave had lasted for two weeks now, driving the people of San Francisco to a quiet madness. Earlier tonight, when Frisco had walked the deck just after dusk, she had been strangely uneasy about the quiet. It had seemed even more oppressive than it had been the past few days, with virtually no one moving among the purple shadows of the waterfront. It was the sort of stillness that seemed to precede a storm, yet there was no sign of a change in the weather.

The grand saloon was set up well in advance for the confrontation. Mike had put water, liquor, and even some ice on a serving cart near the one table that would be used directly beneath the large brass chandelier in the center of the room. Only the lamps of that chandelier were lighted in order to keep the heat at a minimum.

Beau and his seconds arrived promptly, on the stroke of nine o'clock. Frisco suspected him of contriving every possible detail to give himself the advantage in the game, even to his manner of dress. Certainly, she had never seen him look more handsome. He wore a tight-fitting cutaway tailcoat of bright red broadcloth, a red and cream tattersall vest, and tight cream-colored trousers. His stiff collar was gleaming white and starched, beneath a flowing black silk tie. The effect, with his flaming red hair and his pale complexion, was almost overpowering.

Frisco realized that, as long as she was aware this effect was calculated to unnerve her, she could be entirely unaffected by it. She greeted all three guests politely, and ushered them into the grand saloon, directing them to the table in the very center of the vast room. Sally had never been inside Frisco's establishment, and she was clearly awestruck by its size, and its simple grandeur. It gave Frisco a degree of pleasure to be a figure of awe to what she thought was Beau's current affection, but that pleasure was somewhat qualified and lessened by a feeling of pity for the girl's stunted spiritual growth. She knew that it was Beau and Valery who were her real enemies, not the unfortunate prostitute.

After Frisco made the introductions at the table, Mike announced, "The drinks are on the house tonight, ladies and gentlemen. What'll you have?" His question was directed to Beau, but his words encompassed all.

"Nothing for me," Beau said with a wise smile. "But I'm sure that Valery and Sally will have something."

Frisco was disappointed at Beau's response; she had hoped she would at least have that advantage. But apparently he was taking this duel even more seriously than she was. Each time she had some evidence of how much he must despise her, it shook her.

The group was uncomfortably silent while Mike served the drinks. They were all aware that enmity existed, though only Lyuba had the slightest inkling of the full meaning of the rivalry, and only she was immune to the tension in the air. That tension built as they all seated themselves around the small gaming table. Beau and Frisco seated themselves opposite each other; Valery and Sally sat to Frisco's right, with Lillian between them, and Lyuba and Mike sat to her left.

Beau settled into his chair, checking everything for maximum comfort and ease. He glanced up at the glaring chandelier, looked across the table at Frisco and smirked, then reached into his coat pocket and took out an eyeshade, which he fitted neatly onto his forehead.

Lillian removed a deck of cards from the

pocket of her smock and extended it to Valery. "As Beau's second," she offered, "would you like to examine the cards to see that the seal has not been broken?"

"Absolutely," he said sharply, taking them with a flourish of his hand. He made much of examining the cards, then announced, "I'm inclined to reject this deck, but I'd like Mr. Tolliver to inspect them."

Beau took the cards and squinted at them suspiciously. "Mmm-hmm," he mused, and then grunted, "Hunh. Yes, I reject them. They appear to have been tampered with."

"They have not been tampered with," Frisco shot out sharply, "and you know it!"

"Perhaps not," Beau said cynically. "But I would be much more comfortable with the deck Mr. Valery has brought with him."

Frisco bridled. "Our agreement was that my establishment was to supply the cards. If you are not satisfied with this pack, we have well over a thousand packs with unbroken seals for you to choose from."

Having irritated her, Beau grinned in triumph. "Then show me another deck," he said.

Lillian pulled two more decks from her smock and handed them to Valery. He examined them and shrugged, "Either one of them is acceptable to us."

Lillian extended the cards to Mike. "They're fine with us," Mike said.

Lillian broke the seal and removed the stiff, shining cards. "I will repeat the rules of this challenge," she said formally, "so that there is no chance of a misunderstanding. The game is poker, of the type known as five-card draw. This means that each player will be dealt five cards. You may discard up to four cards and draw replacement cards from the deck. However, if you wish to keep your hand a complete secret, you may draw no more than three cards. In order to draw four cards, the card you retain must be an ace, and you are required to display that card. Three hands will be dealt, and the winner of this contest will be the winner of two out of three. Is that understood?"

There were nods all around the table. Lillian split the cards and shuffled expertly. She handed them to Beau to cut.

Frisco was beginning to feel rather strange as the cards were dealt out, vaguely chilled and lightheaded, as if she might faint. It was hot in the room, and beads of perspiration were creeping onto her forehead and her upper lip. Why was she feeling this way? She was not afraid of losing; she had made her decision, and she intended to stick with it.

Her hand shook as she reached out to the table to pick up her cards. She took a deep breath to steady herself, but it did no good.

Her vision was blurred as she gazed down at her cards. She had been dealt the six of diamonds, the six of hearts, the seven of hearts, the jack of spades, and a nail. She blinked her eyes at the last card: it was an ace, but what kind of ace she could not make out, for glowing from the very center of the card was a flaming nail!

She closed her eyes and rubbed them, then looked back. The nail was gone. The card was the ace of spades. But the vision had shaken her. She could not think clearly. Through a ringing in her ears, she heard Beau ask for three cards. That meant he had not drawn a good hand. She had that pair of sixes, but there were two cards toward a straight, and then the jack and the ace were in the same suit. What should she do? She heard herself asking for two cards, and saw her hands reach up and discard the seven of hearts and the jack of spades.

She was given the ten of diamonds and the five of spades. Her heart sank. Well, at least she had the pair of sixes. There was still a chance. She laid her cards on the table. "A pair of sixes," she said, her voice breaking.

Through hazy eyes she saw Beau raise an eyebrow and sneer. "Three kings," he announced.

She stared down at the cards he laid out—the king of spades, the king of hearts, the king of clubs, the two of spades, and the seven of diamonds.

There was a murmur around the table. Mike and Lyuba looked at each other anxiously, then looked at Frisco. She did not hear what they said, but there was concern in the eyes they turned on her.

Sally and Valery were looking at her with mockery in their eyes. But Valery quickly turned to Beau, slapped his hand on the table, and said loudly, "Well, Tolliver, you've won that one! One more hand, and it's done!"

Frisco felt faint. "It's warm in here," she said. "Mike, please give me a glass of water, and put some of that ice in it."

The ice tinkled nervously in the glass as she raised it to her lips with a trembling hand. Her dry throat constricted as the cold liquid touched it, but she forced herself to swallow, and it helped a bit. For a moment, her body felt a sense of relief, though her skin still felt raw.

This time, Lillian handed the cards to Frisco to cut. Valery is right, she thought as she waited for her cards to be dealt. If Beau wins this hand, that's it; I've lost everything.

As she reached to pick up her cards, she flinched. They were so hot, they seemed to burn her fingers. She hesitated a moment, looked across at Beau. There were beads of perspiration breaking out on his face, too. He did not look her way, but simply gazed down at his cards and frowned.

She touched the cards again. They were still hot, but they did not burn her fingers. She fanned them out in her hand to look at them. She

274

flinched. She could see nothing but flames, a roaring mass of fire, leaping and crackling in her hands. She felt faint, and quickly reached for the glass of water to take a drink. It did no good; she could still not see her cards.

Through the roaring of the fire, she heard Beau ask for three cards, then she heard Lillian ask, "Frisco?" There was no way she could ask for cards, because she did not know what she had. "I'll hold," she said. It was the only thing she could do under the circumstances—trust to fate.

Beau slammed his cards down in disgust. "A pair of deuces!"

Slowly Frisco spread her cards out on the table and withdrew her hands to wait for the reaction to tell her what she had. There was an excited murmur, and then a guffaw from Mike. "Three jacks."

After a moment, the flames died down, and Frisco could see her cards—three jacks, the queen of clubs, and again that ace of spades. She heaved a great sigh of relief, and with it let out a faint quivering moan. Fate had given her a chance after all. If she could only get through one more hand.

Lyuba caught her eye, and she sensed that the older woman knew what she was feeling and thinking. The message in those eyes came through to her—trust in your heart; relax and let be what will be.

She knew that Lyuba was right, but she was afraid to relax. She felt so tired, and if she relaxed she might not be able to think clearly, and she had to think. No, she didn't. She had won the last hand without even knowing what cards she held. She had to trust. That was the key—trust and relax.

"Mike," she said suddenly, "please pour me a drink. Some whiskey over ice!"

"Whiskey, ma'am?" he gaped in disbelief. "You?"

"Yes," Frisco replied, "for me."

He obeyed.

Going down her throat, it felt warm and cold at the same time. She shuddered slightly at the bitterness, but then felt the glowing feeling of relaxation creeping over her body. For the first time in the game, she felt she could see with clarity.

Beau cut the cards briskly and efficiently. This time she reached out for her cards with a steady hand. She felt cool, no chills or perspiration. She looked across at Beau. He removed his handkerchief from his pocket and mopped his brow vigorously, a dull look of concern in his eyes as he gazed at his cards. Then he looked up, and his eyes met hers. They spoke to her, but she did not know what they were saying. It was a look she was not accustomed to in Beau, a look of indecision, of uncertainty.

Disturbed, she looked down at her own hand.

The first thing she saw was the Nail, flickering threateningly on the ace of spades. The blasted card had plagued her throughout the game! She felt a surge of anger rise within her breast. What was it fate was trying to tell her? She looked at the other cards—the two of diamonds, the six of hearts, the ten of spades, and the eight of clubs. She could not possibly have had a worse hand than that.

"I'll take one card," Beau said, running his tongue over his dry lips.

Frisco pulled the hateful ace of spades away from the other four indecisively. Suddenly it seemed to burst into flames, burning her fingers, and she dropped it faceup on the table. Lillian looked at her questioningly. Frisco handed over the cards in her hand. "I'll take four," she said.

She took another sip of whiskey, and suddenly an image of the children flashed into her mind—Alex and Natasha dressed for bed, laughing as they put their violins away in their cases. For some reason, Frisco felt a strange longing to be near them, to hug them and kiss them and tuck them into bed.

She reached out to pick up her four cards at the same moment Beau picked up his one, and again their eyes met. There was a question in his eyes, and she did not know how to answer it because she did not know what the question was. Whatever it was, there was nothing hard or cruel in it, and that perplexed her.

She looked at her cards—the nine of spades, the six of clubs, the two of clubs, and the ace of hearts. Her spirit surged. She had a pair of aces! She could win with that. Surely Beau would not have anything to beat it.

She was about to lay her cards down when she was startled by the sound of shouting from up on deck. It was followed by the sound of the outside door flying open and Captain Wellington stumbling downstairs, screaming frantically, "Fire! The town's burning! There are blazes all over the place!"

·26

The hot night sky was filled with the glow. Here, along the docks, the shabby lean-to buildings were alive with flames. To her left, below the slot, there was an eerie light choking with billowing black smoke. To her right, up Telegraph Hill, there was another, smaller glow.

With a terrible sinking feeling, she realized what the Sight had been trying to tell her. It did not matter who won or lost a game of poker, because everything would soon be lost anyway.

Her first concern was for the children. She could not tell where on Telegraph Hill the fire was, but—wherever it was—Alex and Natasha were sure to be frightened, and they might even be in danger. Of course, Julie was there with them, and so were Janet and the housemaids, but

Frisco would not feel satisfied that they were safe unless she were there to see that they were.

"I swear these fires was set," Captain Wellington's voice droned behind her. "They seemed to break out all suddenlike, at the same time all over the city. Couldn't have been spread by the wind because there ain't none. Damned thieves doin' it so they can loot and steal while everbody else is fightin' fires."

The old sea captain was probably right. Incendiaries had been caught before, setting fires for that very purpose; and, of the numerous conflagrations that had destroyed the town in the past few years, almost all had been set purposely. The constant awareness of imminent death and destruction was a part of the price for living in the new little city by the bay. However, Frisco could not help but feel a bitter contempt for the kind of subhuman creatures who valued human life so little that they would cause such a holocaust just to acquire a few trifling material goods.

Captain Wellington rambled on. "Looks like the fire on the hill was set someplace in the tent city." He pointed off toward Telegraph Hill. "But it's beginning to spread upward. Those tents go in no time."

An image flashed into Frisco's mind—the image of Alex and Natasha surrounded by fire, their faces stricken with terror. Somehow she knew she had to reach them before the fire did. While everyone else on the boat stared in shock at the growing conflagration, she quickly turned and rushed down the gangway toward her carriage. She was halfway down the dock before anyone on deck knew that she was gone.

Fear coursed through her veins as she untied the horse and climbed into the carriage seat. Her body responded reflexively to the urgent need of her spirit to be with the children. Her mind in this critical moment was totally uninvolved in her actions. She did not even pause to think which route home would be the safer. She thought only of getting there quickly.

She headed up East Street, which ran along the waterfront, but she quickly became stymied by the crowds. The horse was frightened and confused by the chaos of humanity rushing back and forth between city streets and docks loading all manner of possessions aboard the boats, intending to escape to the sea. It took her almost half an hour to maneuver the clumsy carriage one full block. She would never reach Telegraph Hill at this rate.

At the conjunction of Market and Sacramento, she turned the carriage up into the less-crowded Sacramento Street, and found herself in the very midst of the raging fire. The horse whinnied in fearful protest as she whipped him viciously to make him continue. Smoke billowed all around them, and a sudden gust of wind blew live cinders all over the carriage. From nearby, there was the thunderous crash of falling timbers, and the most bloodcurdling scream Frisco had ever heard.

Then, suddenly, one of the warehouses not far away exploded—clearly from stored gunpowder. The sehock of the sound caused the horse to rear back in protest before plunging straight into the inferno ahead. Frisco knew that fire could cause horses to panic, but she had never realized what that panic meant until now.

There was no longer any controlling the horse. He led her into scorching heat where cinders and fiery splinters rained down unceasingly and the smoke was almost suffocating. Frisco knew that she was staring into the horrible face of death. Any moment might be her last, brought on by the horse's uncontrollable headlong rush through the mass of flames. Her whole life flashed before her in one swift vision of helplessness and foolishness, an instant that was meaningless and purposeless in the blazing light of eternity.

A body rushed past her carriage screaming, indistinguishable as man or woman in its enveloping flames. A woman crouched on the ground moaning helplessly over some charred possession beside her. Frisco did not realize until she had rushed past that the charred heap was the remains of an infant. A bespectacled little man hobbled toward her, a large ornate clock under one arm, a delicate crystal vase under the other. Her horse ran headlong into him, sending his precious possessions flying and knocking him to the ground. The carriage wheels bumped as they passed over his body.

Frisco no longer had any idea where she was or where the horse was taking her. There was only a solid wall of flames ahead of her. As she saw that wall beginning to cave in with a rumbling, crackling, hissing sound, she knew the sound of screaming she heard was her own.

Suddenly a figure on a horse passed her line of vision and grabbed her carriage horse around the neck. The man was coatless and shirtless, and she could see the taut powerful muscles of his back as he struggled to subdue the panicked horse. His skin and hair seemed to glow red from the reflected flames. His own horse seemed docile compared to hers, and—after a moment—she realized why: he had removed his shirt to make a blindfold for the animal.

Through the roar and crackle of the fire, she heard the man shout, "Your petticoat, damn it! Give me your petticoat, and quickly!"

Rapidly, Frisco lifted her dress and ripped one of her petticoats loose, then stood up in the carriage to toss it to the man. Only then did she see the man's face and realize it was Beau. She stood staring in shocked disbelief that he had risked his life to come to rescue her.

"The petticoat, damn it!" he screamed, still struggling with the obstreperous horse. She tossed it to him. Once he had the animal blindfolded, its fear abated. He swiftly tied the reins of his own horse to the back of the carriage, and then leaped up beside Frisco to take complete charge.

He turned the carriage sharply to the right, then slapped the reins to make the horse move more quickly. It whinnied in protest at having to move blindly, but it did obey. Within moments Frisco realized they were out of the worst of the fire and headed up Sansome Street toward the hill.

Until that moment, Beau had been guiding the carriage in grim and anxious silence, and she had been staring in puzzlement at his face in profile against the flaming city. She felt that she had never seen a more welcome or a more beautiful face, even as stained with sweat and soot as it was. It had always been the most beautiful face in the world to her—the high broad forehead, the long straight nose, the proud firm mouth, and the strong arrogant jaw. She ached to touch that face, to kiss those lips, to look up into those cool green eyes and to say, "Thank you." But somehow, under the circumstances, she could say nothing. She could only stare at him and wonder why he had come.

It was he who spoke first, and his voice was cold and harsh. "You stupid little fool," he said. "What could have possessed you to rush off like that?"

"The children," she said. "I have to make sure the children are safe."

"Did you think you could do that by killing

yourself?" he snapped. "You should have said something to me! I can get you there without frying you to a crisp!"

He slapped the reins to get the blind reticent horse to move more quickly. They were out of the worst of the fire now, but they were not completely out of danger. On Sansome Street, they were caught between two infernos, one behind and one ahead on Telegraph Hill. Here, masses of people were rushing about trying to load families and possessions out of endangered houses and onto wagons before the flames reached them. At the moment, there was more danger of being crushed by the mob—or being attacked for possession of the carriage—than there was of being burned to death.

Frisco could still not see how far up Telegraph Hill the fire had moved, but she could see that— so far—Nob Hill was safe, completely untouched. She noted this with irony; of course, that would be the whim of fate—to leave her new fireproof brick building entirely safe from the conflagration. But would it be safe? She wondered. Lyuba's Tarot reading came back to haunt her. "What you have built will crumble," her old friend had said. And, "You must forsake all that you have to gain all that you want."

She knew that part of those prophecies were coming true now, but she still did not realize how accurate the words would be until after she had actually brought them about, not from any desire to fulfill prophecy, but simply by following the whims of her own heart. It was on Sansome Street that she took one step in that direction.

At the corner of Union and Sansome, directly in front of the infirmary, there was such a crowd of people, it was impossible to get through. Wagons filled with the injured had been brought to the infirmary, but they had been left chaotically in the street. At the same time, invalids were being brought out and loaded onto the already crowded wagons, old patients mixed in with the new.

There was much excitement, with people rushing to and fro, shouting instructions and orders. Some of the other residents were trying to get through the crowd with hastily loaded wagons, and they were shouting angrily at the drivers, attendants, and nurses from the infirmary.

One crude-looking young man was being particularly vituperative. He was chewing on a cud of tobacco, and he spat viciously into the crowd below him, shouting, "Get the hell out of the way! Let us through, you sons a' bitches! God-damned do-gooders!"

The object of his curses was a white-haired old man, who was attempting to organize the infirmary wagons. Frisco recognized him as Dr. Bartleby, the doctor who had treated both Beau and Natasha.

He pleaded with the young man. "Try to be patient. We'll get these wagons out of the way as soon as we can. But it's impossible to move them at the moment. There's no reason to panic. There's no immediate danger to this area. The fire shouldn't reach us for another half hour."

Beau edged the carriage as close to the doctor as possible and called out to him. "Dr. Bartleby," he shouted, "what seems to be the trouble here?"

"Oh, Mr. Tolliver," he almost smiled with relief to see a friendly face. "I've never had so many problems all at once, with no way to solve any of them. The authorities have advised us to evacuate the infirmary, but they keep on sending the injured here for treatment. We already had too few vehicles for transporting the patients, but now it's absolutely impossible. And anyway, we don't even have a place to go. There's just no building that's available that's also large enough and in a safe area."

"How big does it have to be?" Frisco broke in.

"Well," the old doctor shrugged, "it's got to be at least as large as this place here." He indicated the infirmary. "But even that's too small for the numbers we're getting in from the fire."

"I've got a place for you," she said impulsively. "It's on Nob Hill, and it's got twice as much room. The only problem is it doesn't have beds."

"That's all right," Dr. Bartleby said gratefully, "as long as it's got walls and floors. Where on Nob Hill is this place?"

Frisco explained, reached into her purse for the key, and gave it to him.

287

"I don't know how to thank you, Mrs. Tolliver," the old man said. "I just pray that the Lord will bless you for what you've done." Then, as they were about to try to drive off through the crowd, he looked wistfully at the carriage. "By the way," he added, "you don't happen to know where we can get more vehicles, do you?"

Beau looked at Frisco with a questioning grin. Frisco nodded. "You can have this carriage," Beau told him. "And we'll see if we can get you some more."

"Thank you, sir," the doctor smiled. "I'll be forever beholden to you."

Beau handed the carriage over to one of the attendants, them climbed onto his horse and helped Frisco to step up into the saddle behind him. Getting rid of the carriage proved to be an advantage for them; they could move much more easily and swiftly through the crowd on horseback, and they felt more secure about entering the fire-stricken area of Telegraph Hill.

There was another advantage that Frisco felt almost ashamed to admit to herself: it had been a long time since she had had a reason to have her arms around Beau, and it felt good to touch him once more, even if it was under the pretext of holding on to keep from falling off the horse. For all the strength and muscularity that Beau possessed, his waist was incredibly slender; for all the sweat and soot that clung to him, his bare flesh was unbelievably smooth and sensuous to touch.

She longed to rest her head on his back, to kiss him and thereby to give up all of her cares and anxieties to him.

But she chided herself: it was wrong to feel so good in the midst of such suffering. She had to restrain her selfish desires, her personal passions. There were others she cared about whose very lives were in danger. Certainly, she must not think about herself before Alex and Natasha were safe.

And even then, she thought, I cannot give in to this passion. I can never give in to my feelings for this man who is not really my husband, not after all I have had to go through to sever myself from him—and not with the hatred he feels for me.

27

A wind had come up, fanning the flames and spreading them to every corner of Telegraph Hill. When Frisco saw the devastation that confronted her and Beau beginning at Filbert Street, she feared that they were already too late to be of any help to the children. The tent city was completely gone, with no trace at all remaining; all there was where it had been was a great sweep of charred and blackened earth, still smoking dismally.

The violent flames were all ahead of them, up on the crest of the hill, the outermost limits of the city, where only recently fine homes had been built, where Beau had built the finest of all the houses for Frisco. It was not much further to the top, and then they would be home—if there was any home left to greet them.

From the side, there was a sudden burst of white flame, as of spirits or liquor exploding. The heat from it singed Frisco's hair and brows, and for a moment she breathed but could find no oxygen in what she inhaled. She gasped and coughed, and then—blessed relief—they were back in a draught of air again. They had passed through the wall of flame, the advancing line of the fire, and there—only a few feet ahead of them—was their house, as yet untouched.

The sky beyond it was dark and innocent, though above it like a curse there was a heavy stratum of black smoke. The house itself stood like a bulwark defying all evil, arrogantly proclaiming its inviolability; but its white walls reflected the approaching flames, flickering pink and orange and mauve.

In their anxious, headlong rush to see to the safety of the children, neither Frisco nor Beau looked carefully at the wagon, laden down with household items, that was drawn up before the house. They both simply assumed that someone had paused there in his flight from the fire below.

Nor did they even think it was odd that the front door of the house was unlocked. Very likely, Janet or Julie had neglected to lock it behind them in their haste to get the children and the household staff to safety.

And so they were taken completely by surprise when they surged into the house and found themselves face-to-face with two total strangers—two rough-looking men with their arms filled with Frisco's priceless possessions, silver and crystal and fine china.

"Damnation!" one of them snarled. "Two more!" And he dropped his treasures to take a swing at Beau.

Frisco grabbed an umbrella from the hall tree and swung it at the other man, while Beau landed a blow on the chin of the first. Dodging repeated swings from Frisco's umbrella, her man finally dropped his load of stolen goods and moved toward the door, crying, "I'm going, lady! I'm going! The fire'll be here any minute anyhow!"

Beau grabbed his man by the scruff of the neck and scuttled him toward the door as well, saying fiercely, "And you'd better do the same! The fire will take all this stuff, but I'd rather it have everything than scum like you!" He literally threw the man down the front stairs.

Frisco moved swiftly into the house, calling out, "Julie! Janet! Is anyone here!"

Beau came up beside her gravely, with the comment, "Our looters said we were 'two more.' That means they've already run into somebody in the house. You look upstairs, and I'll check the back."

Frisco lifted her skirts and rushed up the stairs, taking them two at a time, and calling out, "Alex! Natasha! Julie! Are you here?"

At the top of the stairs, she stopped in shock.

292

The back wall of the house was aflame! And tiny tongues of flame were dancing toward her along the edge of the Turkish carpet.

Natasha's room was at the very rear of the house, the one that would be affected by the fire first. Decisively, Frisco rushed to it, stepping gingerly over the burning carpet, and thrust the door open, calling out, "Natasha!"

The room was empty, except for the thick smoke that billowed out to greet her. Quickly she moved to the next door. It was the nursery, and it was most unlikely anyone would be in there, but she had to check to make sure. It, too, was filled with smoke, but again there were no children.

It was in Alex's room that she found them. All three—Alex, Natasha, and Julie—were curled up in the middle of Alex's bed. Julie was in the very middle, a book in her lap, with one arm around each child. The smoke was thick, and there was almost no air in the room at all. At first, Frisco feared they might already be dead.

But when she screamed, "Wake up! For God's sake, wake up!" Julie stirred, moaned, and coughed.

By the time Frisco reached the bedside, Julie's eyes were open and filled with fear. "What's happened?" she asked. "Where is this smoke coming from?"

"The whole town is burning," Frisco said quickly. "We've got to get the children up and out of here!"

The full impact of what was happening did not register on Julie immediately. "But that's impossible. Only a moment ago, I was reading," she said. "I must have just dozed off."

"There isn't time to explain," Frisco snapped. "We've got to move quickly!" She reached out to Alex and shook him brusquely. "Alex! Wake up! It's Mommy! We have to go somewhere, and we're in a hurry!"

The child moaned and rolled over. Frisco turned back to Julie. "Pick him up and carry him downstairs and out the front," she instructed. "I'll take care of Natasha!"

Julie—still numb from shock—did as she was told, scooping Alex up in her arms and moving toward the door of the room.

Frisco turned her attention to Natasha. She knew she had to be gentle with the girl, who had been through so much tragedy in her brief life. A sudden shock might be more than she could stand. Frisco reached out her hand and touched Natasha gently on the cheek. "Natasha," she said softly. "You have to wake up now."

Natasha's eyes opened immediately, alert and questioning.

It was at that moment that Julie screamed from the doorway. "Oh, my God! The whole place is aflame! We'll never get out of here!"

Natasha sat up abruptly. "The Nail!" she gasped. "I knew it would come, and it has!"

"No, child," Frisco said sternly. "It's not the

Nail. The whole city is burning. It's not just this house."

That glazed retreating look came into the girl's eyes then, and Frisco knew that she was lost. She would not be able to deal with her rationally. She grabbed Natasha rudely by the arm and jerked her to her feet. "I'm not going to stand for this sort of thing now!" she snapped harshly. "You're going to do as I say, or I'm going to slap you 'til your teeth hurt!"

She dragged the child across the room to the doorway, where Julie was still cowering with Alex in her arms. She saw immediately that the fire had indeed already enveloped the hallway, but she knew that there was no other way out of the house. If they could not pass through the fire they were doomed.

Alex had begun to awaken, but his eyes were blinded in that groggy, confused way of small children when disturbed from a deep midnight sleep. "Mommy," he asked, "what's going on?"

"Hush, child," Frisco replied abruptly. "I'll explain later."

At that moment, Beau appeared at the top of the stairs, his face and shoulders barely visible above the flames. "The others are safely outside," he called out. "Though your housekeeper has suffered a pretty bad blow from our looters!" Then he paused to survey the flaming hall. "Do you think you can make it?"

"We have to," Frisco called back.

"No," Julie cried. "It's impossible! You have to do something!"

"All right," Beau replied matter of factly, as if rescuing them would be simple. "Don't move! I'll be right back!"

Frisco was impatient. She did not know what Beau could hope to do, and they were wasting precious time. The flames were advancing rapidly. At any moment the whole floor might collapse beneath them.

Some of what was happening must have finally registered with Alex, because he asked suddenly, "Mommy, if we're going away forever, I want to take my violin."

"There isn't time," Frisco replied. "I'll have to get you another violin."

"No," Alex said peevishly. "I want mine."

There was no time to answer him, because Beau had returned. He had brought with him several large bedsheets soaked in water. Swiftly, he wrapped himself in one of them and dashed across the fiery floor to where they stood.

"You'll have to remove your petticoats," he instructed Frisco and Julie, "and lift your skirts up around your waists and tie them. Then wrap yourselves in these and run as fast as you can." He gestured to Julie. "Here, let me take my boy."

A thrill ran through Frisco at the possessive note in his voice, but she did not have time to savor it. She had to hurry to follow his instructions.

"I want to take my violin," Alex moaned plaintively to his stepfather.

"I'm sorry, son," Beau replied. "We can't. We'll have to get you another one."

"That's what mommy said," Alex told him. "But I want mine."

Julie went first, and she easily made it to the stairs and continued down to safety.

The fire was rapidly consuming Alex's room. The paper on the ceiling above their heads was beginning to break into black circles that gradually expanded, forming red-hot circles at the center, then flaking and falling as ash. There was a thundering, rumbling sound all around them now, as of hundreds of wagons advancing rapidly toward them—all wagons bearing death.

"You and Natasha go next," Beau instructed. "And Alex and I will be right behind."

Frisco did not argue, but gripped Natasha's hand tightly, checked to make sure the child had her sheet wrapped securely around her, and then stepped swiftly out into the flames, dragging the reluctant child behind her. She knew that Beau was following her closely, because she heard Alex's pleading, "Daddy, my violin," directly behind her ear.

She had just reached the head of the stairs when suddenly, inexplicably, Natasha broke free from her grip and rushed back across the hallway and into Alex's room. Frisco screamed then. She knew quite clearly what was happening, because all she could see was the Nail burning brilliantly and victoriously.

Beau thrust Alex into her arms and started after Natasha, but the child was back almost instantly, carrying Alex's violin. With a faint, sweet smile on her face, she kissed the instrument lovingly and handed it to Alex, who took it gratefully.

Beau reached out to take Natasha's hand, but she pulled away, backing into the flames. She shook her head determinedly and let the sheet fall down around her ankles. "No," she said. "It's better this way. I'm the one the Nail wants. Once it has me, you can be happy."

"No, Natasha," Frisco screamed, "don't be a fool!"

Beau lunged into the flames to get her, but she continued to back away from him.

He did not reach her.

There was a loud snapping above them. The walls and floor shook. Then, above and behind Natasha's small frail figure, everything seemed to crash in at once, and she was gone, without even a scream.

Frisco broke into sobs. Silently, Beau took Alex from her arms and ushered her swiftly down the stairs and out into the smoke-filled night air.

28

Little Alex understood and accepted the death of his deep love, and that was Frisco's only comfort. "She wasn't happy here, Mommy," he said softly as they all huddled together in the buckboard like the woebegone remnants of a shellshocked army in retreat. "She wanted to be with the angels, so she wouldn't hurt anymore."

They were traveling the dusty back-country road toward Nob Hill, and soon they would all be safe—all, that is, except Natasha, and she was beyond safety. The fires were all behind them, and they showed no signs of moving toward this farthest outpost of San Francisco. The further they traveled, the less harsh the devastation appeared, the more beautiful the red glow seemed.

Yet Frisco could feel nothing but numbness. And a strange sense of guilt, as well. She had failed Natasha, the last fragile flower of her adopted Rom family, and she was sure she could never forgive herself for that. It did not occur to her that she had done everything possible to help the child; she could think only of the fact that her last words to her charge had been harsh, even cruel.

Natasha had been obsessed with the Nail's curse, yet Frisco was certain that it was that obsession, and not the curse itself that had doomed the child. Or was it? Lyuba's Tarot reading had foreseen death, a death that could not be avoided. If it was Natasha's death, then perhaps it was the curse at work. If not, there would be another death, or even several.

Despairingly, Frisco thought of the boat. In her haste to reach the children, she had abandoned all of the other people she cared about— Mike and Lyuba, and Lillian, and all of the girls who were below in their rooms. Were they safe? Or would the fire claim them as victims, too? Had it possibly already claimed them?

She turned around in the buckboard, her eyes searching the scene behind her. It was impossible to see anything clearly in the enormous canopy of red light and black smoke. The great forest of masts was still there in the bay; some seemed to be burning, and some not. She could not determine precisely where in the bay the *Frisco Lady* had been, because all the familiar buildings and landmarks had been reduced to rubble.

She prayed fervently that all the girls were safe; she could not bear it if they too had been lost by her carelessness. She would break completely under that much guilt. Frisco recognized the fact that she had been willing to forsake them; that had been a part of the risk in her challenge to Beau. But she would never have considered losing them in this manner. She would never knowingly have forsaken them to death.

"You must forsake all that you have to gain all that you want," the cards had said. Was this what they had meant? All that she wanted was for Beau and Alex and her to be united again. And they were all together now, in this buckboard, though they were far from being fully united.

Faced with the fire, Beau's actions had been fine and noble and caring, but after it was all over, Frisco was certain he would return to his bitterness and his cruelty. Perhaps he was behaving well under stress only because his masculine vanity required acts of heroism.

His actions, when they reached the new casino atop Nob Hill, confirmed this appraisal. Dr. Bartleby and his staff already had the place operating as an infirmary, though they still had many patients to transfer, and there were wagonloads of newly injured arriving constantly. As soon as Beau learned what the situation was, he told Dr. Bartleby, "I'll take the buckboard down and see what I can do to help. At least you'll have one more conveyance in operation."

Without a word to Frisco, he climbed back onto the buckboard, and took the reins. After all he had done in the past few hours, she could expect no more, but she could not allow him to leave like this.

She moved swiftly to the side of the buckboard. "Beau," she said softly and with a trace of embarrassment, "I want to thank you. I owe you my life as well as Alex's, and I'm grateful."

"No need for thanks," he said with a superior smile. "I'm simply protecting my investment. We've got a game to finish, remember?"

Frisco stiffened. "Yes," she said, "I haven't forgotten. But by the time we finish the game, the stakes may be all gone."

Beau shrugged. "I have nothing to lose." He released the brake on the buckboard and made ready to leave.

His attitude angered Frisco, but she tried not to show it. "I'll be glad to get back to the game as soon as this is all over," she said coolly. "*If* the game is still there. Since you're so concerned about it, while you're in town, you might check to see if the *Frisco Lady* is still there."

"I'll do that," he said with a grin. Then he slapped the reins and headed off down the hill again.

She felt a twinge of regret seeing him go. He was venturing back into danger, entirely alone, his bare broad shoulders squared, his head held high, the picture of dauntless courage. Only then

302

did it occur to her that she might never see him again. Where he was going the fire still raged, there was still death and destruction, and she knew that he would be risking his life time and again to help others. She stood there on the top of the hill, watching as long as she could see him. Then she turned her attention to the chaotic conditions around her.

Thousands of people had sought refuge on Nob Hill. It was one of only two alternatives that people had when these disasters hit the city, the other alternative being to head out to sea in anything that would float. There was no other town in history that had faced total destruction so many times, and San Franciscans had begun to accept the pattern, knowing well what had to be done in the face of disaster, and doing it.

There was already a tent city spread out around the casino, the people having made their temporary shelters out of whatever was available—canvas, blankets, sheets, scraps of wood and tin, even paper. Some had managed to bring food supplies and household goods with them, and they staked their claims to small plots of ground, which they fenced off with twine or strips of rag. With or without a roof, they set up housekeeping in public view. It was a strange sight to see—here a brass bed, complete with pillows and silk sheets, a couple fast asleep beneath a quilt, with only the sky overhead; there an elderly woman rocking placidly in her rocking chair, watching the crowds move about her while crocheting something delicate and pink; and over there, underneath a scrubby pine, a woman with a tin tub and washboard, busily scrubbing clothes, while her naked children patiently wait for the soot to be removed from their only apparel.

But most of the people had been able to get away with only the clothes on their back, and they were grateful even for that. They knew they could live without material possessions as long as they had themselves and each other. After the first day, food and nourishment might become a problem, but they had faith that they could meet that problem. They could work; they could scavenge; they could even beg if necessary. They had gotten away with their lives, and they considered themselves lucky, knowing that there were others less fortunate.

Frisco was one of these. Her home was gone, and perhaps all her riches with it. Her only possession was a lavender satin gown—appropriate only for evening wear, with its low-cut bodice and its delicate lace trim—now torn and badly stained with soot and ash, its skirt hanging limp against her legs since she had divested herself of her petticoats.

She had lost someone she loved, but she had managed to save another—her son. That was all the reason she needed to keep on living. In fact, it was Alex who set the example for her.

They were wandering almost aimlessly through the crowd, trying to decide where they could find a space to sit down and rest, when an old man called out to Alex, "Hey, boy, what's that you got there?"

He was walking along a few feet behind Frisco at that point, holding Julie's hand in one hand and carrying his violin case in the other. As he replied, "It's a violin, sir," Frisco turned around to look. She was concerned about how her son would feel about music now that Natasha was gone.

"Do you mean it's a fiddle?" the man asked. "You don't mean to say you can play it, do you?"

Alex nodded.

The old man slapped his knee. "Why, it's been a long time since I heard anybody play the fiddle!" he exclaimed. "You wouldn't be willing to play a little tune for me, would you?"

Alex hesitated. Frisco saw the frightened look in his eyes, and she knew what it meant, but luckily the old man did not.

"It would mean an awful lot to me to hear a bit of music," he said genuinely. "You see, I just lost someone I loved very much, and she always liked music."

Gentle tears began to well up in Alex's eyes. Frisco anxiously started to step forward to stop the exchange, but then Alex spoke.

"I lost someone, too," he said. "And I think she would like me to play for you."

He took the violin lovingly out of its case and carefully tuned it. Then he began to play. It was a gypsy tarantella, a wild, free-wheeling dance, and its strains lifted into the night like a plea. A crowd began to gather, coming from all over the encampment, and they began to clap merrily in time to the music.

It was a strange sight to witness. Only a few moments before, all of these people had been frightened and isolated by their private losses, straining to meet the future, painful moment by painful moment. Suddenly they were transformed. They were laughing and smiling and dancing in the face of disaster, looking at each other and sharing in the beauty of life. And all the time, lending its rosy glow from the distance, there was the fire. The effect was awesome, and it caused a slight chill of pride to run through Frisco, not just pride in her son, but pride in the people of San Francisco.

When Alex finished playing the tarantella, there was wild applause. From all over the crowd, people shouted, "More! More! Play another tune!"

Then Alex looked directly into his mother's eyes. "All right," he said as loudly as he could in his thin little voice. "I'm going to play this one for a very special lady they call Frisco."

Even before he lifted his bow, she knew what it would be—Lizst's Hungarian Rhapsody—and she wanted to protest: No! Not that! Not here!

306

Not now! That piece of music had special meanings for her, and they were for the good times, the happy joyous occasions. She could not bear to hear it now, at the very nadir of her life.

But she could say nothing, for fear her child would not understand, that he would be hurt.

The first note, heavy with dignity and power, gripped her soul and shook it. "Remember who you are," it said firmly. "Lift up your head. Open your heart. The pain and loss can be endured."

Tears stung her eyes. She was ashamed of her despair. Her child knew more about living in the face of adversity than she did. He knew, when you can do nothing for yourself, you can still do something for others, and that heals your own wounds. He was giving what he had to all these people, and in return their gratitude was helping to mend his broken heart.

She turned suddenly to Janet and asked, "Will you stay here and look after Alex?"

Janet nodded, a bit puzzled.

She turned to Julie. "You and I are going to go make ourselves useful," she said.

She blew Alex a kiss and smiled at him. He smiled back with understanding. Then she turned away and led Julie up toward the red brick building she had worked so hard to construct without the use of a single nail. Behind her, Alex's music had broken into the second strain—the wild, free, scampering melody that seemed to have no begin-

ning and no end, nothing to hold it tied securely
to the earth.

She knew at that moment that the red brick
building would never be a casino. It would never
belong to her again. It was serving the finest purpose it could ever serve right now, giving refuge
to the sick and the injured. When this was all
over, she would give the property to Dr. Bartleby
and the city of San Francisco to be their new infirmary.

It was not difficult to find Dr. Bartleby. His
shock of white hair stood out from the crowd, as
he moved swiftly and efficiently from one makeshift bed to another.

"Doctor," she approached him, "can you use
any help?"

Despite his fatigue, there was a trace of a smile
on his face as he responded. "Bless you, child,
you don't know what you're asking. I could have
a hundred people working in here and still need
help."

"Neither of us know much about nursing," she
explained. "But we're willing to take orders and
learn."

"All right," he said. "It won't be very pleasant
work, mostly washing wounds and emptying bedpans, but you have no idea how much help that
will be."

They were assigned to a stony-faced nun, who
would give them their orders. Unfortunately the

infirmary did not have extra kerchiefs and aprons, so they would have to make do with whatever they could improvise.

"Perhaps you could tear off some bits of cloth from your petticoats," the sister said primly.

Frisco looked at Julie and laughed. "I'm afraid we don't have any petticoats left," she explained. "But we do have some ruffles left on our skirts."

The nun remarked, "It doesn't matter what you use, but you must have your hair tied securely so that it will not get in your way. Most of what you will be doing will be cleaning and sterilizing."

That was how their work began, but as the night progressed they found themselves performing all sorts of tasks, all of them tedious, exacting, and exhausting. They boiled water, and they cleansed instruments. They made bandages, they emptied bedpans. They made beds out of straw, and they went scavenging among the other refugees for all manner of supplies.

However, at about three o'clock in the morning, their inexperience as nurses no longer mattered. It was at that point that the injured from an explosion on the docks were brought in, and all available hands had to be used to wash wounds, apply ointments, and bandage the badly burned men, almost a hundred of them all at once. By that time, Frisco and Julie no longer considered themselves novices; they had grown accustomed to the screams of pain and to the sickening mutilations. They had passed through their baptism of suffering and were immune.

However, there was one young man who insisted upon talking endlessly as she bandaged, perhaps to keep his mind off his pain. There were burns of some degree over almost all of his body, and it took Frisco a long time to see to all of them.

"It were a ship that did it," the young man told her, whether she wanted to hear it or not. "One of those old hulks down on the docks that had been abandoned and turned into a warehouse. None of us knew it was used to store gunpowder. We just thought to get aboard, cut her loose, and get out into the water to safety. We had more'n two hundred people aboard, I swear, most of 'em dead now, as well as people on the boats nearby. When it went, it looked for sure the whole sea caught fire. I didn't know water could burn, but it did then. That's where I got most of my burns, in the water."

"Oil," Frisco corrected him.

"What say?" he asked.

"If there was fire on the water," she explained, "it must have been oil, not gunpowder."

"Oh," he said, "I wouldn't know about that, but it were an awful explosion. And most of the people thinking they were safe on the boats."

Suddenly she thought of the *Frisco Lady*, and

she was frightened. "What was this boat?" she asked. "What part of the bay?"

"It were tied up on one of the piers off Mission Street," he explained. "You know, the old part of the docks."

Panic seized her. "What was the boat's name?" she asked. "It wasn't the *Frisco Lady*, was it?"

"No'm," he said. "It were a boat called the *Maribou*."

Frisco knew the *Maribou*. It had been tied up two ships away from the *Frisco Lady*, and that was close enough for worry.

It was then that she realized she had not seen Beau return to the infirmary with the buckboard as he had promised.

29

Frisco's mind and body had reached that plateau beyond fatigue, where only total collapse could keep her from going on and on. At dawn, Dr. Bartleby had insisted that she and Julie stop to sleep, but Frisco could not sleep. Her feet ached, her muscles were sore, and her head had that dull insensate feeling of being disconnected from her shoulders by a few inches. But it was too painful to lie down, and closing her eyes brought on a sickening nausea.

But it was her mind's persistent questioning that made sleep absolutely impossible. What had happened to the *Frisco Lady*? Were Mike and Lyuba all right? Were the girls safe, or had they all died in the fiery explosion of the *Maribou*? And what about Beau? Why hadn't he returned? Was he, too, dead? She could not rest at all until she had answers. Until she knew what sort of future she would face when she awakened.

Shortly after dawn, word came to the hill that all of the fires were out. Almost immediately, some of the people had begun to pack their things, planning to return and rebuild. The people of San Francisco may have been crude, uneducated, and uncultured, but they also had to be among the most resilient people anywhere.

As the small trickle of wagons began to descend the hill, Frisco stood at the top and surveyed the incredible scene below her. The dawn had come up gray with soot, and the land that stretched out to the water was a black expanse of rubble. There was nothing left there that resembled a town. It would be much more difficult to clear away the ruins to rebuild than it would be to pick up stakes, move a few miles up or down the coast, and build an entirely new city. Yet the San Franciscans—almost none of whom had lived here for more than three or four years— were fiercely determined that their city would be on this small spit of land lurching out into the Pacific.

She thought she understood their defiance though. In fact, she was like them. She was one of them. As long as she was alive, she would fight and struggle for what she wanted.

She was as determined as the others to return to the city today, even if she had to go on foot— though, as tired as her feet were, she prayed she would not have to do that. There were now very few injured being brought into the infirmary, and more than enough wagons. Perhaps she could ask for the return of her carriage, at least for a few hours.

All of the conveyances were tied up back of the building, being looked after by a few of the men who had been driving them. Frisco walked up to the building and around, in hopes of finding someone in authority who could give her the permission she needed. She did not want to bother the harried Dr. Bartleby with her request.

As she rounded the corner of the building, she saw the buckboard and horse that had taken Beau down the hill. She could not have been mistaken. They were hers. But she had not seen Beau return.

She approached the man who was leaning against it, lazily chewing on a cud of tobacco. "Could you tell me where I can find the driver of this wagon?" she asked, her manner perhaps a little too anxious.

"Why, I am, ma'am," he replied. "Can I help you with something?"

She was somewhat taken aback. "I mean . . ." she stammered. "The man who . . . After leaving me here last night, my husband went down into town with this buckboard to bring more of the injured back. I'm looking for him."

"Oh," the man took off his hat and stood up straight. "You must mean Beau Tolliver. After

314

we got the wagon all loaded up down on Sansome Street, he handed her over to me, sayin' he had some business to attend to. I been drivin' it ever since."

"Then he didn't come back up the hill?" she asked, her voice revealing her dismay.

"No'm," he said. "I'm sorry. He got himself a horse and lit off downtown. That was the last I seen of him."

Of course, Frisco realized, he would have had his own interests to see to. While he had been helping her with the children, his entire business could have been lost. But surely, if he were alive, he would have returned by now. There was really no place else he could have gone that was safe. But her heart did not want to believe what her mind was telling her—that Beau was dead. Her heart was sure there had to be some other explanation.

She looked up at the tobacco-chewing man before her, trying to hold back the tears that were straining to reach her cheeks. "That carriage over there," she gestured to the tattered remains of her once elegant equipage, "was mine before I turned it over to Dr. Bartleby. I wonder if I might get permission to borrow it for a while?"

"Sure, ma'am," he smiled. "If it's really yours, I don't see why you can't have it back. We don't need it no more. It was hard gettin' injured folks in and out of it anyway."

Frisco made sure that Julie and Janet would be

able to look after Alex, and then she set out down the hill toward town, joining the somber procession of evacuees returning. Below them, the blackened rubble still smoldered in places, sending up thin plumes of defiant smoke that bent gently southward with the breeze. Far beyond, across a narrow tiara of sparkling water, she could see the floating city of the other refugees, a helter-skelter armada, composed of almost anything and everything that could conceivably be called a boat. From it too, a few people were returning in small corries and dinghies, cautiously approaching the scene of last night's terror.

In the aftermath of fire, the first sense to be touched is that of smell. The awful, acrid odor had never left San Francisco completely since the first fire, but it took another fire to realize how much the real stench had abated. As Frisco drew near the outskirts of the town, the smell was overpowering. Blue Ruin, the San Franciscans called it, but if anything, that name was an understatement, which gave no hint of the nausea it brought to the stomach or the tight aching to the head.

It was easy to become disoriented amid such devastation, and Frisco quickly lost her way in taking detours to avoid streets piled with litter and debris. There were no longer any familiar landmarks. There would be a chimney standing here, and one brick wall of a building there, but nothing was recognizable as a home or a hotel or a place of business. She continued to wander almost aimlessly, hoping eventually to come upon someone or something familiar.

When she did see a familiar face, it was not someone she would normally have been pleased to see, but under the circumstances she was excited. Albert Valery had been aboard the *Frisco Lady* when she had left, and he was still alive. The small forlorn man sitting desolately atop a set of fine brick steps that led up to nothing did not look much like the proud arrogant little Frenchman, but Frisco could never mistake those dark narrow eyes.

She stopped her carriage and called out to him, and he looked her way with an almost childlike expression of hopeful expectancy. "Mrs. Tolliver!" he exclaimed. "Then you've survived!"

Frisco did not answer the obvious. Instead, she asked anxiously, "You were on the boat, Valery. What happened to it?"

"I don't know," he shrugged. "I left shortly after you and Beau did. I tried to get to my house, but the fire was too fierce." He gestured despairingly about him, shaking his head. "It's all gone. Everything! The house, the girls, everything. The biggest of the fires started right in this area. The girls didn't have a chance at all."

"You didn't go back to the boat then?" Frisco asked.

He shook his head. "No. I managed to get aboard a small fishing boat that pulled out into the bay until the worst was over. Then I came back to try to see if any of the girls had managed to escape. All I could find that was left of the place were the front steps. Then I found a man who saw what happened here. He was from the hotel down the street. He said the girls were jumping out of windows and off the roof, their bodies burning beyond recognition. He said he didn't see anybody get out alive. They're dead, every one of them dead."

In this pathetic moment, Frisco felt all her hatred of this little man melting away. She had wished nothing good for him, but it was impossible for her to be so spiteful as to wish this horror on anyone. It was not him that she hated, but only his arrogance and cruelty. Now that was gone, and he was paying the price in his own private hell of guilt.

But she could say nothing to comfort him. Soon she knew she might be going through the same bitter torment as he, and she knew that nothing would be able to console her. They had both taken on the responsibility for other human lives, and they had both abrogated that responsibility, he through sadistic manipulation and she through carelessness.

"Tell me," she said, "have you seen Beau, or anyone at all from the boat, since last night?"

"No," he shook his head dejectedly. Then his dark little eyes looked up at her, and there was genuine feeling in them as he said, "I'm sorry."

She left him to his misery then, riding on, at

318

least with the comfort of knowing where she was. By guesswork, she should be able to reach the docks from here. If she turned left at any open street, she could eventually get down to the waterfront.

But the debris was much worse here. This was the heart of San Francisco, and there had been a number of three and four story buildings, the large, elaborate new hotels, the banking and business exchanges, many of them of brick. It was the bricks that made her progress down Market Street impossible. Without their supporting timbers, brick walls had caved in and collapsed onto the street.

Finally, she had to leave her carriage and pick her way to the waterfront on foot. It was difficult going. Frisco's boots were of a fine, lightweight leather, and therefore not very sturdy. She twisted her ankles several times as bits of brick or debris slipped and broke loose beneath her steps. At times the debris was so high, she had to bend down and brace herself with her hands to crawl over.

When she did reach the docks, she was completely dismayed. The waterfront was as unrecognizable as the rest of the city. Many of the docks, and the ships that had berthed at them, were gone without a trace. Others were charred beyond recognition. Here and there a boat listed in the water, as if threatening to go under at any moment. A few seemed to have survived with very little damage. The fire had been capricious and illogical in selecting its prey.

Frisco assumed that she was standing at the end of Market Street, but she could not be absolutely sure. If she were indeed where she thought, then the *Frisco Lady* would have been moored about a block down to her right. There were a few ships still in that area, but as she strained her eyes, she could not recognize the *Lady*'s masts among them.

She knew that she could not hope for anything as miraculous as that, but she prayed that she could find some indication that those who had been aboard her were safe. That was all that she asked. She could give up material possessions, but not the people she cared about.

With a resolute admonition to keep up hope, Frisco set off down what had once been East Street. She had not progressed very far, however, when she heard someone call out from behind her, "Graciela!" She had turned before she even realized it had been months since she had heard anyone call her that.

There was a small fishing boat that had just come in. It was being tied up to some pilings that had once supported a pier. There were a number of people on the boat, but one of them was a woman, and she was waving. It was Sarah Royce.

Frisco had not seen Mrs. Royce since attending her ball on California Admissions Day. They were hardly the best of friends then, but since

Frisco's return to work, they had been on different social planes. But crisis can make close friends even out of strangers, and Sarah Royce was delighted at seeing a familiar face.

As soon as she was out of the boat, she rushed up to Frisco and embraced her. "My dear, I'm so glad to see you're alive and safe," she said. "I fear we may never know how many of the people we loved and cared about were lost."

Those words did not cheer Frisco; they merely confirmed what she feared and dreaded. "I know," she replied coolly. "I trust all of your family is safe."

"Yes," she confirmed, "thank the Lord. But I don't think any of us could have gotten out alive if it hadn't been for your husband. My dear, you must be terribly proud of him."

For a moment, it didn't register. But then, hope leaped within her breast. "Beau?" she asked. "Then you've seen him?"

Sarah blushed. "How foolish of me!" she exclaimed. "You probably didn't even know where he was. But he was responsible for saving hundreds of lives down here on the docks. He took charge of the loading of the boats and evacuating them into the bay. There was such chaos before he came along. People were actually being trampled to death. But Beau got everyone calmed down and organized. As far as I'm concerned, he was truly the hero of the evening."

"But did Beau get away?" Frisco demanded

shrilly. "Was he able to get into one of the boats himself?"

Sarah was crestfallen. She looked down in embarrassment. "I'm sorry for chattering like this," she said. "Of course you must be worried sick. I'm afraid I don't really know for certain whether he managed to get away or not. But I'm sure he must have. After all he had done to help others, I'm sure the Lord wouldn't have taken him."

Frisco's faith was not so sure as Sarah's. Tears fought in her eyes to find release. "What time was it when you last saw him?" she asked, her voice breaking.

"Why, I guess it was about two-thirty in the morning," Sarah replied. "It was a short time before that terrible explosion from one of the old abandoned boats. That was a terrible tragedy. So many people burning to death in the water. In the water, can you believe it?" Suddenly she looked up into Frisco's pale frightened face. "My dear, you don't think he could possibly . . . ?"

Knowing Beau as she did, Frisco thought it was more than possible that Beau had dived into the burning oil-slicked waters to try to save lives; it was probable.

The Frisco Lady was gone, without a trace.

30

The *Frisco Lady* was gone, without a trace. After leaving Sarah Royce, Frisco had picked her way through the rubble of East Street, her heart heavy with dread, to find the dock where the boat had been tied up. But she had known that it would not be there. The scene she found at the site was exactly the vision that had come to her— flashing startlingly into her mind—while she had stood listening to Mrs. Royce's prattle.

A piece of the pier was still standing, much of it charred and hanging precariously over the water, as if waiting for time to send it crumbling down. Far out where the end of the pier had been, a few pilings—their tips charred like used matchsticks—stood out of the water to mark and outline the dock. To Frisco's left was the *Falcon,* one of the abandoned ships that had been used for storage. Beyond it had rested the *Maribou*, which had exploded, sending flames across the water. It was clear that the *Falcon* had burned from the hull upward, because its masts—only slightly charred—protruded at a slight angle from the water. To Frisco's right, there remained a small piece of the bow of the *El Dorado*, with only its name left to identify it.

In between, where the *Frisco Lady* had once lain sleek and proud in the water, neatly restored and painted, there was nothing but charred boards and pilings. As Frisco stared at the dark water lapping angrily against the pilings, her eyes were attracted to a piece of rope tied neatly and firmly to one of the pilings. Yes, she realized, that would have been where the rope from the bow was tied.

She stared morosely at that knotted rope a long time before she realized it was not burned. In fact, it did not even seem to be singed. Then the smoke overhead drifted slightly, and a bit of sunlight filtered through, and she saw something glitter against the knot—something metallic.

Curious about what it might be, she carefully began to edge her way out across the blackened timbers. She wasn't sure she could reach the rope itself, but she thought she might get near enough to see what it was flashing in the sunlight. Each step she took placed more of a strain on the fragile remains of the pier, causing it to creak painfully and to sway slightly over the water.

When she drew near enough, she realized it was a nail, protruding from the rope, and . . . it was made of gold.

Impetuously, she moved closer, stepping out onto the very precipice of the burnt structure. It swayed violently beneath her feet, and so she quickly stepped over onto the edge that was still secured to the pilings and sat down next to the rope, allowing her feet to hang down over the water.

It took little effort to pull the nail from the rope; it had not been hammered in with any great force. Frisco held the golden object in the palm of her hand and stared at it. Of course she recognized it. It seemed an eternity since she had last seen it, though she knew in fact it had been only two nights ago. It was the gold nail the strange young miner had wanted to place as a bet—the nail that had so upset her.

Now, holding it in her hand, Frisco knew the nail was harmless. It did not smolder and burn; if anything, it felt cool to her raw skin. Clearly it had not started the fire, because the wood for a few feet around it had not been charred at all.

What then was its significance? Why was it there? The strange, half-mad miner had called it his good-luck piece. Was it possibly some good talisman that would somehow protect from evil?

It was pure gold, and Frisco knew that gold was said to have magical properties.

As she sat there, rubbing the smooth shiny metal object between her fingers, Frisco found herself constructing an elaborate rationalization for hope. Perhaps the young miner had not been so mad after all. Perhaps he had possessed the Gift, and he knew somehow that the *Frisco Lady* was in danger. There had been, now that she thought about it, a slight look of the Rom about him. Perhaps he had known about the Curse of the Nail and this golden nail was a talisman against its destruction. That was the only reason—as crazy as it sounded—Frisco could find for the young miner's determination for her to have it.

Finally her thoughts brought her around to the reason for her rationalization. If all of this were true, then the *Frisco Lady* had to be safe. It must somehow have survived the fire. Only then did it register with her that the rope tied to the piling was not even singed by fire.

Quickly, she tucked the nail securely into the bosom of her dress and then reached out to grab the heavy rope that trailed down into the water below her feet. Tugging, hand over hand, she gradually pulled it all out of the water. The end of the rope was not charred at all. It had been cut neatly with a knife.

Somehow the *Frisco Lady* had been taken out into the bay with all her passengers aboard. She had no idea how it had been accomplished, with no captain and no crew, but she felt certain that it was true. Perhaps it had been towed out by some other craft. Perhaps it had simply been cut loose and allowed to drift with the tide.

Frisco rose to her feet so swiftly and so excitedly that she almost fell headlong into the water. However, she managed to catch herself on the piling and then to step carefully, toe on heel, along the edge until she got back to a sure footing. Then she almost danced with joy as she hopped about on tiptoes, trying to scan the horizon for the familiar masts. But it was virtually impossible to pick out any one craft from the enormous flotilla that made up the seaborne half of San Francisco. The bay was literally filled with boats.

She decided that the only way she would be able to find the *Frisco Lady* was to go out there and search for her, and the only way she could do that was to find a boat that would take her. She spent over an hour wandering up and down the desolate waterfront without success. Men were coming into shore with small craft, but no one wanted to take a passenger back out.

There was finally one man who, seeing Frisco's desperate and plaintive look, had pity on her. "I'm sorry, ma'am, but I got work to do afore it gets too late," he told her. "But you can take my rowboat. I won't be needin' it anymore today."

Frisco looked distastefully at the small dinghy.

She did not relish the thought of rowing herself out such a great distance. Her body was already aching from the strain of so many hours without sleep. But she realized that she had no choice. "Thank you," she told the man. "I'll see that it's returned to where you left it."

"No matter," the man said. "It weren't mine anyhow."

It seemed an eternity of rowing before she approached the closest of the ships. Her back and arms ached from the rhythmical lifting and pulling of the heavy oars. With each release of the tension, she feared her chest would cave in completely and be unable to manage the next pull, but each time she found the strength and determination for another.

She did not realize how difficult her search would be until she reached the enormous fleet. From land, the ships had all seemed so close together, as if she could walk from one to the other. In truth, they were spread out for miles, and it was difficult even to shout from one to the other and be heard. She rowed herself from craft to craft, at each one calling out to those on board, "Do you know where I can find the *Frisco Lady*?"

Always the answer was no.

It was the middle of the afternoon before she put down her oars in despair and began to sob. She had worked all night in the infirmary without sleep; she had gone all day without eating. She felt that she could go no farther; it would be a blessed relief just to lie down in the dinghy and drift, to let the sea take her wherever it wanted. She wept and drifted until she could weep no more, and then she dozed off into sleep.

When she awakened, she was being lifted out of the dinghy by two young men. She did not understand what they were doing, and she protested, crying, "Stop it! Leave me alone!"

"Take it easy, lady," one of them said. "We're not going to harm you. We're just taking you to the infirmary where you can be looked after."

"I don't need an infirmary," she said sharply. "I'm all right."

It was growing dark out, and it took a few moments to register on Frisco that she had been sleeping for hours. She could hardly see the faces of the young men, and she had no idea what kind of a harness they were putting on her until they attached the rope in back and shouted up to someone on the large craft that was alongside, "Tow her aboard!"

As she began to lift into mid-air, one of the men patted her hand and said, "You'll be much safer aboard the *Frisco Lady*."

The *Frisco Lady*? It didn't make sense. Nothing made sense. The two men had been talking about taking her to the infirmary, and now they said she was going aboard the *Frisco Lady*. It was all as confusing as a dream. Frisco was sure she was really still asleep.

329

It still did not make sense to her when she was aboard ship being greeted by Captain Wellington, exclaiming, "Why, I'll be a monkey's Dutch uncle! It's the lady herself! How did you get here?"

"I rowed," she replied nonsensically. "But where am I?"

"On your own boat!" he laughed. "The *Frisco Lady!*"

"But those men," she protested. "They said they were taking me to the infirmary."

"The *Frisco Lady* is the infirmary," he explained. "Temporarily, of course. Just until this trouble is over. Then you can set up business again."

"I'm afraid I don't understand," Frisco said. "I don't even see how it got all the way out here, a ship that hasn't sailed for years."

"That was the easy part," the captain grinned. "You put it back in working order yourself. All I had to do was take command again. Of course some of those fine ladies of your'n still don't know the difference between fore an' aft, but they make pretty good sailors in a pinch.

"The infirmary was that Beau Tolliver's idea. After the *Maribou* blew up, there had to be someplace to take care of the injured, and it was impossible to get them to the one on land. 'Course we don't have a doctor, but a couple of the ladies know something about nursing."

"Beau?" she stared at him incredulously. "You've seen Beau?"

330

"Sure I have," Wellington replied. "I couldn't have done any of this without him. And you can see him, too, if you want to. As I recall, you and him got a poker game to finish."

"Where is he?" Frisco asked stupidly.

Captain Wellington shrugged. "Below deck someplace."

"You mean he's on board?"

"Of course he is," Wellington acknowledged. "Didn't I explain that part? You see, when he was pullin' all those folks out of the drink . . ."

Frisco did not wait to hear the end of the old sea captain's story. She turned and rushed across the deck to the door that led down to the grand saloon. All that had been happening for the past few minutes had such a sense of unreality to it, she had to see for herself to believe what he had said was true. If it were true, there would be bright lights and noise down below; there would be no shadows; she would be able to see faces clearly and distinctly.

But the lights below were dim. She stopped halfway down the stairs and gazed at the grand saloon without recognizing anyone or anything. All of the gaming tables had been moved about and set up to form beds, and lying on them were unrecognizable bodies, heavily bandaged. Somber women in green smocks moved among them silently, tending to their needs. The enormous brass chandeliers were barely lit, to keep from hurting the patients' eyes, and there were small oil-lamps in use beside the beds.

She eased her way cautiously into the room. She was not dreaming; she was sure of that. The moaning sounds were real, and so were the odors of camphor and iodine.

As she stood there staring into the gloom, one of the green-smocked women approached her. It was Laura. "Why, Frisco!" she smiled, and rushed to embrace her. "How did you get here? I thought you were up on Nob Hill."

"I took a rowboat," she said faintly, her hands touching Laura in embrace to prove she was real. "I had to see if everyone was safe."

"We're all fine," Laura said. "Not a scratch on any of us. Except maybe Mike and a couple of the boys, but they aren't badly hurt."

"Is Beau all right?" she asked.

"He's got a few burns," Laura told her, "when he went into the water. But nothing serious." She glanced down at the floor apologetically. "Of course, you may not be very happy about the fact that he's taken over the boat and is running everything, but he insists it's only until you return."

"Where is he?" Frisco asked.

Laura turned around to search the room. "I don't see him right now," she said. "He may be up onstage behind the curtain. That's where we've been keeping the really badly injured."

"Thanks," Frisco said, squeezing Laura's hand and then hurrying off toward the stage, climbing up the steps at the side, then going to center-stage and slowly parting the curtains.

Beau was standing beside one of the makeshift beds, bending over a patient, speaking to the heavily bandaged man with a gentleness she had never known he possessed. Then she noticed that Beau's chest and shoulder were bandaged as well, though he gave no evidence of pain.

When he looked up from the patient and his soft green eyes caught hers, a chill rushed through her. Overcome by a feeling of love for him, she wanted to rush to him, to take him in her arms, to kiss him and hold him and never let him go. But she could not move. She could only stand there stupidly staring at him as if not quite willing to believe he was really there.

"Well, hello, my dear," he said with a mischievous smile. "I didn't expect you quite so soon. But then you're always surprising me in one way or the other, aren't you?"

After her torment, his teasing manner annoyed her. She did not want to speak to him in anger, but she did. "You promised you would be coming back to the hill," she accused. "And you didn't."

"I would have returned eventually," he said. "Were you afraid I would run out on our game?"

The completion of their poker game had been the least of her concerns. That he should think she gave it such high importance irritated her still further. "Yes," she said contrarily. "Until it's over, I don't like having you out of my sight for very long."

"Well, you can rest easy," he told her with a smirk. "You've won the game."

"What do you mean?" she asked skeptically.

"You've beaten me," he replied. "I looked at the cards when I got back to the boat. You had a pair of aces. I had only a pair of eights. You've got your freedom now."

He reached into the pocket of his trousers and pulled out a piece of paper neatly folded in thirds.

"Here's your divorce agreement." He smiled wryly, handing it to her. "I'm afraid it's forged. But that shouldn't matter a great deal, since the marriage license was also forged."

"I don't understand," she gasped, looking down at the document in her hands. "When did you get it? Surely there hasn't been time. . . ?"

"I had it drawn up some time ago," he said. "As soon as I learned how you felt about Tom Blanchard. I've never wanted to hold you against your will. And I have to admit I don't like Blanchard. I despised him for what he did to me, and the way he did it. But I don't begrudge any man his life. Right now he's fighting for his life, and he needs every bit of help he can get. If freeing you will . . ."

"What do you mean he's fighting for his life?"

Frisco cut in sharply. "Has something happened to Tom?"

Beau's eyes were averted apologetically. "He was pretty badly injured when the *Maribou* blew up," he explained. "He was on the docks, on his way to the *Frisco Lady*. Apparently he was trying to find you to see if you were safe."

"Where is he?" she demanded.

"He's here," Beau said, turning to point across the stage. "Over there in the corner. But you must be careful not to excite him."

Frisco rushed past Beau to the darkened corner where Tom lay, being looked after by Lillian. He appeared to be either unconscious or sleeping peacefully, but he was heavily bandaged over all of the upper part of his body, including his face. She bent over his bed to look at him, but there was nothing there she could recognize as Tom.

He had meant so very much to her at one time, and she was still fond of him. She prayed fervently that he would survive; she knew that he was in the best hands he could possibly be in. Lillian loved him as deeply as any woman could love a man; and, if he survived, he would surely come to realize that in time, and he would love her in return.

Frisco turned to Lillian and gave her a gentle kiss on the forehead, then gripped her hand and squeezed it. "How bad is he?" she asked.

There were tears in Lillian's eyes. "If it were only the burns," she said, "I'm sure he would re-

335

cover. But he's suffering more from the shock of it all than he is from the burns. After all he's been through, I'm not sure he still has the will to live."

Frisco smiled affectionately. "With you sitting there beside him, holding his hand, smiling at him, and encouraging him, he'll find that will again. Sometimes people lose sight of what's really important to them, but they can find it again. I know."

She turned then, determined, come what may, to confront Beau Tolliver and to say everything she felt in her heart, but Beau wasn't there. She realized he had left the stage area to avoid watching her with Tom. He was still jealous of her, and to her that meant one thing: he loved her, whether he knew it or not.

She wended her way among the sickbeds, and stepped out between the curtains, her eyes scanning the grand saloon for him. He was nowhere in sight. Apprehensively, she hurried down the steps at the side and found Laura. "Where's Beau?" she asked. "Have you seen him?"

"Yes," she said curiously. "He's gone."

"Gone?" Frisco snapped shrilly. "Gone where?"

"I don't know," Laura replied. "He told me and Mike that you were in charge now, and then he left."

Frisco ran up the stairs and out onto the deck as fast as her feet could carry her.

"Where's Beau?" she demanded of Captain Wellington. "Is he still here?"

"No, ma'am," the old sea captain replied laconically. "He took the little dinghy you came in and headed to shore five or ten minutes ago."

"Is there another boat I could take to try to catch him?" she asked frantically

"No, ma'am," the captain told her with a shake of his head. "Not at the moment."

Frisco ran to the railing and peered off into the night. With the smoke still clinging to the air, it was a blacker night than she had ever seen. She could not see anything beyond a few feet in front of her face. Try as she might, she could catch no glimpse of Beau Tolliver rowing toward shore.

The only way she could possibly hope to reach him was by shouting, so that is what she did. "Beau!" she screamed frantically. "Come back, Beau! I have to talk to you!"

She paused and waited for an answer. There was none. She screamed again. "Beau, please come back! Please! I want you to know I love you! Can you hear me, Beau? I love you!"

She waited for a reply.

There was only the sound of the waves lapping against the boat.

PART SIX

31

The ashes were still warm when the phoenix began to rise again. For only a few brief hours after the fire, the blackened spit of land that had been San Francisco was as silent and as still as death itself, hardly long enough for the shock to register. Then the heavy sooty air was broken by the squeaking wheels of wagons and barrows, by the thumping of picks and shovels and sledge-hammers, and by the sharp, gruff voices of men refusing to accept defeat. Working alongside them was every available woman, each equally as the men.

By the following morning, the flatboats and the wagons had arrived with loads of lumber from the mills, and the rebuilding itself was begun, with the brisk hopeful sounds of sawing and hammering joining the cacophony. It was a ritual these people had performed time and again, growing more automatic with each fire, and they did not stop to complain or to consider its meaning.

Within only a few days, a city began to take shape, the old landmarks returning, familiar yet slightly different, gradually persuading memory that nothing had changed at all. Only the smell of Blue Ruin remained, clinging to the earth and air as a reminder of the horror and devastation that had been. And here and there a builder would use a slightly charred piece of lumber among the new, counting the pennies against survival.

The boat city returned gradually from the bay. The smaller craft—those that could be pulled up on the beach—came first. The larger ones had to wait for piers to be thrown up against the remaining pilings.

The *Frisco Lady* was one of the first of the large boats to be brought into dock, the other shipowners acknowledging the rights of the injured to proper medical care. Who knew: perhaps next time they might be among those in need? That was the firm basis of all charity in the rugged, uncertain frontier—an awareness that even the most secure were truly insecure. They did unto the unfortunate as they would have done unto them in the event of their misfortune.

Frisco worked tirelessly to look after her patients as long as they were aboard her ship, and when they were loaded carefully onto the wagons that would take them up Nob Hill to the new infirmary—the infirmary she had now officially given to the city of San Francisco—she let them go with regrets. After Beau's departure, they had become the center of her life. She had tended them with that total selflessness that is itself a form of selfishness. She had given every waking moment to their care to avoid thinking about her own cares. When the last of them were gone, she was desolated. She could no longer escape herself.

She knew that she should have been happy. She had what she had sought for so long— complete freedom. But she was more miserable than ever. Absolute freedom was not what she had thought at all. She had expected it to fill her very soul with wondrous ecstasy, to elate her with limitless possibilities for her life. But it filled her with nothing. If anything, it took from her more than it gave.

Freedom exacted its price silently and insidiously, virtually unseen and unrecognized. It was true that Frisco now owned herself completely; she owed her soul to no one. But almost imperceptibly, she began to see that she was owned by everyone, that her soul could never really be entirely hers, because it was inextricably linked to the souls of everyone she cared about. With freedom came an almost terrifying responsibility, to herself as well as to others.

That responsibility drained her, depleted her of

her strength, gnawed relentlessly at her will, and gave nothing in return but loneliness. She went through her days and nights guided only by the expectations of others. Until now, freedom had been her lodestar; once it had been gained, her life was aimless, purposeless. She was a ship in port, with no further plans, just rocking slightly with the waves that lapped against her.

She was not, however, like the abandoned ships. If it had not been for the needs of others, she might have been. But to her surprise, the patrons of the *Frisco Lady* returned as soon as the last of the infirmary patients were gone, ready to gamble and drink and relax.

As eager as they were to rebuild, the San Franciscans still had to put away their hammers after nightfall. They worked hard all day, but they played equally as hard for much of the night. And they were—as they had always been— gamblers. A loss, even one as big as the fire, merely increased their determination to try their luck, to test it, to challenge it to change.

Because Frisco did not have to rebuild, hers was the first of the gambling establishments to reopen its doors, and the people flocked in, coming in greater numbers than ever before, filling the grand saloon until it seemed it would burst its walls. They brought excitement with them, and they brought profits.

The girls were happy with the success, and with the attentions they received. It did not matter to them that they had to make small sacrifices to accommodate the changes brought about by the disaster. They felt needed.

And that was something that Frisco did not feel. The *Frisco Lady* was needed—by the patrons, by the girls, by Mike and his boys—but Frisco began to feel that she herself was almost insignificant in the scheme of things. Anyone could serve the function she served; Frisco the legend could be anyone at all.

Of course Alex needed her. He was perhaps the only one who did, but she realized that she was giving him far less of herself than she was capable of, far less than she wanted to give. So many of his needs were being filled by Lyuba and Julie and Janet, all of them simply trying to make up for the time that Frisco had to spend in keeping the business going.

Actually, Frisco was spending more time with her son than she had before. With the house gone, she had moved Alex and the household staff aboard the boat, and they were always near each other even if they were not together. But proximity only heightened Frisco's feeling that she was neglecting the child. At night, he shared a small room with Lyuba. During pleasant days, he wandered aimlessly about the deck or sat and watched the activities on the docks. On days when the weather was bad, he explored the catacombs of the ship, occasionally helping in the cleaning. He spent his evenings in the grand saloon, either performing on the violin or wandering about watching the games at the tables. It was not the sort of life Frisco thought appropriate for a small boy.

Yet she could not find within herself the will or the initiative to rebuild their home. She seemed to be waiting passively for something to happen to change the pattern of days, something from outside herself. Something or someone, she wasn't really conscious of what. She was waiting for Beau. And he never came.

She had been given so many chances to speak to Beau, to tell him what was in her heart, and she had missed every one of them. Now she was frightened that she had been given her last chance, that there would be no more.

Again Beau had disappeared without a trace. This time she had no hope that he would ever return; he no longer had a reason to be a part of her life. The false marriage that had kept her bound to him had also linked him to her. As unpleasant as that link may have been, it had been something to link them, and it had kept him from going his own way entirely independent of her.

Now, Frisco learned, Beau had sold his business, and he had left San Francisco. No one she talked to knew where he had gone. He had apparently cut all ties and disappeared with whatever money he had been able to scrape together.

Mike and Lyuba were the only ones who sensed that there was something terribly wrong in all of this. The two of them were so close, they even jokingly talked of marriage, though they always broke it off with, "Whoever heard of a gypsy girl and an Irishman curbing their free spirits for a calm marriage?"

Frisco was certain that they had pooled their separate bits of knowledge and had managed to piece together a fair semblance of the true story of what had happened between her and Beau. The only point where they had to rely heavily on conjecture was with the reason for the poker game and the meaning of its conclusion.

Frisco did not learn why it was they were confused until one unusually warm night in July. It was long after closing, when Alex and Lyuba and all of the girls were in their rooms fast asleep. Frisco had turned a corner of her office into her sleeping quarters by setting up a small cot. This night, she was restless, unable to shut out the concerns of the day by closing her eyes. To escape the heat of her quarters, she finally decided to go up and take a walk on deck.

She wrapped herself in her dressing gown and slipped quietly up the stairs.

Mike was on guard duty, and he looked at her curiously as she stepped out on deck. "Feelin' a bit restless?" he inquired.

"Yes," Frisco nodded. "It's rather warm below. I thought it might be cooler up here."

"It wouldn't be bad," Mike commented, "if we could get a breeze."

Mike obviously sensed that Frisco wanted to be alone with her thoughts, and—at first—he left his conversation with the bare minimum of politeness, allowing her to wander off to the stern by herself.

It *was* a bit cooler on the deck; the moisture in the air was beginning to form into a low fog hanging over the water, occasionally drifting up to shroud Frisco from her surroundings, making her feel even more isolated from life than she was. She forgot that Mike was nearby keeping watch, his eyes and ears alert.

Her thoughts drifted back to the night Beau had left her. She had stood on the bow of the *Frisco Lady*, looking out into the fathomless night much as she did now, calling out to Beau, pleading with him to return. Weeks had passed since then, yet she had remained unchanged, unaffected by the passage of time. She was like a ghost, haunting a single moment that could not be resolved. She yearned to believe that this was still that moment, that she was calling out to the man she loved, and that in the next moment he would be back and holding her in his arms.

She thought she repeated the words only in her mind. She did not know that she voiced them aloud, to the fog. "Beau! Come back, Beau! Please! I love you!"

She realized it only when Mike stepped up beside her and spoke. "Ma'am, I know it's none of

348

my business," he said kindly, "but it's no good goin' on and on over him like this. He can't hear you."

She smiled at him, rather embarrassed. "No," she said, "you're right. I've made such a mess of things, Mike. I thought I knew what I was doing. I thought I was so smart that I could order my life just the way I wanted. I thought I could control myself and everyone around me. But I've been such a fool. I've come to realize life doesn't work that way. A woman can be given so many chances, and God help her if she lets them all pass by."

Mike shuffled beside her hesitantly, uncomfortably silent, not knowing what to say to her. After a moment, he leaned against the rail decisively, and said, "Beggin' your pardon, ma'am, but there's something I've been wonderin' about for some time."

Frisco looked at him curiously. "Yes, Mike," she said. "What is it?"

He looked out at the fog. "That poker game you and Mr. Beau played," he said. "What was it all about?"

She smiled affectionately. "It was about freedom," she said.

Mike frowned. "That's strange," he said. "It never struck me that Mr. Beau wanted his freedom from you. Entirely the opposite, I would have thought."

"Not his freedom," Frisco explained. "My freedom. If I won the game, I would have my freedom from him. If he won, I would come back to him and turn everything I owned over to him."

"That don't make no sense," Mike said, shaking his head. "If it did, he wouldn't be gone."

"Why not, Mike?" she asked curiously. "After all, I won the game." Then added, "Like a fool."

"No, you didn't," he said firmly. "You only had two aces."

"Yes," she nodded, "and Beau had two eights. He told me so."

Mike shook his head vigorously. "I saw the cards," he explained. "He had a boat."

"What?" she gasped.

"He had a boat," he confirmed, nodding his head, as if to clear up any doubt. "Three eights and two aces."

"Then why . . . ?" Frisco's mind began to race, looking for reasons.

"That's what I been wonderin'," Mike said casually.

Suddenly Frisco understood Beau. He had admitted he had drawn up the false divorce papers long before she ever challenged him to the poker game. He had done that for the same reason he had done this—because he loved her, and he wanted her to be happy, even if it meant being happy with some other man. It had been the same reason he had offered her that "bargain" at the very beginning of their false marriage.

He loved her, but he did not believe that she truly loved him, because she had never really proven it to him.

Decisively, she turned to Mike. "There's something I want you to do for me," she said firmly. "It's the most important thing I've ever asked. I want you to find out where Beau Tolliver is. I don't care how long it takes or how much money it costs. There must be someone, somewhere, who knows."

32

"You must forsake everything you have to gain all that you want."

The words now haunted Frisco day and night. She knew their meaning now quite clearly. She knew what she had to do. Lyuba was right; she did not need the Tarot cards to tell her what was in her heart. There was very little in life that she really wanted for herself. She wanted only the man she loved, her child, and sufficient food and shelter to get by.

If she wanted Beau, she would have to forsake the boat, and all it entailed. She would have to give up the name "Frisco" and return to being just plain Graciela McGee—or, with luck, Graciela Tolliver. That would be the easy part, though. She knew now that, given the chance, any woman could be Frisco, because Frisco was not real. Frisco was a legend, a thing of air, of dreams and imagination, of playacting. She could live on, no matter who played the part.

Lillian could be Frisco without any effort at all. There had been times when she had been running the boat without any help from Graciela at all; and it had, in truth, been her dream they had been fulfilling from the very moment they had begun to plan the reopening.

All Graciela would have to do would be to sign the legal documents that would turn the boat and all the girls over to someone else. It was as simple as that.

There was only one problem at the moment, but it was a minor one. Since the fire, Lillian had had her hands full with Tom Blanchard. His recovery had been slow and difficult. His burns had healed easily enough, but his spirit had progressed by fits and starts. He would do very well as long as he had Lillian by his side, but whenever she would leave him, he would relapse into bitterness and despair. The fire had destroyed the little that was left of his business, and it was a struggle for him to try to begin all over again.

Frisco hoped she had the solution to the problem. She decided to announce her decision to Tom and Lillian at the same time, and she called them into her office together. They sensed from her manner that this was to be an important

353

meeting, and they sat down across the desk from her, waiting quietly for her to tell them why they were there.

She began hesitantly. "I think you both know that I have been unhappy for quite some time," she told them. "I have been torn between my own personal life and my responsibilities here on the boat. I have finally decided that I can no longer continue like this. I have decided that I must leave Frisco's."

A look of fear and dismay crossed Lillian's face, but on Tom's there was merely puzzlement.

"Don't worry," she said to Lillian. "You won't be out of a job. I do not intend to see Frisco's close. In fact, what I wish to propose is that I turn the place over to the two of you. You, Lillian, are quite capable of serving all the functions of Frisco. You, Tom, know all of the financial arrangements necessary to business success. And besides, considering all you spent on furnishing and decorating this place, I've thought of you all along as a sort of silent partner."

"But neither of us can afford to buy Frisco's," Tom interjected.

"I didn't say that I was selling it to you," Graciela amended. "I wish to sign over, free and clear, a controlling interest in the place. The remainder I intend to hold in trust for the other girls." She paused, looked from one incredulous face to the other, then asked, "Are you interested?"

354

Tom looked at her suspiciously. "What if we should say no?"

"Then I would have to find someone else to take my offer," Graciela replied. "I am determined to leave."

"What if Lillian should accept and I refuse?" Tom pursued.

Graciela knew what he was thinking—that she was doing this more out of pity for him than out of careful business judgment—and she had to be careful not to confirm it. "I would accept that," she said, "but with reluctance. I might have to find someone else to help her. She can manage the girls and run the gaming tables well enough, but I don't think she is capable of handling the finances and the larger business decisions." She paused, relaxed, and smiled. "And there's another reason I picked you specifically. Her partner would have to be a man, and I would like to see her avoid the problems I've faced."

Tom fidgeted in his chair. His dark eyes looked first at Graciela, then at Lillian, who was gazing at him with unwavering love. "What do you think?" he asked her indecisively.

"Of course! I'm willing, if you are," Lillian replied.

Tom reached out between the chairs and took her hand. Then he turned to Frisco and announced, "It's a deal."

Once the decision had been made, Graciela felt almost happy. It was as if a great burden had been lifted from her. However, she knew that the most difficult part of her plan still lay ahead—finding Beau and convincing him to believe her.

Mike and his boys had been investigating Beau's whereabouts ever since Graciela had asked him to that foggy night, but they had had no luck at all. Wherever Beau had gone, he had left no trail behind him.

Their first clue came completely by accident, and it came at their very doorstep—from the garrulous Captain Wellington. They were all sitting up on deck one warm night after closing—Mike and Lyuba, Lillian and Tom, Graciela and Captain Wellington. The old sailor was whittling and rambling on as he usually did, when Beau's name came up in the conversation.

"If you want to find Tolliver," Wellington said with authority, "look in the gold fields."

"What do you mean?" Graciela asked. "Why should you think he would be there?"

"Because he once talked to me about it," Wellington said. "A few days afore the fire. He knew I'd been there. Wanted to know how much money a man needed to get a start. What sort of supplies a man would need. Where the best places were to buy 'em. All that sort of thing. Sounded to me like a man who had caught the fever." He paused. "Or else, like a man who just wanted to get off to hisself for a while. Sometimes I think they's one and the same thing."

The next morning, Mike put his men onto this

possibility, and they quickly began to find Beau's trail. They located the man who had sold Beau supplies; they then found other miners who had seen and talked to Beau; and finally they were able to learn where Beau had staked his claim.

It wasn't far from San Francisco, compared to other gold fields. It was out in the direction of Stockton, miles from any town or village, as lonely a place as there was in California.

Graciela was not unaware of the kind of life men led in the gold fields. It was lonely, it was hard, and very often it was filled with failure and despair. She had been there herself, before she had ever come to San Francisco. In fact, that had been where she and her dear friend Wes Falligant had made the money that had built the first Frisco's.

She knew that a woman would have to have a very deep love for a man to follow him to the gold fields, and an even deeper love to stay there with him.

A woman truly would have to forsake everything.

33

Graciela left Frisco's quietly and without fanfare. Lillian wanted to give her a big party, a celebration that would show the gratitude and affection everyone felt for Frisco, but Graciela refused. "You are Frisco now," she said. "You must remember that. The less attention paid to my going, the better. It is only Graciela McGee who is leaving. Frisco remains."

Lillian was a bit disappointed at that response. She had looked forward to festivities, and had not understood what Graciela was talking about. "We're all going to miss you," she said. "You have meant so very much to all of us."

"That's what I'm talking about," Graciela replied. "Frisco has meant much. Graciela McGee has not. You will understand what I mean eventually."

She said her good-byes to each person separately and individually, promising to write and to visit when she returned to the city. She did not say good-bye to Mike and Lyuba, however, for they had decided to go with her. "You and the boy can't go all that far alone," Mike had insisted. "You've got to have a man along for protection."

When Graciela had protested that it was such a long and arduous trip for Lyuba to make, Lyuba had said simply, "Where you and my little Alex go, I go."

Graciela knew that there were other reasons. There was the chance that Beau would not be happy to see her, that he would turn her away, that he would laugh at her for chasing after him. Then she would need friends such as they. She could make the trip out to the gold fields alone, with hope blossoming in her heart. But she could not make the return trip by herself, with failure dogging every mile.

Graciela was aware of that possibility. For that reason she told Alex only that they were going to "visit" Beau, not that they were moving there permanently. She might be able to bear another disappointment, but she sensed that he could not.

It was a beautiful August day when they set out on their journey—the sky a pure deep azure, with a slight cold breeze, and great fluffy cumulus clouds drifting lazily. Leaving the acrid-smelling city behind, with its bright new buildings

359

set neatly and orderly among the scattered patches of blackened earth, Graciela felt good. The weather was an auspicious sign for a new beginning. With the past, she felt she was leaving behind her mistakes. Even though it was likely that she would make new mistakes, there was always the chance that she would not.

They were ferried across the bay, with their newly purchased covered wagon and team of horses; and it was only after they had disembarked on the other side that Graciela felt they were truly leaving. Then she felt the most unexpected surge of emotions. Suddenly, she felt *free*! That freedom she had striven for so desperately and so long came to her with no effort at all, and she understood.

Perhaps it was the gypsy blood in her. Certainly it felt good to be sitting up on a wagon again, behind a good pair of horses, with a sense of moving on to the next adventure life had in store for her. But she thought it was more than that. She no longer had obligations that tied her down; she belonged to no place and to no thing or person. She owned her soul free and clear, without any debts, and she would never give it away. She had deep love, and that she could— and would—give, but it could never be taken from her or bought or bargained for or demanded. It would be given because she was free to give.

At night, they camped beneath the stars.

Lyuba made a fire and cooked their meal in a big pot, humming to herself while she worked. Graciela stared at her and realized it had been years since she had seen Lyuba so happy. Lyuba felt at home here, just as she did. After laying out their bedrolls, and before going to sleep, Lyuba told Alex stories from the Rom. Alex listened wide-eyed with wonder and delight. When Alex and Graciela went to sleep, Lyuba and Mike were still sitting up beside the fire, their voices droning rhythmically like a mother's heartbeat.

Awakening with the sun, Graciela realized she had spent her first truly restful night of sleep in months. She was happy. She spent most of the day riding in silence, drinking in the beauty and grandeur of the stark mountainous scenery.

It was almost dusk when Mike announced, "If I've got my directions right, we should be gettin' to Mr. Beau's encampment pretty soon."

He was right. As they came up over the next hill, they found themselves looking down on a small crude cabin beside a stream. There was nothing spectacular about the scene. It was just a cabin and a stream and a few scrubby trees, with a rocky mountainside behind. But to Graciela, it was the most beautiful sight she had ever seen, because standing not far off, working furiously at repairing a sluice, was Beau Tolliver. His back was turned to them, and she did not see his face, but she knew it was Beau from the broad shoulders and the red hair.

361

She asked Mike to stop the wagon. "Wait here," she advised. "Let me go down ahead of you."

Mike nodded in understanding.

The fading sun was at her back as she walked down the hill, trying vainly to keep her feet from hurrying. Beau had no way of knowing that she was coming to him, and she had no idea how she would be received. Would he be glad to see her, or would he be angry? Would he listen to what she had to say, or would he laugh at her?

She was halfway down the hill when Beau turned from the sluice and saw her coming toward him. But clearly he did not recognize her. The sun was in his eyes, and he lifted his hand up to shield them. She was about thirty feet from him when he dropped the hand and asked incredulously, "Frisco? Is that you?"

It was the first time he had ever called her that, and it shook her slightly. She stopped, hesitating where she was, and said, "No, Beau, it's Graciela. Graciela McGee."

"Well, I'll be damned!" he exclaimed. "You do turn up in the most unexpected places!"

As always, his manner unsettled her. She still did not know how to take that slightly teasing edge to his voice. And so she responded defensively. "You left rather hurriedly," she said accusingly, hating herself for doing so. "We still had a few matters to discuss." That was not what she had intended to say at all, but he did not move to embrace her. He made no gesture whatsoever toward welcoming her.

"What's the matter?" he challenged. "Weren't you satisfied with the outcome to our little poker game?"

He was grinning mischievously, but his words angered her. She replied hotly, "As a matter of fact, I'm not! You lied about that game! I didn't win it! You did!"

"And you came to deliver my winnings, is that it?" he cocked his head to one side, and lifted a dubious eyebrow. "That's a long way to travel, just for that."

She began to tremble. This wasn't going precisely the way she had wanted, but she was growing more furious with each exchange. Finally, she would put up with it no longer. She began to advance on him, her shoulders thrust back, her chin high, her steps deliberate as she continued down the hill toward him.

"You aren't giving me a chance to tell you what I have to say, Beau Tolliver!" she said fiercely. "You've never given me a chance! You're always teasing me and toying with me! You think you know what I think, what I want, and what I have to say! But you don't know half of what you think you know! Well, I am not leaving this place until you give me a chance to say it once and for all!"

"All right," he shrugged. "What is it you have to say?"

"I love you!" she snapped. "I have loved you, Beau Tolliver, ever since the first time I laid eyes on you! I have never loved anyone else, and I probably never will!"

He looked at her, slightly nonplussed, waiting silently for a moment after she had finished. "Is that it?" he asked.

"That's it!" she snapped.

A warm light shined in his green eyes. His manner softened as he reached out his hands to grip her shoulders. "Well then," he said, "I guess I'd better tell you something. You are the most confusing, unpredictable, disarming, beautiful, wonderful, tantalizing, seductive wench I have ever met in my life, and I love you, too. I don't know when I started loving you, but it was a long time ago. And I never at any time thought you could possibly love me. I'm not sure I believe it even now, but if you tell me enough times, maybe I will believe it."

Graciela was shaking. There were tears in her eyes, tears of joy. She threw her arms around him and said passionately, "I love you, Beau Tolliver! I love you! And I intend to keep saying it until the day I die!"

He lifted her face up to his, and she saw that there were tears in his eyes as well. Then he reached down and kissed her. Their lips met with the pent-up passion of eternity.

34

This time they would be married legally, by a padre at a little mission a few miles from Beau's camp. That evening, Beau did everything possible to dissuade Graciela, but she had an answer for his every objection.

"The life in the mining camps is hard," Beau cautioned. "You have to work from sunup to sundown, and usually by the time you go to bed you have nothing at all to show for your efforts."

"I'm used to hard work," Graciela told him. "And I've been in the mining camps before. Remember? I know what to expect."

"You'll have only me for company," he said. "My nearest neighbor is three miles away. And there are no women at all for at least twenty miles."

"You and Alex are the only company I need," she replied.

It was after dinner, and they were out walking alone in the moonlight beside the little stream. Beneath the vast canopy of stars in the still night, there was an absolute peace. Beau paused beside a stunted pine and pulled her into his arms again, as if he still needed assurance that she was really there. He kissed her gently and lovingly, with a quiet contented passion. Enveloped in his powerful arms, Graciela felt an inexpressible joy, a happiness that filled her entire being, a sense that she was finally where she belonged. She was home, and home was wherever her beloved Beau's arms were.

His next words were melancholy, and his fingers caressed her hair and face as he spoke. "You are the most beautiful treasure God ever created," he whispered. "But the sun and the wind out here will dry that hair and make it brittle and coarse. It will turn that lustrous glowing skin to leather. And the work will harden the soft lines and gentle curves of your body, making it tough and sinewy. Can you bear that, too?"

"If you can," she said softly. "I can bear anything as long as I have your love."

"It will only make me love you more," he said, "knowing you have given all that beauty to me." And he kissed her again, now more passionately and desperately, as if every blessed moment counted now.

They decided then that they would be married the following day at the little mission of San Alessandro, with Mike and Lyuba as their witnesses. "But I want you to be certain this time," Beau warned her. "I could not bear to lose you again."

"I'm certain," she said. "I'll never leave you, no matter what."

Early the next morning, they all climbed into Beau's wagon—Beau and Graciela, Mike and Lyuba, and Alex—and set out over the barren, rocky hills towards San Alessandro. Beau was showing Alex how to help him use the horses' reins. Graciela had no idea how the word had spread through the mining camps that there were women nearby, but the men for miles around all seemed to know. There was clearly some invisible line of communication between them, for as their wagon rattled along the rocky tow path men came running up to the crests of almost every hilltop to wave and shout excitedly, "Women! It's Beau Tolliver, and he's got two women with him!"

All Beau had to do was to tell one of the men who came rushing down his hill to get a closer look that he and Graciela were about to be married, and the men all the way along the line got the news. There was already a crowd of dusty, grizzled, sun-baked men gathered around the little mission by the time they arrived there themselves. And more arrived soon after them. It did not bother Graciela to be the object of so much curiosity. In fact, it rather delighted her. She laughed and joked merrily with the men.

It was Mike who was disturbed by all the attention given to Lyuba, and to the fact that she was unmarried. There was much hurried, anxious whispering between the older couple as they got down from the wagon and moved off toward the front door of the mission church. Just as they were all about to enter, followed by the curious crowd, Mike stopped Beau and asked, "Mr. Beau, do you think maybe the padre would be willing to perform two marriages for the price of one?"

Beau grinned. "You mean, you and Lyuba?"

Mike nodded.

"Of course," Beau replied. "But are you sure you want to go through it? You might change your mind when you get back to San Francisco."

"We've decided we're not going back," Mike explained. "Lyuba's determined to stay out here with you folks, and, well . . ." He hesitated. "I've decided I'd like to try my luck to see if maybe there's any gold waitin' for me someplace."

And so it was a double wedding. The other miners were rather disappointed that both the women were spoken for, but they still watched the proceedings with delight.

There was nothing fancy about the ceremony. Graciela wore a simple gingham dress of pale blue, and Beau wore the only good quality suit he still owned, without a tie, but bathed and clean-shaven for the occasion. Father Francis, the white-haired priest, had been taken rather by surprise; he had managed to wash his face and hands, but his cassock was dusty and frayed, and his memory of the marriage ceremony was a bit rusty from not being used in a long time.

But it was the most excitement San Alessandro had seen since a miner had struck a mother lode ten miles up in the mountains over a year ago.

In keeping with the excitement of the occasion, Beau invited all of the miners to his camp that night for a celebration, promising plenty of food and drink, aware that the real attraction would be the vicarious thrill of being near a woman for a night.

They all came, and Graciela and Lyuba prepared a special dinner outdoors over an open fire. After dinner, Alex—his face glowing with unrestrained happiness—took out his violin and played tirelessly while Lyuba and Graciela danced with the men. His music had never seemed to sound so beautiful as it did echoing against the rocky hillsides and stretching upward to the stars.

Later, after all the dancing was done and all the men were sitting contentedly around the fire, warm with drink, Beau took Graciela aside and said, "I think it's time we went to bed. The sun rises early around here, and we mustn't miss another day of work."

"All right," she replied. "If you think your guests won't mind."

"Mind?" he grinned, his green eyes glittering with mischief. "It's what they're all waiting for."

Then he opened the door of the cabin, swept her up into his arms, and carried her over the threshold, closing the door behind them with a swift kick of his foot.

He held her there in his arms for a long time, just inside the door, kissing her hungrily, and then he laid her gently on the bed and began to undress her. She looked up at him, still unable to believe that this was really happening. It was all like a wonderful perfect dream. When she lay completely naked before him, his lips explored the hollows of her neck and breasts while he rapidly divested himself of his own clothing.

There was no other man in the world like Beau. For Graciela, there was no other man who even existed. He was all the beauty and strength she would ever want. He had changed slightly from the Beau she had always known, but the change was for the better, if that was possible. His pale skin had been tanned by the sun, making his green eyes more coolly penetrating than even before, and his red hair had been bleached into a burnished gold. She had never sensed any softness in his body at all, but now it seemed even more hard and firm and muscular, like a great lithe animal as it enfolded her own body. She melted beneath his passion and returned it with an equal passion of her own. Time stopped as they made love, and they savored eternity in each other's arms.

As the sun was rising, they lay contentedly together in the bed, their bodies touching blissfully. But as the time drew nearer for them to get up and set about the business of the day, Beau spoke. "There's one thing that bothers me," he said softly with a trace of apprehension.

"What is it?" Graciela asked.

"You were always so concerned about being owned like a slave," he said cautiously. "That was why you objected to the other marriage license, or so you said. Now, with a real marriage, don't you feel I own you even more surely than before? With all the hard work you're going to have to do as my wife, I'm afraid you're going to rebel again."

"No, I won't," Graciela replied. "Because this marriage is real, and we both have learned from our past experiences and know that neither of us owns the other. I think I can explain it best, if I tell you what Shandor's wise old Rom grandmother taught me."

She closed her eyes and tried to remember the words as she had heard them so many times from Pesha. They came to her clearly:

For those who would share love, this must be
    known,
One the other must never try to own.

True love means caring; it means sharing,
But jealousy and possessiveness will cause
love's tearing.
Love must be held as you would a frightened
dove,
Gently and loosely; if you squeeze, no bird,
no love.
These words are from the Rom, who understand love,
Follow them and you will be truly blessed
from above.

Beau was pensive for a moment, then said,
"Yes, that is true wisdom and very beautiful, my
love. Let's always remember it."

Impulsively, Graciela threw her arms around
Beau, and with all her vibrant zest for life
surging forth from the depth of her being,
she said, "I'm so happy. We have each other and
Alex . . ."

In a burst of enthusiasm, she rose from the
bed, her voice thrilling with excitement as she
cried, "Come, Beau, it's time to seek our fortune!"